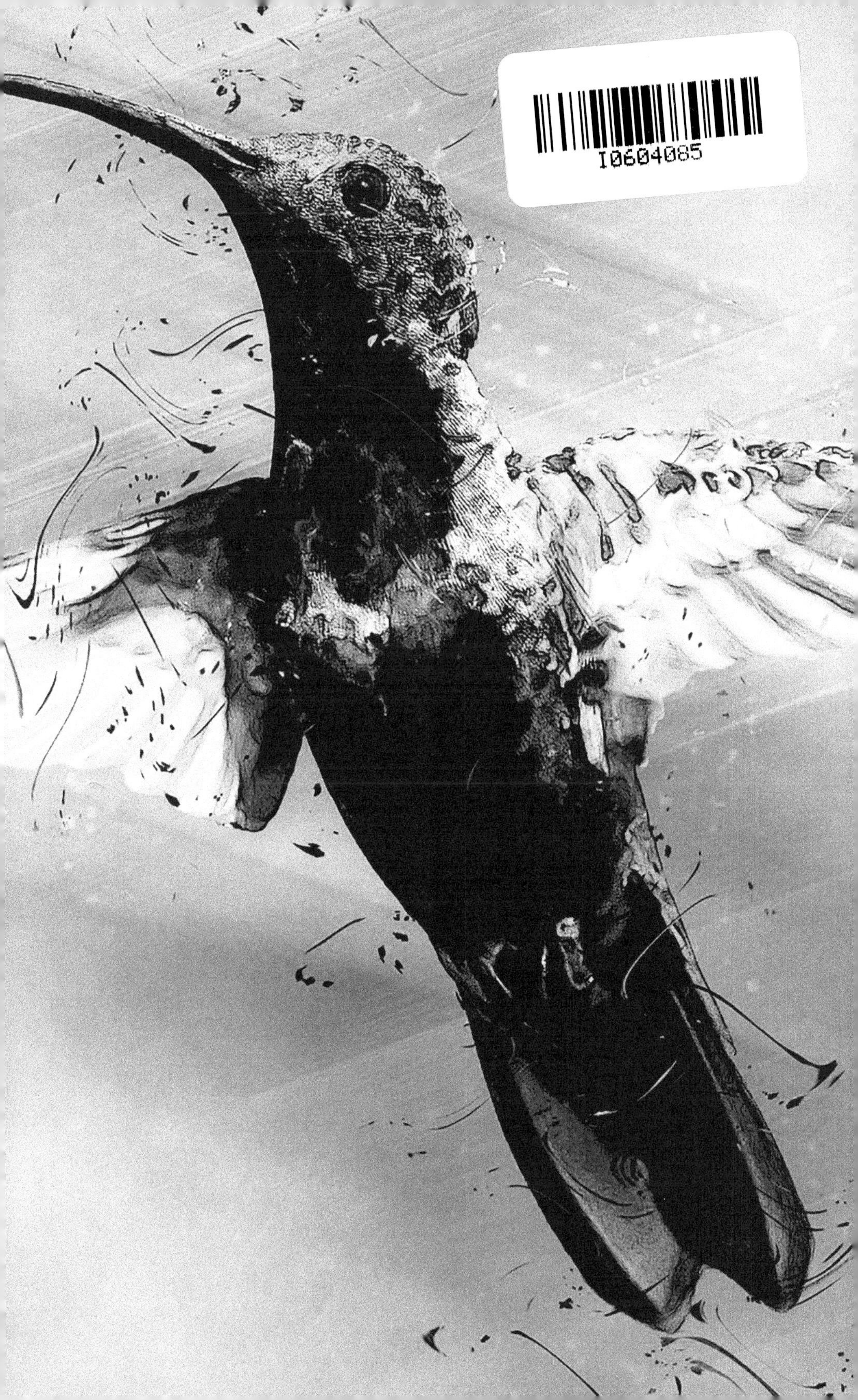
I0604085

HUMMINGBIRD

ALSO BY T. C. PARKER

Saltblood
A Press of Feathers
Salvation Spring
Maiden (with Ward Nerdlo)
The Long Con: An El Gardener Omnibus

<u>The El Gardener Trilogy</u>
The Debt (Book 1)
The Push (Book 2)
The Remembrance (Book 3)

HUMMINGBIRD

A MOSAIC

TC PARKER

FOREWORD BY STEPHANIE ELLIS

PUBLISHED BY NEFARIOUS BAT PRESS

2022

HUMMINGBIRD: A MOSAIC
Second Paperback Edition

Published by Nefarious Bat Press

Copyright © 2022 by TC Parker
Cover design by Kealan Patrick Burke
Interior art by Edward Lorn
Interior design by Todd Keisling | Dullington Design Co.

All rights reserved.

No part of this book may be reproduced in any form or by any electronic or mechanical means, including information storage and retrieval systems, without written permission from the author, except for the use of brief quotations in a book review.

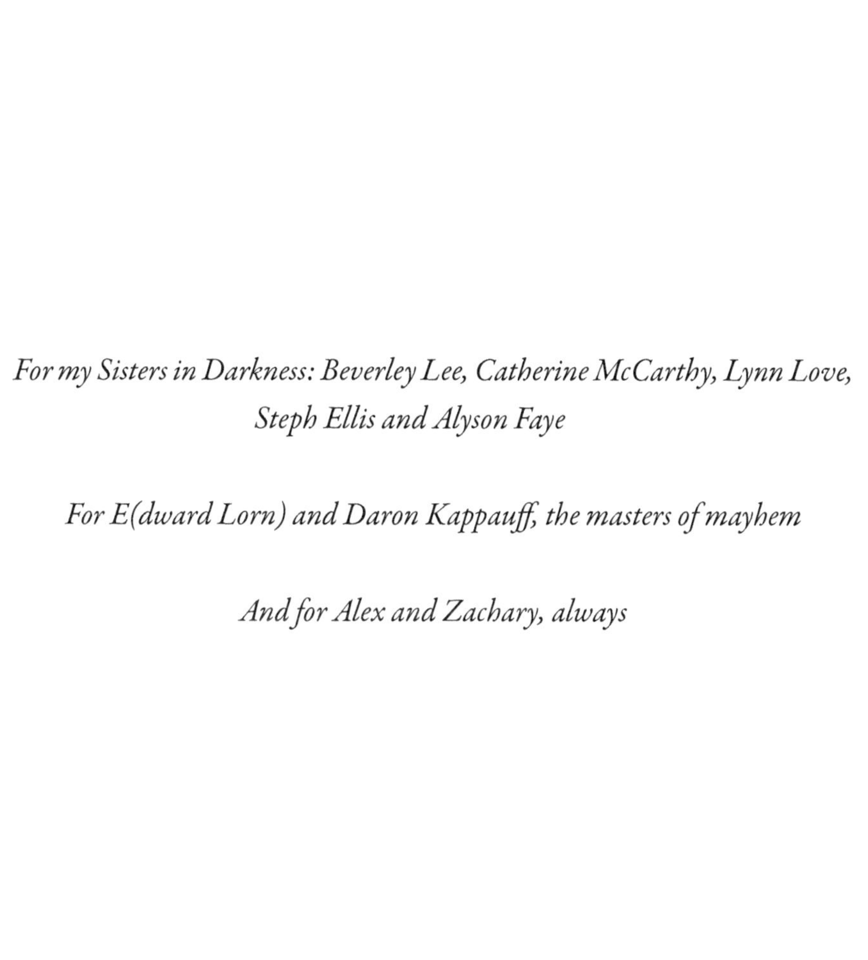

For my Sisters in Darkness: Beverley Lee, Catherine McCarthy, Lynn Love, Steph Ellis and Alyson Faye

For E(dward Lorn) and Daron Kappauff, the masters of mayhem

And for Alex and Zachary, always

FOREWORD

Since time immemorial, man has loved to categorise, to classify and label object or human – and to fit them into neat little boxes. In days gone by, there was no room for any deviation from a norm defined by those in authority; authority determined by religion, wealth or social status. To survive, you had to conform and accept your lot in life. Those shackles of identification became so ingrained, that it is only in recent times people have been able to shake them off and declare themselves in the way they truly wish to be seen. And yet ... and yet there are many, even in this modern and supposedly enlightened age, who see these declarations as something wrong, as a challenge in some strange way to themselves. They become monstrous in their condemnation of the other, fanatical in their opposition, to the point they become a baying mob.

What has this to do with Hummingbird? A horror story with monsters and mayhem? Everything. T.C. Parker leads you by the hand through intertwining narratives to explore the nature of monstrosity. Is it the shapeshifter who could rip another creature to shreds in minutes or is it the group of 'respectable' folk screaming abuse as small children enter their school playground? Is it the person who kills or the person who is killed? And thus she leads us to acceptance, demonstrating how bonds of love transcend the revealed reality of another and the mask of 'monster' fades away. She holds up a mirror to us and presses the point that hatred is a parasite which grows on the fear, bigotry and ignorance of others.

Perhaps Parker didn't intend the story to be read in this way, but the evidence is clearly there. She has delivered an important message in a format which refrains from preaching, which shows the conflict and turmoil to be found in the breast of those who seek to discover their true selves but fear the reaction of others. As revelation succeeds revelation and she takes the narrative in so many completely unexpected directions, digging down and down into the realms of superstition and legend and closing the circle of a story started centuries earlier, she carries the reader with her. You can read this as a straightforward horror story, expertly told and enjoy it simply for that. Or you can recognise the weaving in of the thread of transformation and acceptance and admire it all the more.

I was privileged to have read the first two sections of the Hummingbird story when I published it with Alyson Faye, in Daughters of Darkness II. I could see it was going to be something special then and to me, T.C. Parker has delivered. I have long been an avid fan of her work and I hope that if this is your first introduction to her, it is only the start.

Stephanie Ellis
March 2022

PART I
THE BODY TREE

I

The protesters were blocking the gates again - their handmade banner-slogans (LET KIDS BE KIDS and SAY NO TO BRAINWASHING and PROTECT THE FAMILY *NOW*) ringing in Jodie's ears as she pushed through and past them, Connor's mitten-covered hand imprisoning hers in a death-grip.

He was crying, but that was nothing new: he'd cried every day on the way to school since the protests had started, like so many of the other kids in his class. The ones who were left; the ones whose parents hadn't pulled them out of lessons.

She could hardly blame him. Navigating a path around two dozen angry, bellowing grownups at eight-thirty in the morning was hard enough even for those six- and seven-year-olds who *weren't* being told their own families were a disgrace before God.

A ripple of awkward nods and stilted half-waves greeted the pair of them at the entrance - the other parents, the ones whose sons and daughters were still *in* school, determined to show sympathy for Jodie's situation, even if they'd never go quite so far as to stand with her in actual solidarity. She tried not to hate them for it. They were pleasant people, she was sure, even if there were few of them she'd spoken to long enough to test the hypothesis. They just didn't *understand*, that was all. The protestors and the banners and the shouting - all of it upset them, because it upset their kids and disrupted what should have been the smooth unfurling of their formal education, but none of it *touched* them, not really. None of it called *their* home lives into question, decried *their* marriages as a threat to the moral welfare of under-elevens everywhere.

She kissed the top of Connor's head, pressed the bright green canvas book-bag into his hand and steered him through the entrance and into the waiting arms of his teacher and the classroom assistant - both tough, sensitive women whom she genuinely liked, and who certainly didn't deserve the abuse that had been hurled at them, these past few weeks.

"They're very loud, that mob, aren't they?" said a voice just behind her - a voice like honey and mentholated cigarettes and childhood elocution lessons. A London voice, dripping with inherited wealth.

She turned around and came face to face - or more accurately face to throat - with the voice's owner: a very tall, very thin and very angular white woman with a black riding cape draped around her shoulders, and a shock of short wavy hair dyed an electric red that matched the fire-engine scarlet of her lipstick.

She was new, Jodie thought. She had to be - you wouldn't just forget seeing a woman like that on the school run.

"They've been louder." Jodie looked down at the scuffed tips of her running shoes, reluctant to return the woman's stare. "When the vicar's here, usually. He tends to get them a bit... riled up."

Which was the understatement of the year, she realised as she said it. Tim Howard - born-again Evangelical, recently installed Vicar at St. Stephen's and creator of Exploring Avenues, a church-endorsed "learning experience" designed to bring the faithless back to Christ - was more than a rabble-rouser: he was an out-and-out bully, a charismatic but strong-arming demagogue whom she could easily imagine, a few decades earlier, inciting an army of skinheads to cave in the windows of a Pakistani corner shop. And here, in his new parish on the rural conservative-leaning fringes of the south-east coast, he'd found a ready audience of hitherto-lapsed Anglicans - with more pent-up bile, apparently, than Jodie would ever have anticipated, before.

"I've read about this sort of thing," the woman replied. "This sort of *person*, I should say – religious zealots with a bee in their bonnet about sex education. There was something like this at a school in Canterbury last year, wasn't there? Catholics rolling in at pickup time with placards and loudspeakers and what have you, screaming at anyone who'd *dared* let their progeny stick a condom on a wooden dildo." She paused; dipped her head towards the protestors, her hair and cape both blowing wildly in the October wind. "These are the same, I'm guessing?"

She really *had* to be new, Jodie thought, if she didn't know. If she hadn't heard already about St. Stephen's; if she needed Jodie to fill her in.

"Not exactly." The words came out clumsily, stumblingly; blood flooded Jodie's cheeks, betraying the discomfort she felt at the clarification she'd have to give. "It's the... equality stuff. They started talking to the Year 2s about same-sex parenting, and some of the mums and dads got a bit... upset."

She trailed off, waiting for a reaction; trying to gauge what the stranger would say, how she'd respond. Which side of the newly erected ideological fence she'd fall on.

"Ah. *That*." The woman sucked the air in through her teeth; grimaced, and sighed. "It did strike me that might *also* be a possibility, when I saw the signs. Funny, isn't it, how much energy people like that invest in tying themselves in knots about us? I can't help but feel they'd be happier at home baking lemon slices, or strolling around the golf course, or doing whatever it is they do when they're not out here screaming into the void."

It was the *us* that Jodie focused on: the quiet announcement of solidarity that the woman might not even have been aware she was making, but which put Jodie immediately at ease. At greater ease, in fact, than she'd ever been around any of the other parents at the Hummingbird Academy - even the *nice* ones, the ones who probably thought of themselves as liberal and accepting, as allies to the cause.

"A lot of them are just bored, I think," she said – feeling herself opening up, very slightly, to the stranger who was, whatever *else* she was, at least a little like Jodie. Then, catching sight of the heavily made-up blonde woman at the front of the group of protestors: "Most of them, anyway."

And some of them are in it for the cruelty, she added to herself. Some of them just want the chance to put the boot in with impunity.

"Lemon slices, that's what they need. Something to keep them occupied." The woman smiled at her, red lips stretching to a wider, conspiratorial grin as her eyes held Jodie's. "Listen - possibly this is going to come off as a bit odd, I'm not sure on the etiquette in these kinds of situations, but would you like to come round to mine for a coffee sometime? Sunny and I haven't been here long, and I'm getting the sense it might be helpful for us to know at least *one* person at the school who isn't an out-and-out lunatic."

A part of Jodie wondered, dimly, who Sunny might be: a wife, or a partner, or the child whom the woman had just dropped at the gates. A larger part of her, however, could only reel at having received the invitation - the first she'd ever been offered, by any parent, in all the time Connor had been at Hummingbird.

"I'd love to," she said, without so much as stopping to consider whether it might be a good idea, whether they'd have anything at all to talk about. "When are you free?"

§ § §

"She seemed nice, the woman," she told Laura that night, when Connor was up in his room and they'd bedded down on the sofa with the bottle of red one of Laura's clients had given her for handling the conveyancing on his daughter's flat in Hastings. "Well... friendly, anyway."

"Great." Laura reached for the remote control on the coffee table; switched on the TV, navigated to an episode of something with a laugh track and a New York skyline and settled back into the cushions, half-full wine glass in hand.

She wasn't really listening, Jodie thought. She rarely seemed to be listening at all lately, when Jodie was speaking: the gap between them widening with every extra hour Laura put in at the office, every load of Connor's soaking-wet laundry Jodie pulled resentfully from the washing machine.

"And if she's got a kid in Year 2, then there'll be someone else for Con to play with. Someone we know won't care he's got two mums."

"Sounds good." Laura took a long sip of her wine, gaze fixed to the screen.

Jodie's stomach sank; a dull, increasingly familiar plummeting sensation precipitated not so much by Laura's obvious disinterest as by her lack of effort to conceal it. By the growing awareness that the woman she'd married wasn't even trying to pretend anymore that she enjoyed Jodie's company.

She bit her lip; shook off the tears she could feel building at the corners of her eyes and pulled her phone from her pocket, the text she'd send already half-composed in her head.

2

Miranda. That was the name the woman had given Jodie: Miranda Harper. She lived in a cottage in one of the less populated pockets of the village: a thatched Tudor affair with nothing but fields on either side and a dilapidated glass-walled summer house in the garden.

"I love it," she said, leading Jodie through to the lounge. "No neighbours, peace and quiet... it's bloody perfect. Exactly what I need, especially for work."

"Work?" Jodie asked, lowering herself onto the seat of one of the strange, mismatched pieces of furniture that dotted the room - this one a carved wooden chair in the shape of an outstretched hand.

"Sculpture." Miranda followed suit, curling her own long body into a polished metal rocker fashioned into a crescent moon and stars. "Corporate stuff mainly - the kind you see in hotel lobbies, that kind of thing. If you've ever found yourself in a foyer somewhere staring up at something that looks like a Henry Moore but isn't and asked yourself, *who made that?* Well... it might've been me."

She flashed Jodie a smile, gentler and more self-effacing than she'd seemed the first time they'd met outside the gates, and Jodie felt herself warming to her.

"Sounds fascinating." And it did, in a way: Jodie had managed human resources before she'd left to look after Connor full-time and, secure and reasonably well-paid though she'd found the job, it had rarely afforded much scope for creativity. "Are you working on anything now?"

"I've just started a new project, actually. Out the back."

Miranda gestured with a flick of her wrist to the transparent sliding doors separating *inside* from *outside* - and through them to the summer house that was, Jodie assumed, the place where she made her art, whatever kind of art it was.

"For Halloween, of all things," she continued, seeming faintly ashamed of the admission. "Sunny's been on and *on* at me for *months* about trick or treating and decorating the house with pumpkins and skulls and whatnot, and I suppose the idea of doing *something* to commemorate the occasion must have... seeped in, somehow."

Sunny, Jodie had learned - from Connor, of all people - was Miranda's daughter: an unusually shy and withdrawn child who, at least as Connor told it, had yet to utter a single word to any of the other kids in their class. Perhaps, Jodie thought, the kid was more loquacious at home. All kids were, weren't they? When they were somewhere they felt safe?

Of Sunny's *other* parent, if the girl had one, Miranda had said nothing at all.

"So... what is it, this Halloween project?" Jodie said, the tiny cup of espresso Miranda had made for her warm between her hands. "A giant skeleton?"

Miranda smiled again, her eyes lighting up at the question. She was oddly attractive, it struck Jodie; more so than she'd seemed, that morning outside Hummingbird. Too hawklike to be classically beautiful, sure: her nose too hooked and her mouth too wide and her jaw too jutting. And the stick-thin contours of her body were the absolute antithesis of Laura's lean-muscled solidity - though Jodie hated herself a little for drawing the comparison between them, even in her head. But Miranda was magnetic, somehow, the aesthetic whole of her greater than the sum of its parts, and Jodie was surprised - not to say embarrassed - to find that she wanted her. That she might even, were she a different kind of woman - one whose sexual confidence *hadn't* been so very dented by motherhood and a decade of not always happy marriage - have been tempted to put down her coffee, stride across the room and straddle Miranda where she sat, on her ridiculous crescent-moon rocking chair.

"Would you like to see it?"

Ordinarily, Jodie's instinctive inner-voice response would have screamed a clear, emphatic *no* - regardless of whether she'd felt obligated to acquiesce on the outside, to feign enthusiasm for the proffered viewing. Did any visitor to another person's home ever *really* want to look at their host's artwork - their macramé dream catchers and pen-and-ink sketches of the Bedruthan Steps by night, the haikus they'd cross-stitched onto cotton wall-hangings and had mounted in the upstairs hallway?

But she was curious, about Miranda and about the kind of work a woman like her might produce, and when she nodded and told her *yes, she'd love to*, Miranda's eyes lit up all over again with pleasure.

The summer house *was* her studio, Jodie discovered, as she followed Miranda outside and down the broken-stone path leading down to the bottom of the garden. It was far less dilapidated up close than it had seemed from a distance, and neither transparent nor exactly glass, as she'd assumed on first glance, but rather was coated roof to ground in a backscattering glaze that framed the structure as a kind of geometric mirror - a three-dimensional wave reflector that served, she supposed, to keep whatever was inside cool and out of direct sunlight.

"Brace yourself," Miranda said, opening the door.

Jodie was glad of the warning.

The studio was chaos, a battlefield of tools and timber, stone and vinyl, modelling clay and metal: all the materials, she presumed, that Miranda needed to produce her sculptures. And in its centre, eight feet high and ten feet wide and so jarring, so eye-wateringly *bizarre* Jodie had to look twice before she could really take in what she was seeing, stood the piece that Miranda must have been working on.

It was a tree, of sorts: a birch-like construction, leafless and emaciated, its wire and plywood trunk wrinkled and knotted and coloured silver with what looked to Jodie like spray paint. But its branches were bone - some spotted brown and ivory with age and others fresher and cleaner, as if the flesh had been stripped from them earlier that day. Except... *no*, she corrected herself, as she stared at it; no, that wasn't quite right. Not bone; bone*s*, or rather what simulations of them Miranda must have crafted out of silicone or fibreglass or PVC. *Specific* bones, too: ulnas and fibulas, sturdy femurs and delicate metatarsals, all of them disconcertingly human in appearance.

And that was the *point* of the thing, wasn't it - to disturb, to leave the viewer disconcerted? It must have been: Jodie couldn't conceive of any other explanation for it. For the bones, sure - but for the rest of it, too. For what was *hanging* from the bones.

They were mannequins, or seemed to be: ghost white, bald and featureless, their straight-hipped bodies life-size and their expressions uniformly blank. Six of them in total, bound to the osseous branches above by heavy-duty string and suspended in mid-air like the cast of an obscene puppet theatre. All were clothed: four in brown hessian sackcloth fashioned into dirty, bloodstained tunics, another in a Cenobite leather and dog-collar getup that wouldn't have been out of place in the window of an old-school Soho sex shop, and the sixth covered from shoulder to ankle in something like chainmail. The face of one was obscured entirely by a black hood fixed around its neck with hangman's rope; the head of another was entirely absent, its body not only decapitated but dismembered and its absent arms and legs piled in an untidy heap on the floor below.

"Jesus Christ." Jodie flinched; couldn't stop herself. "It's…"

"Hideous?" Miranda was right there, at her elbow - her breath a low, soft almost-whisper in Jodie's ear.

"Shit. Sorry, I didn't mean…" She flushed, immediately aware of the harsh critique implicit in her loss of words, the reaction Miranda would undoubtedly read as an insult. "It's just… a lot."

"Isn't it, though? I don't know what came over me, when I started it. That happens sometimes, when I'm working, when I'm really in the flow of it. I end up in a kind of… trance. Lasts for hours, sometimes. Then I look up at what I've been doing, and… *bam*. There it is."

"And it's… for Halloween?" Monstrous though the sculpture was, Jodie found she couldn't tear herself away from it; couldn't *not* look.

"Truthfully," Miranda said, stepping in closer - the proximity sending an uncomfortable wave of heat gliding across the surface of Jodie's skin, "I don't know *what* it's for yet. But I daresay I'll find a use for it, somewhere."

§ § §

"Her wife died," Jodie told Laura in bed that night. "She didn't say when or how, but I got the feeling it was… not good, the way it happened."

"Not good?" Laura murmured, half asleep beside her. "When is it *ever* good, when that happens?"

"You know what I mean. It didn't sound like, you know… natural causes." Laura rolled around to face her.

"What, like a car crash or something? Or have you convinced yourself someone murdered her down a dark alley?"

Jodie flinched; the cruelty, the mockery churning her gut and stealing some of the breath from her lungs as it sank in. Had it always been like this, with the two of them? Had Laura always had this much contempt for Jodie, for her thoughts and ideas and opinions, her observations of the world? Or was it a recent development - an unintended consequence of Jodie playing the little woman at home while Laura performed whatever high-powered services she provided for her clients in the City?

"No. I just... she said it was sudden. That it knocked her and her daughter for six."

"The poor woman probably had a heart attack or an aneurysm - it happens, even at our age, and that's assuming she *was* our age and not older. Nothing sinister about it."

What she was saying was logical - Jodie knew that. Laura probably hadn't even intended it to be hurtful; it was just second nature to her now, to dismiss out of hand whatever comment Jodie might make.

But there'd been *something* about the way Miranda had described her wife's death earlier that day, vague and allusive though she'd been - something that to Jodie had suggested violence, a *suddenness* more abrupt than even the most unexpected illness.

"It's been a learning curve," she'd confided in Jodie, when they'd retreated from the summer house and its grotesqueries to the living room and were perched back on their respective chairs, clutching yet more tiny cups of coffee. "For both of us - me as well as Sunny. We're still adjusting."

So it was recent, then, Jodie had thought - another swell of guilt for her attraction to Miranda radiating outward from her abdomen to the tips of her fingers. *Very recent, if they're still getting used to it. Is that why they moved out here, to the countryside? For a fresh start?*

"I didn't say it was *sinister*..." she began. But Laura was already asleep, her back to Jodie.

3

Henry's dad's run off," Connor said, apropos of nothing.

They were almost at Hummingbird – Jodie's eyes peeled for signs of Miranda, just as they'd been every morning of the week that had passed since she'd left the woman's cottage, for an ostentatious flutter of cape or flash of bright red hair that might signal her presence.

"Run off?" she asked him - stopping for a second to adjust his tie and straighten his sweater. "Run off *where*?"

Had Henry's dad been almost any other man, or almost any other woman for that matter, Jodie might have interpreted Connor's *run off* as an unwitting euphemism for *left his wife* or *hopped a plane to Amsterdam before the debt collectors caught up with him*. But neither scenario, nor any like it, seemed to fit the bill where Rick Fielding was concerned.

He was a committed Christian, despite the alternative suggestions offered by his hard-man looks, his kanji and Japanese woodblock tattoos and the collection of Harley-Davidsons he kept in his garage: one of Tim Howard's faithful at St. Stephen's, and an enthusiastic participant in the school gate pickets, although his own child remained - no doubt against the Reverend Howard's advice - *in* classes and not out of them in protest at the curriculum. Jodie wasn't so naive as to believe that Fielding Senior's religiosity would in itself preclude him engaging in the sort of extracurricular activity likely to precipitate a midnight flight from the village, and possibly the country; she'd have put money, from the bits and pieces of gossip she'd picked up in the village over the years, on more than a few of his pew-mates having secret lovers, or a hand in the till, or a decades-long coke habit they'd kept hidden from their wives.

Rick Fielding, though... that wasn't his style. *Running* wasn't his style.

He'd brazen it out, she thought. If he were ever caught in a moment of indiscretion, pecuniary or extramarital, he'd deny it, no matter how compelling the evidence against him; would argue tooth and nail against any accusation thrown his way, and do it publicly. He was a proud man, or so she'd gleaned from the interactions she'd had with him in the days before Tim Howard, back when he'd allowed Henry and Connor to play together - and a *loud* man, if the fervour of his yelling and chanting at the gates was anything to go by.

A man like that... he wouldn't run. He'd stay and fight, even if what he ended up fighting was a losing battle.

"Dunno." Connor shrugged. "Somewhere. He's gone, though. Henry said. Are we having spaghetti for tea?"

There was no point pushing him, she knew; he'd already lost interest, his attention flitting to the next shiny object it had glimpsed. If she wanted to know more about Rick Fielding and what might or might not have happened to him, she was going to have to find out for herself.

He *was* missing, though, she saw as she and Connor approached the school; missing, at least, from the usual-suspect throng of protestors obstructing the entrance with their banners and their caterwauling. They were a smaller crowd than usual today, only eight strong, with Elspeth Palmer leading their number - her foundation densely orange and her pale blonde hair so thick with lacquer it was entirely immobile, even in the wind.

She and Elspeth had never been friends; nor even, as with her and Rick Fielding, friendly acquaintances thrown together by their mutual guardianship of same-aged children. Elspeth, in fact, was a homophobe of old - not a late adopter like so many of the St. Stephen's parishioners, who'd been happy enough to let their children mix with Jodie's before the Reverend Howard's arrival, despite Jodie's undeniable deviance. She'd been chilly with Jodie even before Connor and her own son Felix had started at Hummingbird. Since both boys were in nursery, no less - when she'd first spotted Laura's arm around Jodie's waist in the reception area and, scowling and tutting, had made known her displeasure at being forced to acknowledge the existence not only of lesbians (though that, Jodie suspected, would have been offence enough in itself) but of lesbians who'd dared to reproduce.

It hadn't surprised Jodie in the slightest to find Elspeth spearheading the protests; they were, to her mind, the logical release value for at least some of her antipathy. The only real surprise was the religious angle: she and Laura had taken Connor to the odd Sunday service and Midnight Mass at St. Stephen's in the days before Tim Howard, back when the church's primary political concern was a longstanding boundary dispute with the now-abandoned wool shop down the road, and not once had they seen Elspeth there, not even for the harvest festival events so stripped of Christian connotations they might as well as been secular. Privately, Jodie had wondered whether Howard himself might have been the draw, for Elspeth as well as for some of the other female congregants St. Stephen's had gained on his watch; whether the man's shaved head, deep blue eyes and Hollywood smile coupled with the broad shoulders, muscular arms and tapered waist he wore under his dog collar and clerical vestments might have had as much to do with the expansion of his flock as the content of his sermons.

"Spaghetti for tea?" Connor repeated, tugging at the sleeve of her jacket.

Her gaze, she realised a moment too late, had alighted unconsciously on Elspeth, as her mind had wandered; worse still, Elspeth had *seen* her looking, and was now looking back at Jodie, her thin-lipped mouth twisted into a grimace of sour, unambiguous disgust.

Elspeth whispered something to the short, pixie-haired woman directly behind her and, keeping eye contact with Jodie, raised the placard she was holding - a rigid, foot-long square of white cardboard exhorting its readers to RESPECT TRADITIONAL VALUES - and called out, in a singsong burst of sound so loud it was very nearly a battle cry: "education not indoctrination! Education not indoctrination!"

A brief pause, and the parents behind her followed suit, adding their voices to the chant until the combined off-key weight of their individual contributions harmonised into something like an incantation.

"Really, do they never just *stop*?"

And there, again, was Miranda, at Jodie's shoulder - by her side a dark-haired, freckle-faced little girl in a green and yellow Hummingbird uniform, small and slight and apparently very shy, her head down and stare rooted to the pavement in front of her.

Sunny, Jodie presumed.

Miranda herself looked good, her bright eyes and full lips more disarming than ever and her dark shirt open wide enough to accentuate the curve of her neck. Jodie was mildly alarmed by the intense stomach-flip of excitement that struck her as Miranda threw a cheerful smile her way.

"I'm not sure they're allowed to stop, when they're doing God's work," she replied, rallying - shoving her reaction to Miranda's appearance, and what that reaction implied, as deep down inside her as it would go.

Miranda laughed delightedly at this - her laughter attracting the attention, and immediately thereafter the disapproving scowls of Elspeth Palmer and her minions.

Jodie was, against both her conscience and her better judgement, entirely captivated.

"Mum," Connor asked, snapping her back to reality, "are we going in?"

"I suppose we'd better, hadn't we?" Miranda said, answering for her. Then, taking Sunny by the hand, added, only to Jodie: "Coffee at mine, once we've got rid of these two?"

§ § §

Was it Jodie's imagination, or was Miranda sitting closer to her than she had before? Touching her more often - briefly, casually, on the arm or the knee - while they were talking?

"I just don't understand what they think they're going to achieve," Miranda concluded, with a shake of her head. Her hair was catching the light, Jodie had noticed; even the weak Autumn sun causing it to glow, very faintly. Turning the blood-red of it to copper and back again with every pulse and flicker of cloud. "It's the *curriculum*, for fuck's sake. Do they *really* think that if they shout loud enough and long enough, Tara Blacklock is going to turn around and *agree* with them?"

"They're kidding themselves, if they do." Jodie allowed herself a small, rueful smile of her own. "I've met her wife."

Tara Blacklock - *Mrs* Blacklock by day, in her role as Hummingbird's acting principal - had made her position on both the protests and the teaching materials that had inspired them abundantly clear. She wouldn't, she'd told the parents of the Year 2 kids affected, be steamrollered into submission by a handful of *fringe voices*; nor, more importantly, would she countenance any disruption to the education of the students in her care.

Tim Howard, Elspeth Palmer and their ilk could complain as loudly as they liked; it would have no impact whatsoever on what would or wouldn't be taught to their children. And if they began to make life any more difficult than they had already for *other people's* children... well, then, Tara wouldn't hesitate to call the police and have them forcibly removed from the premises.

"Oh?" Miranda raised a single, amused eyebrow. "And is the good reverend aware of the existence of this wife?"

"I doubt it. I only know her..." Because Laura's firm handled her divorce from the husband she left for Tara, was what Jodie *should* have said. But the thought of Laura entering her exchange with Miranda, even tangentially, troubled her in a way she didn't care to analyse; provoked in her an unhappy mix of guilt and resentment and trepidation. "Through friends," she finished, feebly.

The already-raised eyebrow climbed higher, but Miranda said nothing, leaving the conversational lull between them to stretch out into borderline-excruciating silence, broken only by the metallic back-and-forth of the moon-and-stars rocking chair as it creaked under the pressure of Miranda's body.

"How's the sculpture going?" Jodie said eventually, when she could no longer bear it. "The, you know... bone tree thing?"

The whole of Miranda's face came alive again, seemingly animated by Jodie's interest.

"Well!" she answered. "Very well, in fact. It's coming along nicely, if I do say so myself."

Whereupon Jodie, for no good reason she could think of, asked whether she might go back out into the summer house to take another look.

§ § §

Miranda added another mannequin to the sculpture: a large one, at least six feet long, its body shrouded entirely in a dirty, blood-streaked sheet and its bandaged, mummy-like arms secured to the branches by a set of rusted chains.

The branches themselves had been augmented, too, since Jodie's last visit:

the bone now sheathed entirely in an artificial pink skin so realistic it had short, wiry hairs growing from its follicles, and a thick sausage-like string of what might have been intestines festooning them like tinsel on a Christmas tree.

And there was a smell, one not even the coolness of the summer house could mask: a raw, meaty, chlorine-infused odour that reminded Jodie of the butcher's shop she'd hated to go into with her father as a kid, the glass-fronted store with the misleadingly cheery big top awning and the row of dead, skinned rabbits in the window to tempt passers-by inside. Both the scent and the memory sickened her; made her retch, and audibly.

"Oh fuck, I'm so sorry." Miranda laid a palm, warm and soft, between her shoulder-blades. "I didn't think. Are you alright? Do you need me to... I don't know, prop the door open or something?"

Jodie tried for a smile but managed only a grimace.

"What *are* they?"

She pointed one hand towards the branches; held the other, loosely, to her nose.

"Exactly what they look like, I'm afraid - offal. Animal innards. Pigs', I believe."

"You use... offal in your sculptures?"

"Occasionally. There's a certain shock value, with organic material. It makes people look twice."

"And it... keeps?" Jodie squinted at the tree, at the looping coils of newly added organ meat. They looked... fresh, for now, inasmuch as she was able to determine their state of preservation. But how long could they *stay* fresh, really - even in a room only slightly warmer than a walk-in refrigerator?

"For long enough. But when the rot *does* set in... it'll be rather fitting, for a piece like this. Don't you think?"

It made sense, as an argument; Jodie agreed, in a fashion.

Her capacity to *vocalise* that agreement, however, was significantly diminished in the moment by what she'd seen on the sculpture - or what, perhaps, she'd seen already, but her brain had refused at first to process or acknowledge.

Ink. A patch of blue and white ink, marring the pinkly artificial skin that now circled the bone-branches of the tree - so innocuous she might have thought nothing of it, had she not seen it so many times before, albeit in a somewhat different context.

Tattoo ink.

It was a wave, or a portion of one: a tattooist's interpretation of Hokusai's *Great Wave Off Kanagawa*, the complexity of the original woodblock reworked and simplified into a design better suited to a flesh-and-blood canvas.

A design that its owner, his pride in the body art he'd commissioned bordering on vanity, had shown off to the world at every opportunity.

A design that she was sure had lived, at least until very recently, on Rick Fielding's upper arm.

4

She waited until Laura had finished dinner and Connor was asleep before she spoke up. Waited, although the waiting almost killed her; the story she needed to tell - the things she needed to say aloud, however insane and preposterous they might sound to an audience - bubbling up through her throat and coating the roof of her mouth in a sharp, sour film.

Beyond the most functional of phatics and imperatives - calling Connor downstairs for his tea, asking Laura how her day had gone in the full knowledge that neither one of them cared to discuss it - she hadn't, she realised, uttered a single word since making her excuses and all but sprinting out of Miranda's summer house, and thereafter her cottage: power-walking back home through the village so quickly the balls of her feet began to burn, and spending all afternoon replaying what she'd seen in her head, over and over, in a futile effort to make the pieces fit, to make what she seen make some kind, or *any* kind of sense. And so, when finally she *could* speak, *could* say the things that needed to be said, the things she couldn't *not* say - the speaking itself proved unexpectedly difficult.

"I'm sorry, *what*?" Laura said, when Jodie's first effort at exposition had stalled, the reservoir of language she'd been storing up since late that morning drying to dust on her tongue. "*What* happened at Miranda's?"

She tried again.

"There was... skin." She faltered, doing what she could to rearrange the description into something coherent - something Laura would understand, would find plausible. "She's been building this *thing*, this sculpture out in her garden - a sort of tree, but made of bones, and wrapped in this... skin, I suppose you'd call it. Synthetic skin. Or I *thought* it was synthetic." She paused for breath - saw Laura watching her with the kind of incredulity she knew full well was apt to tip all the way over into irritation, if she didn't get quickly to the point, and pressed on. "There was something *on* the skin, stuck to a bit of the tree. A tattoo. Rick Fielding's tattoo - that big one he's got on his biceps. That Japanese one, you know, with the wave? The one you always see on posters?"

Laura's eyes narrowed, the rounded tip of her nose twitching the way it tended to when she heard something she couldn't quite believe she was hearing.

"Okay," she said, her voice edging into the lawyerly *please note that I'm remaining perfectly calm, even in the face of this immense provocation* tone Jodie found so endlessly infuriating. "Let me see if I have this straight. You're telling me that she showed you this sculpture, this tree, and you saw something drawn on it that looked like the Japanese print some man you barely know has tattooed on his arm?"

"Not just *some man*," Jodie protested. "Rick Fielding. You've *met* him - he's been over here before. Henry's dad, the one with the motorbikes."

"The one who looks like a bouncer?"

"Yes! Him."

"And you thought you saw a tattoo like the one *he's* got on this... *skin* your friend put on the tree-thing she's been making?"

There's no crime *here, Your Honour,* Jodie could almost hear her say. *No evidence. Case dismissed, surely?*

"It wasn't *like* it," she persisted. "It *was* it. And the skin... it was sort of like *Rick*'s skin, when you really looked at it. Sort of... freckly from being out in the sun, the way his was. His *is*."

Laura's face reconfigured itself into concern; into gentleness that might very easily become pity.

"Sweetheart, it's *skin*. How could you possibly know it was his? I couldn't pick *yours* out of a line-up. Tattoos like that... they're ten-a-penny. Every other white guy in Waitrose has an armful of Asian calligraphy. And that wave picture, it's on bloody everything. *I* had a poster of it up on my wall, when I was doing my undergrad."

Jodie was very tired, suddenly - the prospect of convincing Laura of the veracity of what she'd seen filling her with a sick, sad weariness that made her want to take to bed and stay there for hours, days, with the curtains drawn and the duvet over her head.

There was no point arguing; no point struggling to win Laura over, to *get* her to believe. She'd reached her conclusion already: that Jodie was neurotic, or confused, or delusional, or some combination of the three. Or worse still, that she'd made the whole thing up deliberately - concocted the tree and the tattoo-ink and the hanging mannequins, maybe even concocted Miranda herself, in some desperate housewife's bid for spousal attention.

"You're right," she said, because what other option was there? "Sorry. You're right. I must have just... I don't know. Been thinking about Rick too much, him running off."

It was no kind of explanation, really. But it was evidently the answer Laura had been hoping for.

"Are you getting enough sleep, do you think?" The concern she'd been wearing was still there, Jodie thought, but there was something else now too; an inquiring, analytical cast to her expression, as if Jodie were a problem it was incumbent on her to solve before either of them could move forward. "I know things have been tough lately, with the protests and that fucking vicar egging everyone on."

"I'm fine." She turned her head to the window, angling herself away from Laura. "Everything's fine."

"Okay." Laura wouldn't push it, Jodie thought; not now. It wasn't in her interests to push it, to bring whatever darkness Jodie might be battling into the light, if that darkness could be handled. If it could be *managed* – with minimal inconvenience for all involved, and especially for Laura. "But perhaps think about going to the doctor, if it keeps up?"

"If *what* keeps up?" Jodie said, more sharply than was helpful - her face still turned away from Laura's.

"This... anxiety, if that what it is. Worrying about this Fielding man and where he might have gone. Seeing things that aren't there."

And that was how Laura was going to reconcile it, Jodie realised; how she'd square away what she'd listened to, what Jodie had told her. She'd tell herself that Jodie was cracking up; that there was something wrong with her, something best addressed through medical intervention. Through tablets, perhaps, or talking therapy; through learning to reprogram her brain until it was once again the kind of brain disposed to see the world through a sunny, optimistic lens and not a grimy, paranoid fog.

"I will," Jodie said, boxing it up and packing it away, somewhere Laura wouldn't have to look at it or be reminded it was there. "I will."

5

"Has Henry heard anything from his dad?" Jodie asked Connor, as casually as she could muster.

She'd let a week pass without question or comment to her son on the matter of Rick Fielding's disappearance; had bitten her tongue, whenever the urge to quiz Connor had struck, the effort of it once again causing her an almost physical discomfort.

"That's weird," he said, stopping dead in the street. He looked up at her and frowned, his small dark brows knitting together in perplexity.

She stopped too, letting go of his hand.

"Weird?"

"Yeah." He bit his index finger, evidently deep in thought - a habit that was part her, and part Laura. "Did you talk to Freddie's gran?"

Freddie, she remembered - or *thought* she remembered - was another of the kids in Connor's class, though not his immediate friendship group: a squat, bespectacled blond child prone to tears and public meltdowns. His mother, if she *had* remembered correctly, was one of Tim Howard's regulars; an adult-sized version of her child not only physically but emotionally too, if her vociferous, spittle-flecked participation in the protests was any indication. An angry woman, Jodie had considered whenever their paths had crossed, and one looking for a reason - any reason - to get angrier still.

Of the boy's grandmother, however, she knew nothing at all.

"Freddie's *gran*? Why should I have talked to her?"

Connor's brows furrowed further.

"'Cause that's where Freddie's living, with his gran," he told her, as if it were the most obvious thing in the world. "Since his mum ran off with Henry's dad."

If she hadn't been so conscious of needing to modulate her expressions - her *reactions* - around her son, she might have gasped aloud. The implication in the statement, the suggestion Connor probably didn't even know he was making - it was so unlikely, so utterly far-fetched that it was near-on inconceivable. Because *yes*, they might have both been Christians, Rick Fielding and Freddie's mum; and yes, they might *both* have been affiliated with the same weird church, the same mad vicar. But that was where all similarities between them ended.

Rick Fielding... he was a peacock. A little bit vain, and a *lot* proud of himself and all he surveyed - from his inked-up, gym-worked body to his engine collection and the thriving freight business that funded it, the one he'd built himself from scratch. Whereas Freddie's mum, whatever her name was... she, at least from Jodie's perspective, very clearly *wasn't* vain, *wasn't* much invested in clothes or grooming or aesthetics. If anything, she was noticeably plain - from her plastic Rose West glasses to her tartan skirts that reached all the way down to the tops of her equally sensible brogues. Plain, and unlikely to be impressed by the fake-tan flash and new-money appetites of a man like Fielding - if he were even interested in impressing her to begin with.

The odds of the two of them becoming romantically involved, therefore - and *so* romantically involved they'd felt impelled to flee their lives and obligations and run away together - seemed, to her, so slim as to be negligible.

"How do you know that?" she asked Connor - not enquiring but demanding, cross-examining, the interrogatory edge to her voice unlike any she'd normally employ with her own son. He flinched, physically recoiling from her; his mouth trembled, and she worried briefly that he might burst into tears, right there on the pavement.

The contrition was immediate and overwhelming, and she reached for him, pulling him into her and pressing a penitent kiss to the top of his wind-ruffled head.

"I'm sorry, baby." She hugged him tighter. "That came out wrong."

He nuzzled her stomach; let himself be cuddled, the way he always had as a toddler but was less and less inclined towards these last few months.

"Everybody knows," he said, the answer half-muffled by the soft fleece of her jacket. "It's not a secret."

And of *course* it wasn't, a piece of gossip as juicy and salacious as that. What thing ever *was* a secret, really, at Hummingbird? *She* knew things she really shouldn't about the marriages and finances of half the parents, and it wasn't as if she was dropping by at theirs for playdates and coffee mornings.

Only at Miranda's, apparently.

The thought shook her, and she let go of Connor, releasing her grip on his back.

"Want to keep walking?" She studied his face, checking for lingering signs of distress, but found none. He bounced back quickly after an upset; always had.

He nodded, and they walked.

Just six protestors had it made to the gates that morning, she saw - a paucity that *should*, theoretically, have made their passage through and into the school proper more straightforward and less combative than usual.

The six, however, comprised not only Elspeth Palmer and a handful of other St. Stephen's diehards, but Tim Howard himself - his waxed jacket, high-buttoned black shirt and snow-white collar so tight and stiff they might have been painted on. He held aloft a small sign, blue ink on cream-coloured card - KIDS DO BEST WITH A MUM *AND* A DAD - but was otherwise silent, a small and unarguably satisfied smile playing across his handsome lips.

His acolytes by contrast were apoplectic, chanting and hollering and jostling the other parents as they crossed the imaginary picket line separating Hummingbird from the world outside - the parents forming reluctant human shields around their kids as they accompanied them inside.

Jodie put an arm around Connor's shoulders, drawing him back towards her and steering him through the gates and towards the entrance, her body a bulwark between him and the baying mob.

"I just think it's disgusting." A voice, from somewhere close to Howard: a woman's voice, emphatic in its judgement. Elspeth Palmer's. "Two women together, raising a child like that. Did they even stop to think what life'll be like for *him* when he gets older, with no father in the picture?"

Jodie wasn't comfortable with anger, for the most part; preferred to batten down the hatches emotionally, to ignore what couldn't be dealt with there and then. To *suffer in silence*, as Laura sometimes put it in the heat of an argument - not because silence was helpful or preferable, but because she couldn't bear confrontation, even when there was a chance that it would bring some resolution.

A week of doing nothing *but* ignore her feelings, though – and ignore her fears, especially – had left her frayed and ragged; had worn away the lining of the brakes she tended to put on her reactions before they could be read on her face or parsed from her words. And, hearing Elspeth speak, a part of her splintered, and the checks and balances she placed on herself fell away to nothing.

Very gently, she pushed Connor forward, urging him on to the entrance and into the school, away from her.

Spun on her heels, and took five steps forward, out through the gate.

"What did you say?" she said, locking eyes with Elspeth. "What the *fuck* did you say to me?"

Under the orange veneer of her makeup, Elspeth blanched - perhaps, Jodie thought later, because no-one had ever spoken to her quite like that before. Had ever had the temerity to challenge her directly.

"I *beg* your pardon?" she shot back, thin nostrils flaring in indignation.

"You fucking heard me." Jodie took another step towards her; the anger that had powered the initial outburst not dissipating – as it might have done, in more usual circumstances – but whittling to a point so scalpel-sharp she could have used it to draw blood from Elspeth's pansticked cheeks.

"Well... yes. I think we *all* heard you." Elspeth's jaw slackened, her pursed lips resolving into a smirk, and Jodie wanted, unexpectedly but very badly, to knock the straight, capped teeth out of her head and send them clattering to the floor. "But you were mistaken. I didn't say anything *to* you."

A small snigger erupted from the woman next to her – her sidekick, the short one with the pixie-cut and the sign commanding the reader to KEEP GOD IN OUR SCHOOLS.

Jodie snapped.

She'd never been in a fight before, never so much as *slapped* someone before, but she hurled herself at Elspeth anyway, catching the smug bitch square in the chest with the outspread palms of her hands and sending her flying backwards onto the pavement, where she landed – Jodie was gratified to see – on the bony cushion of her arse.

"You *cunt*," Elspeth snarled from the ground – to the great astonishment, Jodie noted, of several of her God-fearing posse, though not of the Reverend Howard himself.

"Language, Elspeth." Jodie strode forward another three steps until she was standing over Elspeth where she lay sprawled – her own legs apart and fists on her hips in an approximation of a wrestler's victory stance. "Not very Christian of you, is it, calling someone a name like that?"

Elspeth's eyes narrowed to slits – and before Jodie could process what was happening, had whirled around on her back like a turtle and grabbed Jodie's left leg with both arms, pulling and pushing until Jodie, too, was borne to the ground.

And then they really *were* wrestling: rolling and tumbling like Judo players, pawing at one another's clothes and avoiding one another's efforts at landing punches to the nose and kicks to the stomach, sweat beginning to bead on both their foreheads and a thick, foamy globule of spittle forming – wholly uncharacteristically – in the corner of Elspeth's mouth.

"I'll fucking *kill* you," she hissed as they rolled, quietly enough that only Jodie to hear.

She bucked her hips, dislodging Jodie from her pelvis – and, pressing her advantage, drove an elbow into the underside of Jodie's jaw, knocking the back of her head against the pavement and sending dull vibrations of pain pulsing though her skull.

Jodie braced herself for a second blow – but none came.

Instead Elspeth appeared to, for want of a better description, float away – her body drifting off Jodie's until she was, or so it seemed to Jodie from the supine position in which she was frozen, simply hanging in mid-air above her.

It took Jodie a moment to understand what had happened; to register Miranda standing directly behind Elspeth, her forearms locked in a vice grip around Elspeth's ribcage, dragging her away from Jodie.

"Leave now," Miranda said, addressing Tim Howard and the other protestors rather than Elspeth, "or I'm calling the police. On *all* of you, not just her."

She indicated Elspeth, limp as a rag doll in her arms - her heels dragging on the concrete and a dazed, uncomprehending aspect to her face that suggested *she'd* been the one just punched in the mouth, and not Jodie.

"And who do you think *you*...?" the pixie-haired woman started – then fell silent, her would-be rant broken off before it had even begun by a pacifying hand signal from the man beside her.

"It's alright, Matilda." The Reverend Howard brought a palm to rest on Matilda's shoulder. "We don't want any trouble."

He turned his attention to Miranda, their gazes meeting for a half-second – hers steely and uncompromising and his, at least to Jodie, tolerant and vaguely amused by the events unfolding around him. And there was something else there too, or so it seemed to Jodie: a recognition, on Miranda's part if not on Howard's.

Did they know each other? Had they met before – before Hummingbird, before the protests started?

Finally, Howard nodded, acquiescing.

"We'll go." His eyes dropped to Elspeth, still sagging against Miranda's breasts. "If you're able to walk, Elspeth?"

Miranda loosened her hold. Elspeth, in response, drew herself up to her full height – 5'2 in heels, almost a full head shorter than Miranda – and, collecting what remained of her dignity, staggered over to Howard, her face a sweat-stained mess of smeared lipstick, streaked mascara and incipient bruising.

He removed his jacket and draped it gently over her shoulders; she, in turn, took the elbow he offered her and, arm in arm, the two of them walked away from the gates, the other protestors following in their wake.

Miranda crouched down on the pavement next to Jodie; snaked a hand around Jodie's wrist and pulled her to her feet.

"Are you hurt?" she asked - nothing but worry in her voice. "Did she hurt you?"

"Not much. Little bit, maybe." Jodie rubbed at her jaw; felt the swelling already beginning to build there. Heard the hint of a slur in the words as she spoke.

"Right." Miranda hesitated, as if she were wary of making too sudden a movement, then closed the gap between them; slipped an arm – one of the arms, Jodie reminded herself, that had only a minute before held Elspeth Palmer in an apparently unbreakable grip – around Jodie's waist to steady her. "Come on. We need to get you cleaned up. I've got the car parked round the corner, so no arguments, okay? You're coming home with me."

And Jodie, all reservations momentarily forgotten, let herself be led away.

6

The compress was cool against her face: the ice cubes Miranda had wrapped inside the tea towel going some way towards soothing the throbbing ache that was beginning to build in her jawbone and the roots of her molars. She'd need to see a dentist, and probably soon.

"Can I get you some more painkillers?" Miranda asked, slipping a fresh glass of water onto the side table next to the bed. Jodie had lost track of exactly how long she'd been lying there, enveloped in soft blankets on the mattress in Miranda's spare room; somewhere between an hour and two was her best guess.

Miranda had been nothing but solicitous, caring even: bringing Jodie fluids and ibuprofen, making sure she was warm and comfortable. Had *looked after* her, in a way she hadn't been looked after by another adult since the few weeks immediately after Connor was born, when Laura had taken a month off work and the three of them had stayed home together, learning – step by tentative step – how to be a family.

Someone who cared like that, Jodie thought – she couldn't be capable of murder, of harming another person. Especially not harming them in the way she'd believed Rick Fielding had been harmed.

Which left only one option: that Laura had been right all along. And what Jodie had seen on the branch of that tree – what she *thought* she'd seen on the branch of that tree – had been nothing more sinister than a pen-and-ink drawing on papier-mâché or a splash of paint on flesh-like silicone.

"I'm fine, thanks," she said, pulling herself into a sitting position. She looked up at Miranda; saw only genuine concern in the fine lines of her otherwise smooth forehead, and felt a twinge of shame that mushroomed quickly into outright mortification.

How could she *possibly* have thought that of her? What kind of woman was *she*, to have leapt so readily to a conclusion like that?

"And you're *sure* she didn't hurt you too badly, that... woman?" Miranda's frown deepened. "When she hit you?"

"I'm good. Really." Jodie picked up the glass; took a long drink of the water. "Probably looks worse than it is."

Miranda sat carefully down on the bed next to her, and – uncharacteristically hesitant – placed the flat of her hand on Jodie's cheek; ran the pad of her thumb, with the tenderness of a lover, over the injured part of Jodie's jaw.

"I hate that she did that to you," she said, so quietly it was almost a whisper.

Scarcely aware of what she was doing, Jodie leaned into the touch; moaned, very softly, at the feel of Miranda's fingers against her skin and then, hearing the sound escape her, pulled abruptly away.

"I should go," she said, almost knocking Miranda to the carpet as she kicked her legs free of the blankets and stood up from the bed. The suddenness of the movement made her head pound and cranked the ache in her jaw up to a hammering pulse, but it didn't matter; *couldn't* matter. She had to leave;

had to get out of the bedroom, out of Miranda's cottage, before the situation between them escalated. Before she allowed herself to be touched again.

Miranda looked crushed; not shocked but devastated.

Jodie's heart sank. But she stepped away, regardless. Left the bedroom, left the cottage, and didn't look back.

7

Elspeth Palmer was reported missing by her husband, Dennis, the morning after she failed to return home from her Tuesday evening Pilates class in Chichester.

Her car, the canary yellow Lotus Elise Dennis had gifted her for her thirty-seventh birthday, was discovered burned to a cinder in a heavily wooded country lane two miles south of the village on Thursday of that week - though no trace of Elspeth herself was found inside or in the vicinity of the vehicle.

By the Saturday morning, at the behest of their Chief Superintendent - a personal friend of both Palmers - two startlingly young police officers from the local station had shown up on Jodie's doorstep, determined to make just a few, informal enquiries about the nature of her relationship with Mrs Palmer and any animosity there might have been between them.

"Are you honestly suggesting that my wife might have had something to do with Elspeth's disappearance?" Laura asked them - irked, Jodie thought, as much by the disruption of her weekend routine as by their calling Jodie's honour into question.

"We're not suggesting anything, Ms. Campbell," the smaller of the officers said, his box-fresh tactical vest rustling as he shifted position on the sofa. "We just want to understand what happened between your wife and Mrs Palmer before she went missing."

"Nothing happened," Jodie said quietly.

"But there was an altercation?" The other officer tilted his softly-buzzcut head quizzically towards her, in a way that was obviously intended to intimidate but created the impression instead of a timid rodent testing the air with its nose before making a beeline for the dustbin. "Outside your son's school last week?"

Instinctively, Jodie touched a hand to her still-bruised jawline; winced, although the swelling had receded, and with it the residual soreness.

"She's already *told* you there was," Laura interjected, before she could speak - ever the lawyer, even at 9am on a Saturday in her dressing gown and slippers. "And she's already *told* you how it happened. Wouldn't your time be better spent grilling that church crowd of Elspeth's? They're the ones harassing people in the street, outside a bloody *primary* school no less. And I imagine they'd be a lot more use to you than Jodie, if you're trying to work out who might have had it in for her."

"We'll be speaking with them too, Ms. Campbell. In due course."

Which was a lie, Jodie thought; a half-truth, anyway. They'd already talked to someone at St. Stephen's – they must have done, or how else would the police have known to talk to *her*? Who else but one of Tim Howard's congregation would have mentioned her fight with Elspeth at all?

She was largely monosyllabic for the remainder of their visit: answering only when spoken to directly, and letting Laura direct the conversation, cutting any potentially thorny lines of questioning off at the pass with the same rigour and deftness she might have applied to the defence of one of her paying clients.

Eventually the officers left, their frustration barely masked by a thin veneer of professional politeness.

"We need to get you a real brief," Laura said, when the men had manoeuvred their car out of the driveway in a hail of gravel and a flurry of blue and neon yellow. "In case they come back. These local plods, they're like a dog with a bone, especially when they think they're onto something. I should think one of those God-botherers picked up the phone to drop you in it the second they heard that bitch was missing. Them, or that friend of yours, Miranda. She was there too, wasn't she? When Elspeth Palmer took a swing at you?"

"What? Miranda? No. Absolutely not. She wouldn't."

An odd and wholly unanticipated sensation of protectiveness swept over Jodie at the suggestion – the very *possibility* that Miranda might ever do that, might ever conspire to hurt her that way.

Miranda, who'd come to her rescue when not one of the other parents at Hummingbird had bothered; Miranda, who'd looked after her, who'd literally tended her wounds.

Miranda, who would have kissed her, if Jodie had let it happen.

"Fine – if you say so." Laura studied her – half-sardonic and half-mystified. "I just meant, you barely know her. And while I'm inclined to agree that those fucking church people are the most likely candidates, I wouldn't *entirely* dismiss the possibility that it was her who passed your name along."

"No." Jodie was adamant, still. "Just... no."

Laura pulled the cord of her dressing gown tighter; took a slow, contemplative sip of the cooling tea in her hand.

"Just be careful," she said. "You barely know her. So just... be careful."

8

Jodie thought of very little but Miranda for the rest of Saturday: her kindness, the warmth of her smile, the timbre of her laugh. The handmade furniture that struck Jodie now both as deeply strange and as perfectly, idiosyncratically *her*.

She *shouldn't* go to see Miranda, she knew that; not after what had happened the last time. What had almost happened; what might, but for the faltering strength of Jodie's will, happen again, and more.

But *shouldn't* wasn't the same as *wouldn't*, and certainly not the same as *didn't want to*. It was with a sense of inevitability, therefore, that she set off for Miranda's cottage the following day, a few minutes after Laura had left for football practice with Connor – the Champagne fizz of excitement in her stomach counterbalanced by a leaden pre-emptive guilt at the moral crime she was already well on her way to committing.

Nobody came to the door at first, when she rang the bell. And then there, just as Jodie was ready to turn around and leave, was Miranda: wild hair pulled back from her face with an Alice band, a pair of gardening gloves over her hands and a brown leather apron-bib covering the remainder of her long, lean body.

"You're here," she said, slightly breathlessly – as if she couldn't quite believe it, despite the evidence of her eyes. "You came back."

"I'm sorry." Jodie gestured to the gloves, the apron. "You're busy. I can come back."

"No." Miranda shifted her weight from one foot to the other; nervously, perhaps. "Don't go. Please."

"I don't want to disturb you, not when you're working."

"You're not disturbing me. Not at all."

Invite me in, Jodie thought. Invite me in, and let the chips fall where they may.

"Do you want to come through to the studio?" Miranda added instead. "See how it's shaping up?"

"The sculpture?"

Miranda nodded, and it occurred to Jodie for a second that maybe it was *Miranda* who was trying to play it safe; trying to stop them doing something they might both regret by restricting Jodie to the summer house, and not the cottage proper.

And maybe that was sensible, after all.

"I'd love to." Jodie nodded back – just that bit too quickly, too vigorously. And Miranda smiled.

They went around to the garden through the side-gate, avoiding the inside of the cottage.

"Did you get any more mannequins?" Jodie asked, as Miranda fiddled with the handle on the entrance to the summer house.

"Mannequins?" Miranda said, and pushed open the door.

The smell was overpowering. Not the blood-and-chlorine butcher's shop odour of Jodie's last visit, but something infinitely worse. The necrotic stink of a charnel house; the gut-churning foetor of a maggot-ridden animal bursting and liquefying in the midday heat.

It wasn't the first thing she noticed, though.

The tree sculpture itself looked, to her, much as it had the last time. Bone-branches still protruded from its artificial trunk; were still wrapped in skin, or something approximating the same. Thick loops of reddish-pink intestines still coiled *around* the branches – albeit more of them, and denser, than there'd been before. Eight figures hung there now; the original six, and two more besides, neither one hooded or masked.

She recognised both of the new additions.

Their bodies – their dead but undeniably *human* bodies – had been damaged beyond the point of identification: skin flayed from the flesh, neck to toe, and midsections eviscerated, the organs and gastrointestinal tracts of both removed wholesale from the emptied hollows of their stomach cavities. One had breasts and a vulva, or what remained of both below the skin, and the other the bloody, tubular remnants of a penis, framed by the jellied sac of what scrotal tissue had survived the removal of its epidermal layers.

One, the larger and more badly decomposed of the two, wore Rick Fielding's face, and the other the face of Freddie Tate's mother. The eyes of both had been scooped from their sockets; though Tate, she saw, still sported the wide-lensed, plastic-framed glasses she'd had in life.

And there was more.

In the left corner of the summer house, chained by the wrists to a hardwood plank laid horizontally across the treated glass wall, was Elspeth Palmer. Bruised and soiled, her hair matted with blood and designer clothes crusted in filth, but alive. Unequivocally alive.

9

so hoped you'd come back," Miranda said, from right behind her.

Slowly, the better part of her surprised that shock hadn't rooted her to the spot, Jodie turned around.

The gardening gloves were there, just as they'd been before, and the leather apron: a butcher's apron, Jodie understood now. There was a cleaver in Miranda's hand: stainless-steel silver, the sharpest points of the blade caked in something Jodie couldn't quite convince herself was rust.

She was smiling, still.

"What have you done?" Jodie sounded distant even to herself; her voice distorted, *submerged*, as if she were speaking from deep underwater. "What have you *done*, Miranda?"

But did she need to *ask*, really? The tableau spoke volumes – the picture it painted clear and vivid and utterly irrefutable.

In the corner, Elspeth groaned: a guttural, rattling keen that might have been a failed attempt at speech.

Miranda ignored it.

"We couldn't just let them carry *on* hurting us, could we?" she told Jodie, the question not really a question at all but a statement of fact. "And really, what did they expect? That they could come for us and come for us, and we'd never defend ourselves, never fight back? Never just stop and say, *enough*?"

Well... *yes*, Jodie thought – the reply bubbling up angrily, traitorously through the photic zone of horror and disbelief that overlaid it. *That was exactly what they expected, what they always expected: that they could shout and scream and beat us over the heads with their bile and their placards, and that we'd take it, that we'd* have *to take it. Because they were right and righteous, and we were wrong and wicked, and wickedness... it can't win, in the end. Can't ever be allowed to triumph over virtue. That isn't how the story goes.*

"You can't just... do this," she murmured. But it was weak, the weakest of protests – weaker by far than it ought to have been, given what she was seeing, the atrocity laid out for her consumption.

"But... it's *done* already." Miranda seemed puzzled; thrown off-course by Jodie's response to the scene. As if she'd been expecting a different reaction altogether. "*Almost* done, I suppose."

She turned her gaze briefly to Elspeth, in her chains, then looked away again, apparently disgusted by the sight of her.

"You can't keep her here." Jodie closed a little of the gap between them, despite the presence of the cleaver; finding, again to her surprise, that she wasn't the least bit afraid. Neither of Miranda, nor of what Miranda might do to her. "You have to let her go. Clean her up and let her go."

Whereupon, she thought, *she'll run straight home to her husband, who'll call the police. And the police will come here, straight away if Dennis Palmer's friend the Chief Superintendent has any say in the matter, and they'll see what I'm seeing, and you won't even have time to ask for a solicitor before they're leading you away in handcuffs. And Christ knows what'll happen to you once they've got you in the cells. What'll happen to your daughter, for that matter. Because who's going to look after Sunny, if you're doing life in Bronzefield?*

"I thought you knew." Miranda's words were small, forlorn, and Jodie felt a surge of remorse at having disappointed her, having caused her distress in spite of the damage Miranda had so obviously done, in spite of the blood still fresh on her hands. "Or... suspected, at least. That you'd figured it out. That you understood."

Jodie stared at her; saw nothing in her but a shadow of genuine grief. Self-recrimination, perhaps, for having misjudged Jodie; for having misread her so completely.

Except... *had* Miranda misread her?

The bodies, the body *parts*, the disfigurements... they were horrific. They appalled her; revolted her. But she couldn't say, hand on heart, that the deaths themselves – the murders, the purging of these two particular human beings from the wider community, from the world – were what troubled her, what turned her stomach to acid.

Rather, she considered, with growing awareness of – but diminishing concern for – what it might imply about her character or her ethical compass: it was the state of the bodies *in death* that revolted her. The look of them; the smell of them. The inescapable, all-permeating *rot* of them.

Because, after all: did two dead homophobes deserve her tears of mourning? Two dead homophobes who'd decried her and her family as abominations, day in and day out? Who'd have no qualms at all about taking her son – her *own child* – away from her, to better serve his moral welfare?

She turned, as Miranda had, to Elspeth Palmer. Saw her bound and bloodied and weeping pathetically in her corner – and felt nothing. Not empathy, nor any desire to rush to her aid; not even a triumphant sense of satisfaction, of justice having been served.

Though, actually – that wasn't quite accurate, wasn't quite right. She *did* feel something; if not quite the something she might have anticipated she'd feel, on seeing another person shackled to a wall like a pig in a slaughterhouse.

Anger. The same hard, unyielding thing that had spurred her on to attack Elspeth at the school gates; that had catalysed her every buried resentment into a knife point sharp enough to cut with.

That told her now, with absolutely certainty, that whatever indignities Elspeth had suffered already, whatever price the woman had paid – it wasn't enough.

"Maybe I do," she said, under her breath.

"You do what?" Miranda asked – and in the question, Jodie thought, there was a kernel of something like hope.

"Understand." She reached out; placed a bare hand over Miranda's. Over the fingers that held the cleaver.

Miranda's eyes widened – in shock, or awe, or both.

"Here," Jodie told her, prising the cleaver from Miranda's fingers and letting her own fist tighten around the handle. "Let me."

PART II
UNDESERVING

1

The food was really very good, Tanya thought. You tended not to get much of a spread at these things – mostly nothing more appetising than a stack of too-moist egg and cress sandwiches, covered in clingfilm and washed down with a cup of weak orange squash and a handful of own-brand salt and vinegar crisps. But whoever was in charge of today's smorgasbord – and it was Elspeth, it *had* to be Elspeth – had really outdone themselves.

There was chicken satay, hummus and pitta; avocado on ciabatta topped with chilli paste; Mediterranean couscous salad with sun-dried tomatoes and feta, bookended by pink lemonade and wide-lipped jugs of sweet iced tea. *Organic* food; food from the better class of supermarket. Food announcing its procurer, loudly and clearly, as willing to go the extra mile – and shell out the extra twenty or thirty pounds – in pursuit of buffet perfection.

But that was Elspeth all over, wasn't it? Always happy to whip out one of her husband's credit cards to make herself look good. Especially if doing it made someone else look bad.

A scraping of chair legs and a muted round of throat-clearing drew Tanya's notice back to the circle: the loose Alcoholics Anonymous-style arrangement of seats Rick and Gavin had laid out in the centre of the hall, away from the draft of the fire escape.

"Everybody ready to get started?" Tim asked – shooting Tanya a look that suggested he *knew* her mind had wandered, and would forgive her for it this once, but would be grateful if she could focus *now*, please, on the matter in hand.

"Ready!" she answered, just that bit too vigorously. Elspeth glanced over at her; shook the solid blonde bouffant of her head at Tanya, sadly, and followed up the gesture with a sigh of disapproval.

Mortified, Tanya dropped her eyes momentarily to the parquet, feeling her neck and cheeks begin to redden and her glasses start to steam up from the embarrassment.

"Good," said Tim. He waited for Tanya to lift her head again, to look him straight on, then graced her with a flash of his straight-toothed, film-star smile – the one that had her wondering, whenever she caught sight of it, just how much money he'd spent at the orthodontist to achieve the effect. "Good."

He took a breath, drew back his shoulder in preparation to deliver what she was sure would be another of the sermons he so often favoured at these Exploring Avenues sessions – but didn't rise to his feet. Only shuffled his hindquarters onto the furthest edge of his uncomfortable plastic chair, cupped his chin in one hand and leaned further in towards the rest of the group, his body curling in on itself like a Rodin statue.

"I thought we'd open with some good news." The voice was mellifluous, as it always was – mellifluous and magnetic, at once sincere and self-aware, intimate and performative. A voice as comfortable preaching to a huddled throng at a revival meeting as to a little old lady in the cool of her sitting room. "Elspeth, did you want to fill us in on some of the progress we've made at Hummingbird?"

Elspeth beamed, revelling in the spotlight of his attention.

"Thanks, Tim." She was pleased with herself – though her obvious delight at having been picked out of the crowd quickly settled into something more serious, more *weighty* as she spoke. "And I'd say it's *great* news, actually. The protests outside the gates... I understand they've been a bit awkward, a bit uncomfortable, especially for some of us with kids still at the school. But they're *working*, they really are. Just yesterday I heard about another member of staff who's gone and got herself signed off with stress – Mrs Ballard, who does Year 5. Which makes four of them down now. And I appreciate that *sounds* bad – but actually, if you stop to think about it, it gives us a lot more leverage when it comes to negotiating with the Head about that filth they've been forcing on the little ones. Tara Blacklock's stubborn, and she's nailed her colours to the mast on this gay marriage business, but she's a pragmatist at heart, and she knows as well as we do she can't keep the school running without teachers. So that tells me that *we* need to *keep on doing* what we've been doing, until she's got no choice but to get rid of the whole PSHE program – just chuck it all out and start again, properly. We need to keep protesting, keep petitioning, keep talking to the papers. Keep making ourselves heard, basically."

She stopped, unnecessarily abruptly Tanya thought, and for a few seconds there was silence. Then:

"Well said, Elspeth," Rick chipped in, bringing his meaty pink hands together in ebullient applause. "Bloody well said."

Gavin and Matilda followed, their clapping only a little less enthusiastic than his, and in twos and threes the others did the same – their approval, tacit though Tanya knew it was, at least in some cases – swelling and echoing across the hall.

And Tanya clapped too, of course. There was really no means of avoiding it.

Only Tim demurred.

"It's great stuff," he said, running an index finger thoughtfully across his dog-collar. "Really great stuff. But also, if we pan out a bit, take a step back from what's right under our noses... what it shows us, I believe, is *how much more there is for us to do.*"

Elspeth frowned, the Botoxed immobility of her forehead only drawing the eye to the pig-like upturn of her nose.

"More, Tim?" She sounded altogether more girlish now than she had even a minute earlier – more ingratiating. Just listening to her turned Tanya's stomach. "How so?"

Tim didn't look directly at her when he answered, Tanya noticed. Instead, he leaned in closer still to the rest of them, his gaze unfixed but contemplative: a cowboy in a Western gearing up to tell a tale around the campfire, one guaranteed to spellbind.

"I'm going to ask you a question," he said. "It's a question for all of you, and it's this: what is it you think we're doing here, at St. Stephen's? What's our mission, our end goal?"

"To witness." Gavin didn't miss a beat; seemed to have the answer already locked and loaded on the tip of his tongue. "To find the lost and bring them back to Christ."

"Hmm." Tim seemed to chew this over. "And if they're *not* lost?"

"What do you mean?" Gavin asked, confused.

"Exactly what I say. What if they're *not* lost? What if they know the truth of Christ, and they carry on sinning regardless?"

No one spoke.

"We talk," Tim said, slipping into what Tanya increasingly – though privately – conceived of as his Sermon On The Mount Mode, "as if everyone is deserving of God's grace, irrespective of their sins. But if someone sins, and sins, and sins, fully cognisant of the truth but refusing to pay it heed – isn't that person just spitting in His face? Isn't he, or she, essentially declaring themselves *undeserving* of His mercy, His forgiveness?"

Again, there was silence.

"Our job," he continued, "is to deliver those who can be saved into the arms of the Lord – and to intercede on behalf of those too young to know the difference between right and wrong. And it's a worthy job, a job we absolutely need to keep doing. But when we're confronted with *unrepentant* sinners, ones so proud of their sin that they insist on extolling the virtues *of* that sin to others... well then, surely, our responsibilities are rather different."

A low-level murmur of non-specific approval oscillated through the circle.

"All of you," he looked back and forth across the group, "have people like this in your lives – on the peripheries, and at the centre. Unworthy people. Undeserving people. And you tolerate them, accommodate them – *facilitate* them. I know, I *know*," he added. "They're your friends. Your family. People you've known for years, people you care about. But what does it say in Proverbs? *He who justifies the wicked and he who condemns the righteous, Both of them alike are an abomination to the Lord.* That's a pretty clear moral imperative to me. Justifying wickedness, it's a sin in itself. An *abomination*, no less."

Where, Tanya wondered, was he going with this? What *responsibilities* did he have in mind, exactly?

"What is it you're wanting us to do, Tim?" It was Rick who piped up again: Rick the bullish Alpha Male, Rick whose insistence on taking charge of every conversation and steering it his way usually grated on her nerves like salt on a paper cut but for which, right now, she was grateful, if only because a straightforward question would force Tim to make plain whatever point it was he was dancing around.

Tim breathed in through his nostrils and pinched the bridge of his nose: a pair of tics Tanya had noticed tended to manifest most when he was losing patience with an audience slower on the uptake than he'd like.

"To be blunt: outreach." Another deep breath; another pinch of the nose. "We're so proactive, so very proactive about *some* sin – the situation at Hummingbird, for example – but we need to be proactive closer to home.

We need to be talking to those sinners in our lives: those who've fallen by the wayside, and those who've chosen quite deliberately to spit in the face of God. We need to tell them, very clearly: there's a way back, if you want it. If you're willing to work for it, to make the right changes.

"But we also need to remind them that, if they *don't* want it, if they're *not* willing to put in that effort... well, then there are likely to be consequences. Very serious, very long-term consequences. Because, after all, *their portion will be in the lake that burns with fire and sulphur, which is the second death.*"

He reached into the inside pocket of his blazer and pulled out a folded piece of greyish, blue-lined paper, so strikingly institutional it could have been torn from the pages of a child's exercise book. Slowly, he unfolded it.

"The challenge I'd set to each of you," he said, "is this." He glanced down at the paper, and then back up again at his audience. "Make contact. These people, these *undeserving* people – extend a hand to them. Pick up the phone. Nip around to theirs for a coffee. *Talk* to them – *tell* them what it is they need to hear. Give them a chance, one *last* chance, to spare themselves."

"They're never easy, these chats. I'm very conscious of that. So... I put together a little script for all of you to follow, to guide the conversation. Just a few of the more salient points to cover, a few of the notes you'll want to hit. Shall I read them out to you?"

A chorus of nods and *yes*s greeted him in response, Tanya's included – mortified though she was at even the *prospect* of proselytising, a practice she associated more readily with the Seventh-Day Adventists and the Jehovah's Witnesses than with an Anglicanism that had never asked her, at least before Tim Howard had landed at St. Stephen's, to do anything more radical than organise a fun-run or whip up a Victoria sponge for a charity fête.

"Alright, then." Tim brought the paper closer to his face, his eyes scanning whatever he'd written there. "Here we go."

He spoke, of course he did. How could he *not* have spoken? She distinctly remembered, afterwards, that his lips had moved, that words had spilled from them, smooth and rhythmic, the way they did when he was holding forth in the pulpit. But what the hell those words *were*, she couldn't have said, not on pain of death.

She remembered the *sensation* of them, right enough: the feel of whatever he was saying washing over her, lulling her. Sending her spiralling down into a borderline-hypnotic state, though she'd never agreed with hypnotism as a practice; never let any stage magician trick her into clucking like a chicken on-stage, or tried to shift a few pounds under her own steam by putting herself into a trance at home.

But of the words themselves, there was nothing. Not a trace.

And then Tim was talking again – properly talking, in language that had meaning, sentences that *stuck* instead of ricocheting off her conscious mind with the unstoppable velocity of a rubber ball against a wall.

"That would be my suggestion, anyway," he was saying, tucking the little bit of paper back into his jacket pocket.

"Sounds good to me," Rick said, after a beat – speaking for the rest of them, too, if the follow-up round of head-nods was any indication. "Sounds *very* good to me."

He was blinking, Tanya saw; his eyelids twitching up and down, like he'd stared too long at the sun. Like he'd woken up from a midday nap he hadn't meant to take.

"Excellent stuff." Tim smiled; cracked his knuckles and rubbed his hands together, a man steeling himself to do some heavy lifting. "They're just words, I know. But you'd be surprised how effective even words can be, if you say them with conviction."

For you, maybe, she thought. *I couldn't even tell you what they* were*, so how you expect me to be able to regurgitate them at will...*

In the end, though, as it happened, that was no kind of problem at all.

2

Tanya was making tea for Freddie – sausage, oven chips and beans, two thick slices of bread and butter on the side – when the urge to ring Kenny struck her.

It came more than a little out of the blue; they hadn't spoken in months. The last time, as far as she recalled, had been at Christmas, when she and Freddie had gone for Boxing Day lunch at her mother's in Arundel and Kenny had been there at the table, one hand wrapped around the stem of a glass of Australian Chardonnay and the other resting, defiantly, on the kilted knee of his equally Australian partner: a dark-eyed, cropped-haired fashion designer named Tomasz whom Kenny had met, her mother had confided in Tanya later, on a trip to Melbourne that Easter.

It had been a somewhat awkward encounter: Kenny's desire to show off his younger and to Tanya's mind far more attractive trophy boyfriend crashing up against her need to shield Freddie from the kind of spectacle she'd rather he not be exposed to, at his age. And that was what it always was with Kenny, what it always *had* been, ever since they were kids: spectacle.

Then again, they were all like that, weren't they, men like him? Always wanting to make a scene, to shove things in your face.

Her mother had played the peacemaker, steering them all towards more benign topics: the weather, the new slow cooker she'd just bought herself, the power cuts they'd been having in the next village over. But things had stayed tense, regardless. And when it finally dawned on Tanya that Kenny had no interest in leaving early (in *letting her win*, as he'd probably have put it), she'd made her excuses, pulled Freddie away from his second helping of yule log and driven the pair of them back home.

Why she'd feel so suddenly – so *undeniably* – compelled to call him now, therefore, was a bit of a mystery.

She'd decided more or less from the moment she'd left the meeting at the church hall the night before that she'd be ignoring Tim's insistence they *reach out* to people they knew to spread the word. (Or was it The Word? She was never sure). She'd been happy to get involved in the protests at Hummingbird, if it meant throwing a spanner in the works for that headmistress and her determination to foist God only knew *what* sickness on Freddie and the little ones in his year. But trying to *convert* people, like some sort of bloody street preacher? No; no, thank you. That wasn't Tanya's style.

So, it couldn't be *that*, could it, that had her so keen to give Kenny a bell?

Whatever the reason: once Freddie had finished up his dinner and was washing it down in front of the TV with an ice lolly he'd stolen from the freezer, she sloped up the stairs and into her bedroom, lay down on top of the bed and scrolled through the contacts on her phone – people from St. Stephen's, most of them – until she found Kenny's number.

He answered on the third ring, the sound of his greeting muffled by a cacophony of laughter in the background. *Bitchy* laughter, she thought; male, but bitchy. A gaggle of old queens, cackling uproariously over someone else's misfortune. Perhaps he'd told them already who he was speaking to, who was calling him: his dullard cousin out in the sticks, so dowdy she couldn't even stop her husband from leaving her for a girl from the office.

"Tanya?" he said, apparently surprised to hear from her. "Is everything okay? Is your mum alright?"

Fine, was what she intended to say. *Everything's fine.*

But she didn't.

She opened her mouth to speak, and something else came out instead, something other than the terse reassurance of her mother's health she'd intended to give.

They were sounds, not words: raw and guttural and rising up and through the phone line from somewhere lower and deeper than her throat. Like rusted cogwheels, grinding; like a blunted sword drawn slowly across sandpaper by a shaking hand.

And then a crack, opening and spreading across the surface of the world.

The noise came first: a hissing and a whispering, the impression of voices. *Judging* voices: ones privy to her every secret, her every hidden impulse and suppressed desire, though she couldn't have said how she knew that this was so. Voices parsing and unknotting even the longest-buried threads of her shame, then carefully evaluating each one until she was stripped bare, her dignity ablated.

Thereafter came the eyes, bulging and then bursting through the wallpaper like pustules through pox-afflicted skin. Eyes alien and disembodied: twelve of them or more, the size of footballs, their irises vertical slits of serpentine green, the pupils darting back and forth and up and down with the measured regularity of metronomes.

Then the smell, like woodsmoke and dung, so acrid she felt her eyes begin to water.

Finally, texture: the sheets and mattress underneath her turning from firm to soft and pulpy, yielding unpleasantly under the weight of her hands and body. She thought of spoiled fruit, rotting below the rind, then – worse

– of putrefying flesh, its organs liquefying in a rock-hard girdle of bone and blood-starved muscle.

She swallowed.

"Yes," said Kenny, from however many miles away. "Yes, I understand."

The call cut out, the blue-light screen of her phone fading to black, and the crack in the world began to heal: the voices lowering to silence, the eyes receding back into the walls, a sane solidity returning to the place below her fingertips.

Less than an hour later, though she wouldn't know it until morning, Kenny was dead.

3

Tanya was familiar with the story of the martyrdom of Saint Peter; had gleaned from it that it was at least possible, if not exactly straightforward, to be crucified upside-down.

She *hadn't* known, however, that it was possible to crucify *oneself* in a similar manner.

Nevertheless, according to her mother – left hysterical to the point of incoherence by the news – that was precisely what Kenny had done, almost immediately after he and Tomasz had said goodbye to the guests they'd had over for dinner the previous evening.

"It's called a saltire cross, Tomasz said," her mother had told her – embarrassment briefly overwhelming her grief and hysteria. "Like the sort you'd see in church, but in the shape of an X. Evidently he and Kenny kept it up in the loft for, you know... sex and things. You tie someone up to it, and, well..."

"Yes, I get the point," Tanya had interrupted, nose wrinkling and lips thinning in disgust. "You don't need to hammer it home."

But *hammering it home*, ironically, had been more or less exactly what Kenny had done, or what Tomasz had *said* he'd done, once he'd seen their visitors off in a cab. He'd waited for Tomasz to hop into the shower – then, when the coast was clear, had gone upstairs and locked himself in the attic with a toolbox.

He was a trained carpenter, Kenny, Tanya remembered; had known his way around a mallet. He'd even made the cross himself.

(*Of course* he had, Tanya had thought, as her mother related *that* little detail. It was hardly the sort of thing you'd go out and *buy*, was it? Not if you had even an ounce of pride left in you).

"There were... straps on it," her mother had continued, through her tears and mortification. "Leather things, you know? To... hold you up, and whatnot. He fastened his own feet so they were up the top, and his head and arms were hanging to the floor, and then he must've... must've..."

She'd broken down then, leaving Tanya to plug the gaps in the narrative. *Driven the nails through his ankles*, was what she'd meant to say, or so Tanya had deduced; crucified himself, just like Peter.

"That wasn't it, though," she'd added, once she'd pulled herself together. "That wasn't what..." She'd trailed off for a beat. "Once he'd nailed himself up there, he took the mallet and he... oh, God, Tan. It's horrible, so bloody horrible. I can't even stand to think about it..."

And she'd cried again, louder and harder; wept like child, like Freddie whenever he took a tumble and scraped his knees on the pavement.

Eventually, Tanya had managed to piece together the rest of what had happened, up there in Kenny's attic.

Nailing his feet to the cross – to his *parody* of a cross, she mentally corrected herself – hadn't been enough for Kenny. Once suspended from the wood, he'd taken the mallet – presumably still in his hand – and pounded it, over and over, into his own skull: the cumulative effect of the strikes wearing away first his sparse reddish hair, then the skin below it, and finally the skull structure itself, the hole he'd created leaving exposed both his brain and the cerebrospinal fluids that had, until that moment, cushioned it.

When Tomasz, panicked into action by Kenny's sudden vanishing and the cacophonous hammer-blows coming from the loft, had eventually picked the lock on the door, what he'd seen had caused him first to vomit, and then – or so Tanya's mother insisted – to faint: Kenny, dead and disfigured almost beyond recognition, blood dripping down the swollen trenches the nails had dug into his ankles and a pink-grey puddle of organic sap and brain matter pooling on the floorboards, inches from what had been left of his shredded head.

"Is that even possible?" Tanya had asked. "Can you even *do* that to yourself?"

"What the hell sort of thing to say is that?" her mother had snapped back. "He's *dead*, Tan. Have some respect, for God's sake."

So Tanya had quietened, though her doubts had remained.

The circumstances of Kenny's death might have raised more questions still, had any clear memory lingered of what she'd seen and heard and smelled in her bedroom the night before, when she'd last spoken to him. But none did. Rather her mind, ever resistant to phenomena it preferred not to understand, had guarded itself against attack by *blotting out* the hellscape with which she'd been fleetingly presented – the eyes, the rot, the whispering – until not a trace of it remained.

She'd rung Kenny; she remembered that much. But the brief discussion they'd had, as far as she was concerned, had been wholly benign: an exchange of pleasantries, cut short by Kenny's need to return to his dinner party and an insincere promise on his part that he'd return her call and they'd talk properly, just as soon as he had time.

"I can't think why he'd do a thing like that," her mother said, when she came around to see Freddie the next afternoon. She was still in shock, Tanya saw – her cup of milky tea shaking so violently in her hand that half of it had spilled out onto the saucer. "I know you can't ever *really* know what's going on in someone's head," she visibly flinched at the word, "but he wasn't even *depressed*, was he? Tomasz is sure he wasn't taking anything from the doctor – any medication, I mean. And he said he seemed fine all that night, Kenny did – talking and laughing, not a care in the world. It makes no sense to me, him doing what he did, no sense at all."

"And he's spoken to the police, has he, Tomasz?" Tanya hoped it came off casually; an honest enquiry and not an accusation, not a hint at the scenario she'd been mulling over that morning. Because how sure could anyone be, really, that it *was* suicide, that Kenny really *did* do it to himself? And if Tomasz was the only one in the house with him that night, didn't everyone only have it on Tomasz's say-so that things played out the way they did, up in that attic?

"Of course he bloody has!" Her mother slammed down the cup and saucer on the coffee table, and for a second Tanya worried both of them would shatter. "A scene like that, and you think they'd let him walk away without interviewing him? I love you, Tan, I do – but can you *hear* yourself?"

And Tanya had dropped the subject, again.

4

She'd have preferred not to go to the protest, the following morning: she was tired, and her back ached, and her mother's patience for looking after Freddie during the day was beginning to wane. But Elspeth, who seemed to have a sixth sense for these things, had turned up on her doorstep at 7.30 with a banner and a flask of hot Cappuccino, and had more or less frogmarched Tanya out to the car and onto the mile-long stretch of road that led from the house to Hummingbird.

Gavin was there at the gates, and Matilda and Daria and a smattering of the others. But not Rick, though Tanya distinctly remembered him saying he'd be coming.

"Where is he, do you know?" she asked Daria, once they'd moved into position: Elspeth and Matilda leading the chanting as the kids and their mums and dads started pouring in, all trying their best to avoid looking Elspeth in the face even as they brushed past her on their way to the double doors leading into the reception.

The lesbian was huddled in with them, Tanya noticed – that Connor boy's mum. *One* of his mums, she supposed, though even the thought of *that* arrangement left a bad taste in her mouth. What was her name again? *Jodie* something?

She didn't *look* much like a lesbian; Tanya would give her that. She *did* look troubled, though. Tired and anxious, like she could've done with a good night's sleep, and eyes darting hither and thither, as if she was scanning the crowd for a lost friend.

Ah, well, Tanya told herself. *Not my problem, is it?*

"Who, Rick?" Daria said, sounding peeved. "*No* idea. But I owe him a bit of a talking-to, when he shows his face. He was supposed to be picking me up this morning, and he never turned up. I had to get my Ian to drop me off on his way to work. And no Tim today either, I see," she added, lowering her voice, presumably so Elspeth wouldn't hear her complaining.

Gavin heard, though – his greying, velvet-cropped head swivelling towards them with whiplash speed at the mention of Tim's name.

He didn't look so great either, now Tanya stopped to consider him: his skin like ash, dark circles ringing his brown bushbaby eyes and his lips red-raw, like he'd been chewing on them. And fearful, too, she realised: not just exhausted, but *haunted*. A man who'd seen a ghost, then had that same ghost reach out for him with a putrefying hand, grab him by the throat and squeeze until he choked.

"What's wrong?" she almost asked him – but bit her tongue before the sounds took form. Whatever it was, he wouldn't want to share it within earshot of Elspeth. He was scared of her; even more so than the rest of them. The last thing he'd want would be her turning that unforgiving gaze of hers on him.

And Tanya... Tanya had always had a soft spot for Gavin. Always felt protective over him. There was something so vulnerable about him, so *lost*. It made her want to mother him, to pull him in for a cuddle, the way she did with Freddie.

Later, she thought. She'd talk to him later.

The last of the kids had gone in and Elspeth was leading the rest of the St. Stephen's lot away from Hummingbird on foot when she finally got him on his own – slowing her pace to fall into step with him behind the others as they headed back together for the usual post-protest debrief session at the coffee shop down Squire Lane.

"Something bothering you today?" she said, making sure to keep her own voice low. "You don't seem yourself."

He didn't answer at first. And when he *did*, he didn't look at her; just stared straight ahead, blankly, and down at the tarmac.

"That script Tim gave us to follow, the other night." A long pause. "Did you use it?"

Her stomach lurched, inexplicably; she felt the motion of her body slow, the air around her thicken to treacle.

"No," she told him, though that felt... not quite right, now she said it aloud. Not quite *true*. "No, I didn't. Did you?"

Another pause, even longer than the last. Then:

"Yeah. Yeah, I did."

"Oh? On who?"

It was blunt of her, asking him outright like that; she knew it was. But he was being so taciturn, so *unlike* himself, and she had a sense that going at it anything *but* head-on would be like getting blood out of a stone. Would likely make him clam up together.

"Did I ever tell you what I was like, before I came to God?" he said eventually. "What I used to be, how I used to live?"

He hadn't, not directly. But she'd heard anyway: bits and pieces of gossip she'd picked up from Elspeth and Matilda, whom Gavin had made the mistake of confiding in when he first joined St. Stephen's.

He'd been... well, he'd been *gay*, before. A flag-waving, card-carrying homosexual, out and proud. He'd even had a boyfriend, as she understood it, somewhere down in Brighton. And while she didn't know what *precisely* had happened to bring him into the church, to make him turn his back on that lifestyle – and had never felt comfortable enough to ask, in spite of her affection for him – she'd assumed that it was something serious, something dramatic: a death, or a loss, or a health scare. A brush with his own mortality, sufficiently significant to push him towards re-evaluating who he thought he was, and who – more importantly – he wanted to be.

"You didn't," she said, edging around the question. "Not exactly."

But you never needed to, because I knew anyway. That was the subtext; unspoken, but so clear to them both anyway that she might as well have added it aloud.

"Well, the person I called... it was someone from back then. *He* was someone from back then. A... friend."

The boyfriend, then, she guessed. Or *ex*-boyfriend, rather. The one Gavin had given up, when he'd made the change.

"Oh?" Was that casual enough? Was she giving herself away, more than she had already? "And what happened?"

As if she couldn't take a stab at *that* already. Because it was obvious, wasn't it?

Gavin had actually *listened* to what Tim had said, to the instructions Tim had given, and had taken it upon himself to *reach out* – and she still shuddered at the phrase – to the person he'd loved the most, the one he most desperately wanted to save from the fire.

And evidently, it hadn't gone well.

"You're going to think I'm mad," he said quietly. "That I've lost my mind."

"No." She risked touching his arm for a split-second; long enough, she hoped, to reassure him. "I never would, Gav. You know I never would."

For the first time, he turned to look at her.

"I shouldn't make promises, if I were you. *I'd* think I'd lost my mind, if I were listening to me talk. But I'll tell you, if you want to know. God knows, it's been killing me, keeping it in." He hesitated. "It's funny: I didn't think I even remembered what was *in* that script, after he'd read it out to everyone. It was like it just... fell out of my brain as soon as I heard it, you know what I mean?"

He'd intended the speech tag rhetorically, of course. But she *did* know; knew *exactly* what he meant. And that was odd, in itself. Wasn't it?

"But then, I got home that night," he continued, "and I sat down to have dinner, and as soon as I'd started eating I had this... urge to ring him. John, that is. My... friend. We don't really talk anymore, not since..." He trailed off; had to visibly gather himself before he pressed on. "Anyway. All of a sudden it was like I *needed* to call him, like I *had* to. So, I picked up the phone, and he answered, and then..."

She knew what Gavin was going to say before he said it: knew the scene he'd describe, the disorienting sensory input he'd relate. Because, she realised – or perhaps more accurately, she *remembered* – in that moment: she'd seen it all herself. Seen, and heard, and smelled it; felt the corruption of it under the palms of her hands.

"They were like eyeballs," he was telling her, his own eyes misting over at the recollection. "Just... floating there. Watching me, from all around the kitchen. And it was a bit like... like they were *judging* me. Weighing me up, you know? Like I'd been put on trial for something, and they were sat in the jury box trying to decide what sort of sentence I should get. But then John put the phone down on me, and they just... disappeared into the ether. I thought I must've dreamt them up."

That wasn't the end of it, though.

John, Gavin's friend – Gavin's *ex-partner*, more than likely – hadn't just finished up his own supper and gone to bed after the two of them had spoken.

Instead, as Gavin had learned from John's sister when – cognisant of how deeply her brother had cared for Gavin, despite their estrangement – she'd phoned to break the news, John had pulled on a jacket, hopped on his bike and cycled the three miles from his flat to the nearest petrol station.

There, he'd made what would have been, in other circumstances, several entirely ordinary purchases: two plastic fuel canisters, five litres apiece, and a box of matches.

On the forecourt of the garage, still armed with his credit card, he'd filled both canisters to the brim with diesel; left his bike on the rack where he'd chained it and, without so much as a glance up at the CCTV cameras mounted above the sliding doors, crossed the road that separated the petrol station from the unkempt, beer-and-condom-littered patch of grass directly opposite.

Sequestered on the grass, with scarcely a passing car in sight despite the relatively early hour, he'd fished the matches from his pocket and begun to strip: removing first his cycle helmet and jacket, then his t-shirt and jeans, and finally his underwear, his shoes and his socks. Cautiously, he'd unscrewed the cap of the first canister; raised it above his head, and emptied its liquid contents onto his naked body, dousing himself in petrol from scalp to heel before repeating the process with the second can until he'd saturated not only himself but the ground below him.

And then, apparently satisfied with what he'd done, he'd struck a match, touched it to his skin and let himself burn.

5

Tanya didn't trust the internet. She was half-convinced that Freddie's computer and the laptop they made her use for work – and her own mobile phone, for that matter – were spying on her; monitoring what she said and did and bought and searched for.

Nevertheless, her initial instinct when she came home from the café, after the most cursory of stays and no more than three sips of a bitter Americano, was to go online and look up... something.

Except, when it came to it: what exactly could she look for?

"Local suicides"? "Unusual deaths in the south-east"? Both were vague: too vague to get her any closer to an answer, to help her understand whether what had happened to Kenny and to Gavin's John – on the same night, after both had had the same uniquely unmemorable script recited at them by two people sharing, by all accounts, the same hallucination at around the same time – was an especially bizarre coincidence, or the beginnings of a pattern. The start of a phenomenon that might have affected, say, the friends and relatives of some of the other members of the St. Stephen's congregation.

And in any case: if they existed, these suicides, if there were any of them for her to find... who knew if they *would* be local, if they *would* be in the south-east? The St. Stephen's lot had friends and family all over the country, presumably; possibly all over the world.

What exactly, then, was it she was meant to search for? "Unusual deaths," full stop?

Her best bet, she supposed, would be to actually *ask* someone else from church if they'd had a similar experience; though how she'd construct *that* enquiry tactfully, God alone knew. *Evening, Matilda. Lovely to see you. Tell me, have any of your nearest and dearest taken a hammer to their own heads or set themselves on fire lately? After you had a chat with them, maybe?*

So, with Freddie still at her mother's and Elspeth and the gang still – with any luck – trading gossip over coffee and cake, she set off for St. Stephen's.

Tim wouldn't be there, or so she hoped; not that early in the day. When he wasn't at the school leading the protests, he was out all morning on his community visits: at the hospital, or the old people's home in Malham Edge, or the women's prison in Gilmortenden.

Lettie Pye, however, *would* be.

Lettie had no official role at the church, as far as Tanya knew; certainly no *paid* role. But she'd never married, had no children or close relatives to speak of, and since her retirement from the bank had spent much of her time, Monday to Saturday, serving as a kind of volunteer caretaker: cleaning and tidying the halls and the chapel, and cooking up vats of tomato soup and oxtail stew on a Friday for Rick to drive to Bournemouth and give out to the homeless.

She attended every meeting, every prayer group, every planning session. And, while her arthritis and the biting Autumn chill had thus far precluded her physical participation in the Hummingbird protests, she was certainly a passionate supporter of the cause – and, perhaps just as importantly, of Tim himself.

There was no doubt in Tanya's mind, therefore, that Lettie would have done what Tim asked – would have put in a call to someone she knew, to talk them through the error of their ways. And assuming she *had…* then maybe, *maybe*, she'd have a story to tell, too.

The parish hall was locked, Tanya found when she got there; chained and bolted, a padlock binding the external doors together. Which was unusual, but not unprecedented – especially not if Lettie's joints were playing up, and she was taking her time dusting around the pews and altar.

The church itself was open. Open, but empty; neither sight nor sound of Lettie or her vacuum cleaner anywhere.

It was faintly eerie, actually, it struck Tanya: the emptiness, the absence. But that was churches all over, wasn't it? Warm and lively when they were full of people singing and praying together, but uncomfortably close to sinister when they were nothing but stained glass and crosses on the walls and the echoes of old services, old masses and communions.

She walked up the aisle towards the pulpit, conscious of the echo of her every footstep on the marble tiles below, her breath coming quick and shallow as her pace increased.

"You spoke to Gavin."

She whipped around, hunting for the source of the phrase she couldn't quite believe she'd heard, for the *how* and the *where* of it.

The *who*, though, she knew perfectly well. There was no mistaking the contempt below the thin patina of friendliness in that voice, that sugar-coated sneer.

Elspeth.

She was in the pews, at the far end of one of the benches, back rigid as a measuring rule against the wood.

Had she been there the whole time, waiting for Tanya? And if she had: how had she managed to make it there from the cafe *before* Tanya? How had she even known that Tanya would go to St. Stephen's?

"You scared me," Tanya said, trying to summon up a smile – something, *anything* to plaster over just how scared she really *was*, how much seeing Elspeth there had shaken her.

Elspeth didn't return the smile.

She rose from the pew and, eyes trained on Tanya, slid out into the aisle.

"You spoke to Gavin," she repeated. "Earlier, on the way to Squire Lane. I heard you talking to him. Asking him questions."

There was something... not quite right about her, Tanya saw now. Not quite real, not quite *still*, though she wasn't moving.

She was... blurry; there wasn't any other word for it. All of her, her whole body – it was out of focus at the edges, as if Tanya was viewing her through a sliver of distorting glass or a pair of those 3D glasses you sometimes got at the cinema.

How, moreover – how in the name of *God* – had she managed to hear what Tanya had been saying to Gavin, and vice versa, when they were walking to the cafe? She'd been at least ten feet ahead of them, absorbed in a conversation of her own. And Tanya had been whispering, half the time.

"We were just catching up." Tanya took two steps of her own to the right, moving diagonally away from the place where Elspeth had positioned herself. "Having a chat."

"Don't lie to me, Tanya." Elspeth licked her lips – smearing waxy red lipstick around the corners of her mouth until she looked, to Tanya, like she'd just finished chewing on a bloody steak. And was there something wrong with her tongue, too? Was it longer than it ought to have been, than it had been before? "I know now, when you're lying to me."

The claim made no sense; not a whit. But Elspeth *believed* it, Tanya thought. She was absolutely certain of it; so certain that Tanya felt her forearms start to prickle and pimple, the sensation of Elspeth's eyes on her akin to the feel of an x-ray passing over her body.

"What does it matter to you what I was talking to Gavin about, anyway?" she said – going pre-emptively on the attack.

Now Elspeth smiled. And there *was* something wrong with her, something *very* wrong. Her skin wasn't just blurring, under her fancy leather jacket and Armani denim cut-offs: it was *rippling*, thick snake-like ropes of... *something* visible to Tanya immediately below the surface, as if Elspeth's slightly-built frame was struggling to contain them.

"You asked him about the words. Tim's words." She licked her lips a second time, more slowly, allowing more of that too-long tongue to show. It was bifurcated, Tanya saw; forked at the tip, like a lizard's. "And he told you something, didn't he? Told you a... story."

There are candlesticks on the altar, Tanya told herself. *Heavy, brass candlesticks. If she comes at you, charges you, you need to grab the nearest one you can find, lift it as high as you can over your head, and...*

"Pretty ungrateful of you, I'd say." Elspeth stepped forward – though really, Tanya thought with the bit of her brain still prepared to accept what she was seeing as fact, it was more of a *slither*, a reptilian shift of the spine and slip of the feet along the marble. "Tim lets you in on the secret, gives you a way to finally *do* something about sin, something real – actually *tells* you how to rip it out at the source, root and branch – and all you and Gavin are worried about is how *bad* it makes you feel, how *frightened* you are by what it showed you. By the *gift* Tim gave you."

Tanya sidled left, placing herself a few inches closer to the candlesticks; her legs acting almost of their own accord.

What was it that Elspeth was saying, then? That Tim's script was some sort of... holy weapon? A burning sword he'd got them using to cut down evil where it stood?

And if it was *that: what did that make what Tanya had seen and heard, what she'd* felt *in her bedroom the night she'd called Kenny? What Gavin had seen, too, when he'd rung up his ex? Some sort of... look behind the veil? A glimpse of heaven?*

It certainly hadn't *seemed* like that, to Tanya – or to Gavin, from what he'd said. Quite the opposite; the scene much nearer, the way she remembered it, to something out of Bruegel or Hieronymus Bosch.

Elspeth caught her movement; smiled wider, and mirrored it, gliding along like the corresponding piece to Tanya's on a chessboard.

Tanya saw *inside* her mouth, then. Not just her tongue, but her teeth. The neat, capped incisors - and beside them the fangs, sharp and pointed as a werewolf's.

"What's *happened* to you?" she said. Couldn't help herself.

Elspeth's head tilted to the side – her joints, Tanya noticed through the heat-haze of her terror, more flexible, more *mobile* than they should have been, than they *used* to be.

And she laughed – baring yet more of those teeth, of the thickening calcium leading up and into the jutting pink gums.

"*Happened*? Honestly, you say that as if all this is a *bad* thing." There was a definite sibilance to her words now; so much so that Tanya couldn't believe she hadn't picked up on it before. It was like listening to the hiss of a steaming kettle on the stove. "It's a *blessing*, what he did for me. A gift, really."

It was Tim, Tanya realised. Whatever it was that she was seeing, whatever Tanya was turning – had already *turned* – into... it was Tim's doing.

"What did he do?" she asked – quietly, so quietly, though Elspeth seemed to have no trouble at all understanding her.

"Nothing I didn't want him to. Just... how can I put it in a way you'll understand? *Deputised* me. So... I'm that bit more like he is. Not a *lot* like he is," she added, as if to stop Tanya leaping to an erroneous conclusion. "Only a little. Enough to make me more... effective, when I'm out doing His work."

Tanya spread an arm outwards and right, until her fingertips were very nearly touching the cold metal of one of the larger candlesticks.

Now, she thought. Get it now, and fast, before she gets her hands on you.

Because that was what Elspeth wanted, she was sure of that. To reach out and touch her; grab ahold of her, and do... who could say *what* once she had her. Change Tanya into something, maybe. *Turn* her, like a vampire spawning a sire with nothing but a bite to the throat.

"I'm leaving now," Tanya said – more as a distraction, as she took the base of the candlestick in one clenched fist, than because she genuinely believed the statement would do the trick. That Elspeth really would let her go without a fight.

Elspeth darted forward. Quickly: so quickly, there was no time for Tanya to strike out with the candlestick, let alone to use it to defend herself.

A whiff of musk and that same faint tang of smoke and ordure Tanya had registered the night she'd spoken to Kenny hit her as Elspeth's mouth opened and her body bore Tanya's to the ground.

And, at exactly the moment Elspeth drove those fangs into the gristle of her neck, that sound again: the grate and wheeze of cogwheels, grinding slowly together.

6

She stumbled out of St. Stephen's in a daze: not quite sure of where she was or of what had happened. Aware only of a throbbing pain radiating through her body, and a taste like vinegar on the roof of her mouth.

In the graveyard, she faltered, almost losing her balance before she could lower herself to rest on a moss-covered headstone.

Closed her eyes against the sun.

"Are you quite alright down there? Do you need help?"

She looked up. Saw a woman, tall and rangy, her hair an unnatural red and the upper half of her body sheathed in an odd black cape that made her look like she'd got lost on her way to a fox-hunt.

There was something familiar about her, too; something that made Tanya wonder if they'd met before somewhere. At the school, maybe?

"No," Tanya said. "No, I'm…"

Another dizzy spell came over her, and she lost her balance a second time, pitching forward towards the unmown grass. The woman caught her by the armpits, mid-fall.

"That settles it," she told Tanya, tugging gently at her arm until they were both upright again. "You can't stay here. I dread to *think* what might happen if you were to topple over again and hit your head. I'm only up the road – why don't we pop over to mine and get a cup of tea in you? See if that does you any good?"

Tanya blinked; choked back saliva and licked her lips with a tongue that felt too big and too heavy for her mouth.

Tea, she thought. Yes. A cup of tea, and I'll be right as rain.

"Thank you," she said, her weight still pressed against the woman's side.

The woman smiled – a kinder and altogether friendlier smile than Elspeth's had been, if only Tanya could have remembered it.

And together, arm in arm, they left the graveyard.

PART III

TIES

1

She was making coffee and toast for Laila when the post came: milk and sugar over filtered caramel grounds, butter and a brick-thick coat of lemon curd on three slices of a tiger loaf so undercooked it was indistinguishable from the bread it had been. And all of it exactly the way that Laila liked it.

It meant something, Tara thought, that she *wanted* to bring Laila breakfast in bed. That three years into their marriage, it still delighted Tara to wake her up like that; to slide the plate and the Kandinsky mug she knew was Laila's favourite onto the nightstand, drop the lightest of kisses to whatever expanse of skin was exposed on her neck and wait, patiently, for her to open her eyes.

Over a decade she'd been with Mark, eight of those with a ring on her finger. And not once, not *once* had she ever felt inclined to assemble toast and jam, or a bacon butty, or so much as a bowl of cereal for him at six forty-five in the morning for no other reason than to make him smile.

Probably, on reflection, that meant something, too.

Coffee brewed and toppings duly spread across the tiger bread, she crossed the hallway to retrieve the mail from below the letterbox where it had fallen. *Bulkier* mail, she saw immediately, than would ever normally have come through the door: a fat brown envelope, her name and address handwritten on its front, bookended by two of the flimsy grey utility bills she was more used to receiving.

Handwritten in black marker pen, she noticed: the wide-nibbed kind, not unlike the ones they used at school. The writing itself she didn't recognise – the letters bold, upper-case and so featureless they betrayed nothing at all of the identity of the writer.

And no postage mark or stamp on the envelope.

She picked it up from the mat, intrigued; carried it back to the kitchen with the duo of bills and laid all three on the island in the centre of the room, face up. Stared quizzically at it for it a second and then, impatient, tore it open.

There were photographs inside, a half-dozen of them: full-colour shots on heavy gloss paper, the scenarios each one captured blown up to A5 size, vivid and irrefutable.

Photographs of her. But not *just* her: her, and Laila.

Curiously, given the scene each photograph captured, it was the immediate environment she zeroed in on at first glance: the crisp white linen, sloping ceiling and rustic wooden beams of their room at The Estuary, the hotel they'd stayed at on the trip they took to Cornwall one half-term earlier that year. A lovely place, or so she'd thought at the time: quiet and relaxing, its clifftop location managing somehow to afford them both a panoramic view of Porthcurno Beach and the illusion of utter privacy, absolute seclusion.

And evidently it *was* an illusion. Because the photographs, taken without her knowledge, without her *consent*, in that same hotel room… they couldn't have been more invasive. Couldn't possibly have left her more exposed.

In the first two images, she was naked and bound, with Leila above and straddling her; bound, and gagged, and spread-eagled across that same white linen, her wrists and ankles tied with soft purple Shibari rope to the four posts of the sturdy oak bed they'd chosen for that very purpose, the bed that had been – as far and she and Leila were concerned – one of The Estuary's primary selling points.

In the third and fourth, their positions had shifted: Tara on her hands and knees on the bed, her face turned away from the camera – which must, she inferred from the angle of the shot, have been mounted somewhere high on the opposite wall – and Leila behind her, driving into her; the black dildo she wore secured to the curve of her hips by a polished leather harness.

The fifth and sixth showed Tara kneeling *in front* of Leila: the same black dildo now in her mouth, and Leila's delicate, long-fingered hands gripping the back of Tara's head to hold her in place.

Both of them lost in the moment; both of them oblivious to whatever concealed lens or hidden photographer was, right then, documenting every closed-eye moan of pleasure, every bead of sweat and tight, tensed muscle.

(But none of the *feeling*, she'd think later, when the initial shock had passed. None of the tenderness, the gentleness, the *aftercare*; none of the gossamer thread of respect that passed between them, of necessity, when they played out a scene. Only the facts of their bodies and of what those bodies had done in that particular time and place, presented stark and decontextualised. A few snatched lines of visual dialogue, chosen at random; not the bigger story of a marriage of which those lines formed part).

She opened the hand she'd clenched around the paper and let the photos flutter to the floor. Made it to the bathroom sink, just, before she vomited.

When she'd cleaned herself up and felt steady enough on her feet to walk again, she made her way back to the kitchen; scooped up the photos when she'd dropped them and slid them back into the envelope, where she wouldn't have to look at them.

And saw the note: a thinner slip of blue-tinged writing paper she must have dislodged from the envelope along with the pictures, smelling – or so it seemed to her – of steel and clay and citrus fruit. Then on it, the message, set down in the same tidy but anonymous block capitals that decorated the face of the envelope.

Like the envelope, it was addressed directly to her.

Ms Blacklock, it read,

I didn't take the photographs contained herein, nor did I instruct that they be taken, although I apologise for the distress that seeing them may cause you.

I know who <u>did</u> take them, however. And while I'm reluctant to deploy a word like blackmail in this instance, I believe I know what it is they want from you. What it is they aim to extort <u>from</u> you.

It's possible therefore that I may be able to help you. More specifically, that I may be able to help prevent them – that is, the photographs – from becoming public knowledge, and prevent in turn the reputational damage such exposure would likely inflict on you and your wife.

I'll be feeding the ducks on the western side of Wyevale Park this (Saturday) afternoon at 2pm, on the bench overlooking King Edmund's Lake.

Perhaps you'll join me there?

There was no signature: neither name, nor initial.

No way at all of knowing who'd sent it.

2

I t was something to do with Mark, Tara thought. It had to be.

Who else would want to hurt her like that?

She took a seat at the kitchen counter. Dry-swallowed the paracetamol she hoped would see off the tension headache beginning to build at her temples and thrust the envelope and its ticking time-bomb contents down into the pocket of her bathrobe – the small part of her now consumed with the *who* and the *why* of the photographs mentally scouring the house for a better hiding place.

The divorce had been difficult, protracted. Exactly as difficult and protracted, in fact, as she'd anticipated, when she'd finally told him she needed them to separate.

He hadn't understood, was the problem. Couldn't comprehend why, with no acrimony between them to speak of, she'd want out of a marriage that was, as far as he'd been concerned until that moment, entirely happy.

She'd been reluctant to tell him about Laila; about the thunderbolt succession of revelations – about herself, and her life, and the way she'd been living it – that had assailed her over the course of the day she and Laila had met, at an otherwise uneventful symposium on child development and pedagogy in Bloomsbury. But by his third protestation that *nothing was wrong*, that *things were fine*, her resolve had ruptured under the weight of his certainty, and the truth of it all had coming tumbling out of her, relentless as a rising tide.

He'd rung his solicitor that same afternoon. She'd been the one to move out, of course, and had spent that night, and many nights thereafter, at a Holiday Inn near Gatwick making plans of her own: where she'd live; how (and whether she even *ought*) to access any of their joint finances; when she'd be able to run back to the house to collect the few things she'd need to take with her.

They'd spoken only twice since then, both times over the phone: calls that Mark (she assumed against the advice of his lawyer) had instigated, and that he'd subsequently terminated, slamming down the landline receiver in both instances with a growled *fuck you* and a warning, paradoxically, to never contact him again, not even when she realised what a big mistake she'd made and was desperate for him to take her back.

He hated her, he'd said; she'd destroyed him, torn his heart right out of his chest, and he'd never forgive her, not for as long as he lived.

She'd taken him at his word.

A lot of time had passed since then. But he'd always been good at nursing a grudge, and she could well believe him capable of taking covert pictures and planting hidden cameras; of gathering a binder full of what he'd no doubt consider damning evidence of her moral unfitness to teach – let alone run a school – and passing that binder, anonymously, along to the board of trustees, the local council, even the press. It would be utterly illegal, of course – but she couldn't say for sure that would bother him. Especially if something had happened at his end to push him over the edge: a redundancy, say, or the breakdown of another relationship.

The bigger question was: if Mark had taken the photos, and was intending to use them against her... who sent her the letter? Who was offering to help her, and what could they possibly have to do with any of it?

§ § §

She didn't tell Laila where she was going, when she took off for the park after lunch. There was no sense in worrying her needlessly, not yet – not until she understood the lie of the land and what steps would need to be taken. Besides, Laila was working all weekend, locked away in the study pulling together the first hesitant draft of a consultation document for the Department for Education; she probably wouldn't notice Tara was gone, as long as Tara made it back home for dinner.

Wyevale was as busy as it ever was at weekends, its thickets and clearings crammed with cyclists and dog-walkers and young families out for a picnic in defiance of the cold. The west side of King Edmund's Lake was miraculously tranquil, though; quiet, but for the squawking of the ducks and geese and the flap and flutter of the swans.

Empty, but for the woman on the bench.

Tara caught sight of her in profile, at first: took in the sharp jawline and high-set cheekbones, the Roman nose and ruby-red hair, the hooded travelling cape that could have come straight out of a fairy tale about ravenous wolves and endangered grandmothers and little girls lost in the woods.

She wasn't someone Tara had met before. If there was one thing Tara could pride herself on, one attribute that had served her well in a school of nearly five hundred kids, it was a memory for faces.

So, who the hell *was* she?

Tara briefly considered the possibility that it was a coincidence, her being there. That the woman on the bench – feeding the ducks and geese with one hand, Tara saw as she looked closer, from a small plastic bag of birdseed dangling loosely from the other – really *was* just a stranger; a Saturday stroller who'd wandered unwittingly into the scene of a clandestine meeting that had nothing to do with her at all.

But then she turned her head a fraction, and then a fraction more, until she was looking straight at Tara, and Tara *knew*.

"Won't you sit down?" she said, patting the unoccupied section of bench beside her.

And, in the absence of other options, Tara sat.

3

 really am sorry for getting in touch that way," the woman said, before the backs of Tara's thighs had even grazed the bench. "It must have been so jarring for you, seeing... what I suppose you saw, when you opened that letter. I did *think* about calling, but I couldn't be sure you'd be ready to listen, if you hadn't *seen*."

She wasn't local; Tara knew that. To someone with a duller ear, someone blessed with senses less acute than Tara's, she might have sounded like a Londoner. A well-to-do Londoner, more Kensington and Chelsea than Bow Bells, but a Londoner just the same. One who travelled a lot, perhaps; whose accent had absorbed the flavours of the other, global-cosmopolitan cities she'd visited.

But Tara knew better.

The accent, whatever it was supposed to be, was feigned; an imitation, not the real deal. The sort of thing you might hear from a well-trained American actor making a bid for an Oscar in a Regency romance.

She smelled like the envelope she'd sent, like modelling clay and lemons, and below that, like nothing at all.

"Who took them?" Tara said, because she needed to know. Would drive herself mad hypothesising if she didn't ask, if the woman didn't tell.

"The pictures?" The woman dug her fingers into the plastic bag; pulled out another handful of birdseed and threw it towards the shoreline, scattering the ducks in a paroxysm of loose feathers and excitement. "Technically, no one, as far as I know. From the angle, I'd say you were looking at a hidden camera on a timer, something like that. Not a paparazzo hanging from the rafters with an SLR around his neck."

"And who *put* the camera there?" Tara could feel her temper fraying; feel the fury building behind her eyes, bubbling up through the crust of anxiety that had formed around her since the moment she'd picked the bloody envelope up off the mat that morning.

The woman swivelled abruptly around on the bench, squinting at Tara with deep-set green eyes that seemed, for just a second, to glow as red as her hair in the pinkish autumn sun.

"Who do you *think*?"

The reply, rhetorical as it was, was delivered so matter-of-factly that it brought Tara something like comfort. She'd been right, then: it *was* Mark, had *been* Mark. There were no other enemies out to put a target on her back, no nameless nemeses waiting to leap out at her from the shadows when she dropped her guard. Just him.

"What is it he wants?" she asked, the momentary relief morphing into exasperation at the very real prospect of having to engage with him, *deal* with him again. "I'll say this for Mark: he's got follow-through. When he tells you he's going to hurt you, he really bloody means it, doesn't he? It might take him a while, but he gets there in the end."

"Mark?" The red-green eyes narrowed, apparently thrown off course. "Who's Mark?"

Tara's stomach lurched at the implication: that it *wasn't* Mark, was nothing to do with him at all.

In which case: who the fuck *was* it? Who else could possibly feel so strongly about her, want to damage her so badly that they'd go to those kinds of lengths to get the job done?

"It wasn't him?" The words rose thick and soupy from her gullet, as if she was choking on them. "Then who?"

Now the woman really *was* puzzled, Tara thought. It was coming off her in waves.

"Howard," she said, like it was the obvious thing in the world. "Howard and the St. Stephen's people. Who else?"

That, Tara hadn't expected.

She'd never met Tim Howard personally; only seen photos of his perfectly symmetrical face when she'd looked him up online. But the protestors from St. Stephen's had been a thorn in her side for months: blocking the gates outside Hummingbird with their bodies and their placards, badgering the parents (and occasionally even some of the students) and driving half a dozen of her teachers to the GP's surgery with anxiety and depression and incipient panic disorders. That was *all* they'd been, though, a thorn: persistent and infuriating, an indefatigable generator of stress and the current bane of her professional life, but fundamentally toothless.

Not *harmless*: what they were doing, their obsession with gay sex and their ADAM AND EVE, NOT ADAM AND STEVE banners... it was infinitely damaging, it was. For community cohesion as much as for the mental health of her staff and the kids and their families. But not exactly dangerous, either – not, at least, in the immediate term.

Something like blackmail, something *illegal* – it just wasn't in their wheelhouse. They were too cautious, too middle-England. Too afraid of the consequences even low-level criminality might bring to their door.

Besides which: what would be the *point*, from their perspective? She'd made it clear to them enough times that it was the trust board and the governors, not just *her*, who decided on the curriculum, on what they did and didn't teach in sex and relationship education – although she had more than a suspicion that they hadn't really listened, that they were selectively deaf to any statement that didn't fit the narrative they'd constructed for themselves. Made it clear as she could manage over email; in the letters she'd had sent out to what felt like every adult with a school-aged child within a twenty-mile radius, and then again to Elspeth Palmer and Matilda Larson when they'd ambushed her one evening outside her own bloody house when she was taking out the rubbish.

(And thank God it had been her and not *Laila* they'd managed to corner, she'd thought at the time – Laila who, despite her job, had no patience for diplomacy, no interest in pacifying those whose behaviour she considered wilfully idiotic. Especially when they'd trespassed on her property at eight o'clock at night with the sole intention of harassing her wife).

"Don't be ridiculous," Tara said. "Tim Howard? He's a bloody vicar. He's a pain in my arse, they all are, but he's a man of the cloth. He must have *some* ethics."

"You don't know him." The woman's unplaceable voice went up an octave, suddenly. "He's not who you think he is. He doesn't abide by any rules but his own."

"Then who is he? Who is it I need to be worrying about? And what does he want with me?"

The woman jabbed her fingers back into the seed bag – more aggressively than before, Tara thought.

"I don't believe Howard was responsible *directly*." Another flick of the wrist; another scattering of maize and sunflower seeds. "He wouldn't lower himself to extortion, even in the service of a… larger end. It'll be one of his lackeys who arranged for the photos to be taken. Elspeth Palmer, if I had to guess."

"Her?"

Another surprise. Palmer was a gossip and a troublemaker, no question; a bored, entitled housewife with a moralistic streak and an appetite for the spotlight. Tara had known that long before she and Larson had rocked up at the house with their list of insane demands; before they'd refused to take no for an answer when Tara had told them, absolutely truthfully, that she was neither able nor especially inclined to meet with them. But a *blackmailer*? A blackmailer with the strategic vision – with the *dexterity* – to plant and then retrieve a hidden camera in a hotel room three hundred miles away?

"Her. And if *not* her, then one of the others – Larson, or Daria Morrison, or Gavin Ford. One of Howard's inner circle. Someone else he's infected."

A strange word for the woman to use about an idea, Tara thought – *infected*. She'd had it hurled at her before, in adjacent contexts: from religious zealots preoccupied with the spiritual corrosions precipitated by modernity; from diehard atheists inclined to frame faith as the cognitive equivalent of an STI; from the St. Stephen's protestors themselves, paranoid as they were about the dual contagions of an inclusive curriculum and a liberal-minded head circulating in Hummingbird's classrooms.

But a metaphor like that... it tended to go hand in hand with histrionics, in Tara's experience. With melodrama.

And this woman, with her Cold War espionage demeanour and her matter-of-fact delivery... she didn't seem the sort for moral panic or overstatement. She was too measured; too poised.

That's a pretty definitive assessment of someone you've known two minutes.

She could almost *hear* Laila's voice in her ear; could feel it nearly as acutely as she might, were they sitting opposite each other at the kitchen table. The phantom Laila, who interposed herself in Tara's thoughts as Tara went about her day – counterpart to the phantom Tara, who was given in turn to reminding the *actual* Laila to eat lunch and stretch her legs and get to bed before midnight when she was absorbed in a project.

I mean, who even is *this woman, anyway? What's she got to do with any of this? And what does she want with* you?

"What's your interest here?" Tara asked the woman. "You're right, I don't know much about Tim Howard, but it's not as if I know you either, is it? And I don't see why you'd be helping me out of the goodness of your heart."

"He ruins people." The hand stilled, halfway back to the seed bag, though the woman's face stayed as inscrutable as the Mona Lisa's. "He has a cause, a crusade – a holy war to wage. And he *believes* in it. What you might have seen from him or heard him say, it isn't posturing, the way it is with someone like Palmer. Sin, what he conceives of as sin – it's a very real thing to him. A physical thing. All he wants is to… strip it away."

"That isn't an answer."

"No, it isn't." With two deft twists of her fingers, the woman tied a knot in the bag and brought it to rest in her lap. "I have my own issues with Howard – my own… score to settle, you might say. He hurt me once, a great deal, for much the same reason he intends to hurt you – because he believes us both to be innately sinful. And while I wasn't in a position back then to help *myself*… I may be in a slightly better position to help you, now."

Tara didn't press the point. The woman was telling the truth, she was certain of it – the truth as she believed it, anyway. There'd been no chemical change in her as she'd given her explanation, no surge in catecholamines; none of the lactic acid or urea in the air around her that Tara had come to associate with the guilt and anxiety of a lie spilled under pressure. No: whoever the woman was, chances were she really did have a grudge, and she really was using Tara to work through it.

Which was fine by Tara. Self-interest was a lot more reliable a motivator than altruism.

"How do you know it was them, Elspeth Palmer and her friends?" Tara said, though she could have taken a stab at a response herself. If there was bad blood between the woman and Tim Howard, and the woman had been looking for an opportunity to get even for whatever he'd done to her, then it seemed to Tara reasonably likely that the woman had been following him. Keeping tabs on him, and by extension on his congregation, Palmer included. She might have seen them poring over the hard copies of the photographs they'd taken; handing them back and forth to one another in their church hall with the sort of breathless titillation they could pass off as scandalised outrage, if they had to.

Might even have seen them *taking* the photos – setting up their camera in the hotel room before they scarpered, if she'd been watching *really* closely.

"I just know. Much as I know what it is you'll have to do, if you don't want them to tear your life apart and leave your career in tatters. Which they will. They'll go to the school board with the pictures first, I would have thought – if only to give the appearance of propriety, to make it seem like they're committed to doing things through the proper channels. But they'll take them public eventually, especially if the board don't fall into line. Post them out to the tabloids. Have them leak onto the internet."

"And *what* will I *have to do*, in your opinion? Break into St. Stephen's and steal the photographs? Hack into their computer and delete the files?"

She'd intended it sarcastically; a tongue-in-cheek acknowledgement of the absurdity of a woman like her – a headmistress, a pillar of the bloody community – forcing the lock on a church door, rifling through filing cabinets, guessing at the password that would grant her access to the contents of a battered office desktop. But, the woman offered not so much of a hint of a smile in acknowledgement.

"Of course not," she replied, briskly business-like. "Who's to say how many copies of the images they've made, or where they're storing them? No, you'll have to kill them – Palmer and Larson and the rest, if not Howard himself. It's the only way to stop them speaking out. I appreciate it's been a while since you did that sort of thing – decades, perhaps. But really – does one ever lose the knack?"

4

The takeaway Laila had ordered for a lunch so late it might as well have been dinner was waiting for Tara when she got back to the house, still boxed and steaming on the countertop: half its contents eaten, and the remainder left for her to polish off in front of the television while Laila chipped away at her report.

It was pizza, because it was always pizza. Laila avoided Indian on ideological grounds ("I'm not paying thirty quid for something my mother could have cooked, and better"), and suspected the owner of the Chinese restaurant in Battle Hill of harbouring misogynistic inclinations, so tended to default to Italian when the need for food delivery arose.

Tara liked pizza, as a rule. But not here, not now; not with her mouth dry and her stomach curled in on itself as tightly as a clenched fist.

How had she *known*? The woman, whoever she was – how had she known about Tara, about who Tara had been before Laila and Mark and Hummingbird? Before she'd gotten out, made the change?

She hadn't answered, when Tara had asked her; just tucked the – by then nearly empty – bag of birdseed back into the folds of that ridiculous cape and walked away from the bench, from Tara. It would have been infuriating, had Tara's thoughts not been entirely elsewhere.

"Everything alright?" Laila shouted from the office; her voice, usually so soothing, ricocheting along Tara's newly resensitized nerve endings like a bullet through an echo chamber.

"All good," she replied, through force of habit. Then: "Think I'm going to head out for a walk in a bit. Might be a while, is that okay?"

§ § §

Clearing her head, she told herself. That was all she was doing: clearing her head.

No matter that she'd driven herself – on autopilot, certainly not consciously – to Hummingbird. No matter that she'd left the Range Rover in the car park and the keys in the ignition; that her feet had carried her, of their own accord, in the direction of the Georgian townhouse Elspeth Palmer shared, Tara happened to know, with her husband and her son Felix and a pair of French bulldogs so selectively bred they could barely draw breath.

She was clearing her head. Walking, and clearing her head.

The lights were on and the blinds open in every room of the Palmer house visible from across the street – the kitchen, the lounge and an open-plan, wood-panelled space between the two that Tara took, from the Steinway and the drum kit in the corner, to be the music room; even from a distance of thirty feet she could see inside, as clearly as if she'd had her nose pressed up against the window panes.

It was comforting, in a way, to know *that* hadn't faded with time: the acuity. That her vision was as sharp as it had ever been, even in the dark.

Especially in the dark.

The rooms were empty, or they seemed to be. But there were people in the house; she could sense it, feel the top notes and heart notes and base notes of them calling out to her through the glass and limestone. Two people: a woman, all oud and heavy spice and hair spray polymers, and a man, or something almost like a man, like rust and burning wood and animal decay overlaid with something more recognisable, a well-scrubbed interplay of shaving foam and laundered linen.

Elspeth, then.

And, following after her as she entered the music room, to Tara's surprise: Tim Howard himself.

He *looked* human – human and innocuous, with his blandly handsome face and neat lapels. If she hadn't smelled him first, she might well have assumed that he was.

"Can I get you a drink?" she heard Elspeth ask him, her back still turned to him – the tinny traces of her nasal voice penetrating the brickwork as readily as her scent. "Something to eat?"

He didn't respond; appeared not to have heard her, or to have been so disinterested in anything she had to say that not a syllable had registered.

Something was going on with him, though; with his shape. Something, like the smell of him, that was to Tara both alien and familiar.

He was changing; that was it. Re-forming the contours of his body even as he moved himself further into the centre of the room and closer to Elspeth: muscle fibres twisting and expanding and reshaping in his face and neck and hands and under the heavy cottons of his shirt and blazer, threatening to tear both skin and fabric to ribbons as they swelled.

Changing into *what*, Tara couldn't guess; would have to wait and see. But, the change itself, the process of it – that she knew, and all too well. Watching him, she felt her own muscles twitch and shift in a kind of sympathy; felt her nose and upper lip stretch and lengthen into the beginnings of a muzzle, her back teeth tapering to carnassials, her pores dilate to accommodate the coarsening hair that sprang from them.

A quick, sharp shriek rose abruptly from her throat; she bit it back, just in time, clamping the thickened pad of one hand across her mouth to stifle any more that might come after.

No; no. She wouldn't let it happen: not here, not now. She'd worked too hard to keep things in check, to avoid the triggers that might send her spiralling. Make her lose control.

She dug the unfurling claws of the other hand into its corresponding paw until the blood came, the seductive richness of it insinuating itself into her nostrils, swirling and tightening around her organs like sentient smoke until her stomach howled, audible enough to startle anyone in earshot.

"I never understood why you fought it."

The change was still on her as she turned around – her bones and tissues caught between two states, auburn fur warring with olive skin and claws extending from her knuckles.

He took her in, but none of it fazed him. In fact, he smiled.

He'd not aged, not where it showed. His black hair was as dense and wiry as ever, betraying not so much as a hint of grey; his sun-weathered skin no more lined or pouched than it had been since she'd seen him last, decades earlier. The thick, unruly eyebrows perennially arched above his wide-set eyes gave him a feral, predatory look; and though she couldn't see his teeth, behind the close-lipped smile, she knew they'd be – still – every bit as sharp as her own.

Her instinct was to ask him what he wanted, what he was doing there – whether he'd been following her, how long he'd been following her *for*. The questions were redundant, though, every one of them. Because she knew. Just as she'd known, from the second she'd sensed him behind her, that it wasn't Tim Howard – whatever else he'd done, whatever else he *was* – who'd taken the photographs of her and Laila, nor any of Howard's acolytes at the church.

Though she could well believe that Howard, too – or perhaps Elspeth Palmer – had received a thick brown envelope through the post, much like the one that had fallen through her letterbox that morning. And that whichever of them had opened it had danced for joy, on seeing its contents.

"Blackmail, Jimmy?" she said, feeling the muzzle contract and the fur on her face soften back to a middle-aged woman's peach down, until she was very nearly herself again. "Bit sophisticated for you, isn't it?"

"Who's blackmailing?" he replied, with the same infuriating nonchalance he used, way back when, to signal how absurd he found her, how ridiculous and *overwrought* he thought she was being. "You think I'm after your money?"

He'd taken the same tone with her the day he'd knocked on the door of her caravan to tell her they were getting married, the two of them: that he'd squared it with her father and her uncle, got all the right permissions, and they'd be having the wedding in December. Treated her to that same smile, too; the one that told her he was in charge, he was handling the things that needed to be handled, and that she'd only embarrass herself if she challenged him. If she did anything other than roll over.

"Then what?" She wouldn't defer to him now, no matter what dirt he thought he had on her; wouldn't give him the satisfaction. "What *do* you want?"

He tilted his head, quizzical, as if surprised she even felt the need to ask.

"To bring you back with me," he said. "What else?"

5

She was going to tell Laila – tell her everything. Or almost everything.

It wasn't a conscious decision on Tara's part; didn't even really feel like a choice. But, despite this one – and, she was forced to concede, rather glaring – exception, she and Laila didn't *do* secrets, didn't lie to each other or swallow their feelings or keep under wraps any genuinely salient details of their lives, past *or* present. It was the biggest of the promises they'd made, the day they married: not inside the Town Hall in Marylebone in front of the registrar and two of Laila's sisters, but earlier that morning in bed, when they'd looked over at one another and confirmed that *yes*, they wanted to do this, couldn't imagine *not* doing this.

Tara had done enough hiding with Mark, Laila had told her. Ten years of hiding and evading, of bundling the better part of herself away in a lockbox with no key. It was time to stop all that now. If she wanted to.

And Tara had agreed she did.

Quite *how* to tell Laila was another matter altogether, a problem with no clear solution. There were no roadmaps for discussions like the one she knew they'd need to have, no step-by-step guides or user manuals to memorise. And no right moment – because when would ever *be* the right moment for Laila to hear what Tara had to say?

It struck her, as she drove back to the house, that it might be wise to wait; to hold off speaking to her until the morning, when they'd have the whole of Sunday to sit with what Tara had said, what Laila had heard. But then Laila was *there* in the hallway, waiting for her as she walked through the door, and Tara couldn't stop herself from talking, from letting the whole of the thing pour out before they'd even made it through to the kitchen.

"I need to tell you something," she said. "About my family. My parents."

"Your parents?" The statement caught Laila off-guard, which was perhaps no surprise at all. As far as she was concerned, Tara's parents were dead. Were *long* dead: the specific circumstances of their passing a still-raw nerve that Tara had requested – tacitly, never aloud – that Laila refrain from inflaming with questions.

There were other relatives, of course; there was no way to avoid admitting *their* existence, even if Tara had been an only child. But they were estranged, Tara had said; had peeled away from her in the aftermath of her divorce, the life-choices they perceived she'd made sitting uncomfortably at odds with the view they took of the world, of men and women and the ways they ought – and ought not – to behave with one another.

This, Laila had taken at face value; had moved on, without pressing her for details. She'd lost family of her own that way; had a network of friends and colleagues and acquaintances for whom the same was true. It was an old, old story.

"They're alive." Tara let her body drop into a chair. "And they've come to get me. They've *sent* someone to get me."

"To *get* you?" Laila shook her head – not in denial of what she was hearing exactly, or so Tara imagined, but to clear the jumble of her thoughts, to reshuffle the composite pieces into clean coherence. "What does that even mean?"

"We don't leave." It was a strange place to begin, without the necessary context that might lend it that bit more sense. But she started there anyway, and hoped the rest – the *really* unbelievable parts, the parts no amount of context or exegesis could make explicable – would follow. "Where I come from, the *folk* I come from – we don't leave. We aren't allowed to leave; it isn't something that happens. And I *did* leave, a long time ago, and I thought it was done, but I suppose I was wrong, because now Jimmy's here to take me home with him, to *drag* me home with him, by hook or by crook… and saying no, it isn't an option."

§ § §

Gypsies, people would call them, when they rocked up to another town, another village with their horses and their caravans. *Gyppos. Pikies.*

The inaccuracy of the slurs amused them. There wasn't an ounce of Romani blood in any one of them, nor so much as a drop of Irish. They were… something else.

Among the other things they were, they were performers: acrobats and aerialists, jugglers and tightrope-walkers, their somersaults and tumbles and twists and dives as fluid as Leotard's and as bold as Blondin's. They stayed in each town, each village no longer than a fortnight, playing two shows a night out of a single big-top marquee pitched in whichever park or patch of waste ground would accommodate them: the younger ones selling tickets to the locals from the back of a wagon, advertising that evening's entertainments by way of a megaphone or a pair of small hands cupped around a bellowing mouth.

Tara's parents were fire-dancers, as their own parents had been before their retirement from the ring; Tara, it was assumed, would gravitate to fire-dancing herself as soon as she came of age. Just as it was assumed that, when the time was right, she'd pair off with a suitable boy from within the community, the son of a stilt walker or a rope climber, and produce thereafter sufficient offspring to perpetuate the bloodline.

It was always blood, with her people; blood, and purity, and what she'd come to think of later as *endogamy*, but which then she thought of only as *what you did* and *what you had to do*.

Your duty. The obligations there was nothing to do but fulfil.

The suitable boy, in the end, had turned out to be less a boy than a full-grown man, one of the ones who tended the horses and put up the tent and set to any carpentry work that needed doing, in and out of the caravans.

Jimmy.

She'd been sixteen, the day he came knocking to break the news; a young sixteen, in many ways, but old enough to realise Jimmy – wild-eyed Jimmy with his wrists like knotted ropes and a snarl in his smile – was the last thing she wanted in a husband, in a mate for life.

She'd argued the case against the match, with her dad and her mum and her uncle Aric. But they'd held firm.

Jimmy was strong, they said. Powerful, and vicious too, when he had to be. He'd defend her to the death, and all of them besides. And the children he'd give Tara – the sons – would be just as strong, just as cut-throat. Just as capable of seeing off threats to the family, to the pack.

A Möbius strip of a future with Jimmy and their notional progeny had unwound itself before her, suffocatingly infinite, and she'd known: she couldn't do it. Couldn't live, if what she'd been offered were the choices.

So, she ran.

§ § §

"I had no idea what I was doing," she told Laila, picking at the skin around her fingernails. Laila's face was entirely still, in disbelief or dawning horror or something of both; her eyes burning into Tara's with an intensity Tara found a little frightening. "I didn't know anyone outside the community. I had no friends, no network. No education."

"No *education*?" Now there was a note of anger in Laila's voice, a flush of outrage rising in her cheeks. "Sixteen years old, and you weren't in school?"

Nobody was, my love, back then, Tara thought, *unless you were very rich or very clever. And our way of living hardly lent itself to sitting the eleven-plus.*

"It wasn't considered a priority for us. Boys *or* girls," she continued, before Laila leapt to any conclusions. "Gender didn't come into it. We just… weren't a going-to-school kind of people. The feeling was that we'd pick up what we needed on the road."

And in the graveyards and the alleyways at night. In the clearings, with blood hanging thick in the air and the taste of meat between our teeth.

Laila closed her eyes and breathed in deeply through her nostrils: absorbing the words, the implications. Building the bare bones of a timeline in her head and steeling herself for the pieces that would flesh it out to fullness before – ever the analyst – she decided on which position to take, which emotion to lead in with.

"Where did you go?"

Deeper into the woods, at first, and on four legs rather than two. Not sleeping; laying false scent trails to evade the searchers she was certain they'd send after her. Eating nothing until the seventh day when, in search of shelter in the stable of a small farm on the edges of a town that would eventually be Telford – frightened and confused, delirious with hunger and exhaustion – she found a young man resting in a hayloft, a labourer, and she took him. Fell on him in a frenzy of claws and saliva until there was nothing left of him but bone.

"London," she said, skipping over the lost time, the dark time. "Took me a while, but I got there. And once I *was* there, I knew I could disappear. Just… melt into the crowd."

More young men, more hunting and eating and stealing. More of the regret she found was beginning to follow in the wake of all three, the further she moved from her caravan and kin. And then she had money enough to buy herself at least a few of the trappings of personhood: a name, a birth certificate, a satchelful of dresses.

A cheap room in a run-down boarding-house. Access to the learning that would see her, eventually, all the way to university.

Laila could have been sceptical; Tara half-expected that she would be. She could have scoffed, snorted, raised a disbelieving eyebrow at the revelation; could have pushed for details of the *how* of it.

The *when.*

She didn't, though. Instead, she reached across the table for Tara's upturned palm and held it, gently, between her fingers.

"You can tell me the rest of it later," she told Tara, voice soft and low and – improbably – understanding. "But for right this second – baby, nobody can *make* you do anything. I know you know that. Whoever's found you, whoever's come to *get* you – this Jimmy person… they haven't got a hold on you, not now. You're not sixteen anymore. They try to force you into anything, try to take you somewhere you don't want to go, and we'll call the police. Hell, I'll call bloody Hanif in to sort it out if I have to, he'd be over the *moon* to send a bloke like that away with his teeth in a bag."

Hanif was Laila's cousin: a retired boxer turned restauranteur with some very clear and very specific views on any man inclined to lay hands on a woman. Laila found him, as she put it, *problematic.* Considered him sexist – a dinosaur with a saviour complex, a good old-fashioned chauvinist in white-knight armour. They exchanged cards at Eid, small inexpensive gifts on birthdays, but were far from close. If Laila was willing to ask him for a favour, Tara thought, then she was taking the issue of Jimmy very seriously indeed.

"It's not that simple," Tara said, and talked some more. About the photos in the mail: the leverage they represented and the hold over her they gave Jimmy; about the very real possibility that Tim Howard and Elspeth Palmer would take them to the governors or the Daily Mail or both, that they'd use them – in the very *best* case scenario – to force her quietly out of Hummingbird.

What she'd seen and felt through the windows of the Palmer house – what she'd seen Howard becoming in that music room, while Elspeth had her back to him – she omitted altogether. It was a problem, there could be no doubt about it. But perhaps, given the immediacy of Jimmy, a problem for another day.

And there were miles to go with Laila before that particular footnote to the story would sound anything like plausible. Confessions to make, and sights to show.

"No." Laila was angry now, halfway to furious, her pupils dilating and nostrils flaring with the effort of keeping that fury in check. "*No*. I'm your *wife*. It isn't a fucking secret. You can fuck me anywhere you want to, any *way* you fucking want to, and it's nobody's business but ours. This Jimmy and Tim fucking Howard and his army of desperate housewives... they can't just, I don't know, *revenge porn* you into doing what they say. Even if they *did* go public with the pictures – so what? *You haven't done anything wrong*."

"It's not that simple," Tara repeated. "And it's not just about the photos, not with Jimmy involved. He'll use them against me, and he obviously intended them to be his first port of call, if he went to the trouble of rigging a camera to take them... but they're not all he's got on me. He's... dangerous. Tough and clever and dangerous. Not even someone like Hanif would do much to stop him."

Laila's anger turned to puzzlement.

"Wait. You said he was older than you then, right? You were sixteen and he was, what, thirty? Thirty- five? He must be an old man by now. Not exactly at the top of his game. I don't care how much of a hard man he thought he was back in the day – someone like Hanif could wipe the floor with him, even if you *didn't* get the police involved. Which you should, by the way. He broke about six different laws getting hold of those images, and that's before he got started on the blackmail. You could probably get Howard and Palmer arrested too, come to that, if they've knowingly hung on to them. Kill two birds with one stone."

"He's... aged well," Tara said. "There's nothing frail about him."

It was the meat that did it: kept them young, kept them strong. Kept them from growing old quite so quickly as the people in the places they passed through, who seemed to Tara – when she'd compared them after every return visit with her own people – to move from glowing vitality to decrepitude as rapidly as mayflies.

The meat, and the physical change required to obtain the meat: to snatch the boys and girls and men and women without the sense to leave the tent at speed on the final night before the circus left their towns.

She discovered this early on. Once she'd made the decision to forsake it – to fight the change and the hunger when they came upon her. To live the life of a girl like any other in a big, anonymous city.

They were subtle at first, the signs. Not seismic, but slow and incremental; so slow and so incremental that anyone not studying the contours of her face in the mirror each morning over a period of years – anyone not blessed with Tara's keenness of eye – would probably have struggled to catalogue them.

A roughening of the skin across her cheeks and forehead. An opening of the pores around her nose and chin. The finest of fine lines, spiderwebbing out from the corners of her mouth.

Sixteen she'd been when she left, and sixteen she stayed looking for a decade after, complexion soft and eyes sparkling. As the 1960s became the '70s, though – then into her thirties, and eleven years without the meat that once sustained her, sustained them all – she was passing for twenty-one; by the time she met Mark, in the mid-2000s, she was claiming to be thirty-two, and going largely unchallenged.

So it took its toll, the abstinence. But she'd never regretted it; not once.

"I don't care how tough he is," Laila insisted. "He can't just rock up here and threaten you until you let him club you over the head and drag you back to his cave. That isn't how things work, not in the real world. You *know* that, Tara. He's just a man. Just an angry man with a chip on his shoulder and some very fucked-up ideas about marrying in."

"He's not a man." It came out as a whisper, a confession.

"What?"

"Jimmy. He's not a man. Not the way you're thinking."

She expected Laila to argue, but was proved wrong again.

"Of *course* he is, baby." She gripped Tara's fingers harder. "I get how he must seem to you, with all the history you've got with him. But he is – he's just a man, an *old* man. We can deal with him."

She didn't understand, Tara thought – how could she? How could she possibly, until she'd seen for herself?

"Get up," she told Laila, rising from the table. Because it was now or never, wasn't it? If Laila was going to know, going to *really* know – and Tara wanted her to know, *needed* her to know, she realised that now – then she'd have to *see*. "And go and stand against the counter. I have to show you something, something that'll make all this… make a bit more sense, and it's going to come as a shock, and I don't want you losing your balance or falling off the chair and hurting yourself. So… go and stand back against the counter."

Laila didn't move; didn't speak.

"Please," Tara added.

Laila shook her head again; stayed quiet, for a beat.

Then she stood up from her chair and shuffled backwards across the kitchen floor until her back hit the countertop.

"I'm sorry," Tara said, unbuttoning her shirt with one hand and reaching down to unzip her skirt with the other. "I should have told you sooner."

And then her clothes were off, pooling around her ankles on the floor, and for the first time in five decades she was willing the change to come.

6

The photographs were worn and faded at the edges: some 35mm stills in black and white, the older ones yellowing snapshots captured on a Kodak or a Brownie, and the oldest ones of all much closer to daguerreotypes, tinted portraits sealed in velvet frames no larger than her palm.

In each image, the same subjects. A man and a woman, or at least two figures who appeared to be, both somewhere between twenty-five and thirty: the man square-jawed and broken-nosed, the woman small and slight as a ballerina. Their costumes were identical in every shot: silk Zhongshan suits, dark and sleeveless, their mandarin collars buttoned to the neck and material cut tightly to the very different contours of their frames.

Costumes. Fire dancers' costumes – the ones they'd worn in the ring virtually every night of their lives. The ones, for all Tara knew, they wore there to this day.

There were animals resting at their feet in all but one of the photographs: canids, a cluster of them, their colour made indeterminate by the monochrome inks. Too big to be foxes or domestic dogs, but the wrong shape for wolves: muscles lean and ears triangular, their brush-like tails fanning out behind them on the ground. In the final shot – the one Tara knew to *be* the final shot in the collection, chronologically – the animals were gone, replaced by a small child: a toddler, chubby and grinning from the woman's lap, her tunic a miniature replica of those clinging to the bodies of her adult keepers.

Tara remembered the morning it was taken. How happily she'd smiled for the camera.

§ § §

Laila hadn't fainted. She'd screamed, and sagged back against the countertop, but she'd stayed more or less upright – her eyes fixed on Tara with more fear in them than Tara had ever seen.

Nor had she asked any of the more obvious questions: *what are you?* or *what just happened?* or *what the fuck did you do with my wife?* She was too smart, too observant; it was plain from looking what Tara was, and what had just happened.

What she *did* ask – in the hoarsest of whispers, when eventually she found her voice – was: *has this always been you?*

Tara couldn't speak, then; the constraints of the new-old form meant she could communicate only in howls and barks, growls and screams. But she'd bowed her head, twice – *up and down, up and down* – in an approximation of a nod.

"This man Jimmy," Laila had said, struggling for words but pressing forward regardless, the tenacity and pragmatism that had propelled her into Whitehall and a thousand steering committees and think-tanks outweighing even the terror Tara had known she felt, could *smell* she felt in the moment, "he's aware of this about you?"

Another dipping of the ears and bowing of the head; another affirmation. *Yes. Yes, he's aware.*

"And he's... from your community." She'd been figuring it out even as she talked; solving the puzzle Tara had given her. "So he's... like this too? Like you?"

No, Tara had told her later, when she'd hauled herself back into her skin, her *real* skin – crying but vehement, begging and pleading for Laila to listen, to believe her. *No. I'm nothing like him. Nothing at all.*

§ § §

There were sketches, too: pen-and-ink line drawings on yellowing paper, suspended in the polypropylene pages of a leatherette album and sandwiched between the photos and the scraps of silk cloth that were all Tara had taken with her when she'd fled.

She'd kept them in a lockbox in the attic, just as she had in the home she'd shared with Mark – sneaking up occasionally in the middle of the night, to stare into the faces in the photos or to run a thumb over the edges of the silk. To remember.

She tended not to look for long at the sketches; invariably found herself unsettled, in a way she couldn't quite explain, by the scenes they set, the tales – or the histories – they told.

She looked now, though.

All three showed a similar tableau, detailed impressions in blue and black: ten or more of the wolf-shaped foxes from the photographs, crouched like cattle before a storm, their large heads bowed in submission – or in supplication – before an even larger beast; one that stood fully upright on its four thick legs, its own muzzle turned upward to an unseen sky in the beginnings of a howl.

It was twice the size of its siblings, at least. If each not-quite-fox was as big as a wolf, as the photos suggested, then the animal they prayed to was as tall and as broad as an African lion – albeit with the same pointed ears, brush tail and vulpine profile as its acolytes.

Aglaeca. That was the name her grandmother and great-grandmother and the other older ones had given it, when they'd talked about it at all in her hearing.

Giant. Devil. King.

There was some disagreement among the women exactly what it was: myth or monster, legend or historical fact. Whether it was something like *them,* only bigger – a biological anomaly, a chromosomal quirk lying dormant in the bloodline – or whether it was something different altogether, something greater and more powerful. A kind of deity; a leader, a messiah.

Nor could the ones who argued that it *had* existed and that it *was* a creature much like them agree on how it might have come to exist in the first place, on whether it was something *born* or something *made.*

Sacrifice, Old Lamia had said – though she'd been, now Tara thought about it, a good deal younger-*looking* than Tara was now, the skin taunt around her muscles and her hair blue-black, without a thread of grey. Only her voice betrayed her; the pulse of it, the prosody a relic of another time, another place. *That's what brings it forth, what calls to it. And not just any sacrifice, mark you. The true sacrifice. The flow of the blood and the gift of the marrow.*

And there it was again: *blood.* Did they ever think of anything else? They'd built a world on it, a credo; a civilisation in miniature on a carmine Tiber.

She could taste it, still.

§ § §

"You have to kill him, then," Laila had said – the shock still fresh, but the edges of it blunted by a tumblerful of single malt, and then another.

She'd been able to look Tara in the eye by then, across the table, though they hadn't touched; Laila's hand, the hand not occupied with conveying drink to mouth, resting quite deliberately on her knee, away from Tara's.

There'd been no further questions about the *what* of it, of Tara; whatever information Laila might have needed to process what she'd seen to her own satisfaction, Tara assumed she'd done so already. That what she'd been given was enough. Was more than enough.

"I'm sorry?" Tara had answered her, certain she'd misheard, misunderstood. Because a stranger on a park bench telling her to kill, telling her that killing was even an option – that was one thing. But her own wife doing the same was another altogether.

"Kill him." Laila had filled the glass a third a third time; kept her gaze fixed on the bottle. "I don't see what else you can do. He won't stop until he's got what he wants, and it doesn't sound like anyone else has the wherewithal to do it – anyone who's not like you lot, anyway. So, it'll have to be you, won't it? You'll have to do it yourself."

You lot. Tara had felt it coming, had *known* it was coming, but it had stung anyway: the distancing, the cleaving of what had been the whole of she and Laila into separate parts. Into a *you lot*, not an *us lot*.

"I can't." She'd wanted Laila to reach for her across the table, the way she had before; to let Tara know that she was safe, that she wasn't alone. But Laila hadn't; wouldn't. "He's stronger than me. Faster. I wouldn't stand a chance."

A pause, long and painful, while Laila thought this through.

"You'll have to be smarter, then, won't you?" she'd said. And, to Tara's disbelief, had added: "I suppose we both will, if it's going to work."

§ § §

She returned the sketches to the album she'd taken them from, as delicately as she might a set of stamps; closed the cover, stacked the photos back on top and laid both onto the silk that lined the bottom of the lockbox.

Fastened the box shut and slid the key under the loose section of floorboard, where she kept it.

There was no phone number for Jimmy, that she knew of. No way to contact him, that wasn't seeking him out in the flesh. There'd *been* no phones, no *mobile* phones, when they'd last lived side-by-side; no email, no text messages, no digitised data flying invisible overhead.

Evidently, he'd got to grips with new technologies in the decades since she'd known him, if he'd managed to find a way to rig a hidden camera in the ceiling of an unfamiliar room. But his engaging those technologies to communicate, to *speak* to people – it felt to her unlikely. Because what use had he, had *any* of them, for casual conversation outside of the community, much less for the hardware that might facilitate it? It would serve no purpose; meet no need.

If she wanted to find him, she'd have to look for him. To pick up the flavour of him in the dark.

The taste.

7

She tracked him to St. Edmund's Lake on Wyevale Park. Not quite the spot the red-haired woman in the cape had chosen for their rendezvous, but close enough for Tara to wonder whether Jimmy had gambled on her coming and had led her there deliberately, or whether the universe – ever inclined to mischief – was planning yet another joke at her expense.

On tracking him down, she waited; let thirty minutes elapse, then forty, before she made her approach.

He stood barefoot at the shoreline, looking out into the multi-layered blackness of the lake. Briefly, she considered the possibility of an ambush. Of barrelling into him from behind, driving an elbow or a knuckle into his liver until he dropped to his knees, then pushing his face down into the water until he choked on it. But quickly decided against it. The element of surprise would get her only so far. He'd hear her, pick up the scent of her, no matter how sudden her movements or unexpected her attack; would understand immediately her intentions, and would make her pay for them.

"There's bodies in here," he said, pointing down at the water's edge but not turning around. "Old ones, and fresh ones too. Three of them at least, that I can tell. Could be more again, further out."

She stopped dead – six feet from him, from the stillness of the lake. Slowed her breath and her heartbeat to a speed less likely to betray her shock.

"Of course there aren't," she told him, summoning the tone she used with students, with the Year 4s and 5s who tried to convince her they *hadn't* stolen paint from the art room, *hadn't* kicked that Year 2 boy in the shins. "That's absurd."

Except... *was* it absurd? *Was* there something there, under the water, now she thought about it: the memory of something, playing at the margins of her senses? A rot, perhaps – fleshy, corporeal – below the overarching reek of algae and substrate and small-animal decay?

He'd be better equipped than she was to detect it, if there was: his perception keener, his sensitivity to taste and smell that much more acute than hers was now. That was the meat, too. It that had kept him young, and kept him sharp, while she'd aged and withered and dulled to the bluntness of a serving spoon.

"They're in there, and you know it." He craned his neck around to look at her. It took all of her willpower not to launch herself at him, to wipe the grin off his face with both fists. "You ask me, you should be grateful I've come to get you. This place you've pitched up in – there's something odd about it, very odd. Smell of burning on the wind and bodies in the water, when it wasn't you who put them there. It's not right, Tion. Not right at all."

She winced instinctively at the name – the one she'd been given, not the one she'd chosen for herself. The one, most likely, she'd be answering to still, but for Jimmy.

"Who are they?" She nodded towards the lake, towards the dead men and women who – yes, he was right, she really *could* smell it now, the green-black bloat and peel of them – floated somewhere just beneath.

"Couldn't tell you." He shrugged, indifferent – and perhaps that shouldn't have surprised her, after all. What did it matter to him who they were, these decaying bits of muscle and organ washing up on the slopes of a place he'd never visited before and would probably never have cause to return to? "But they're not *our* worry, lover. I can promise you that."

He turned to look at her, the cotton of his open shirt rustling in the breeze as he moved; sniffed deeply, taking her in, and winked, the gesture a leering obscenity that turned her stomach to ice.

"That your woman I can smell on you, is it?" he said.

It better be, she thought. *It just bloody better be.*

§ § §

They'd taken pains to lay the trap before they left the house. Another false trail: Tara dousing her skin in the sweat-and-jasmine odour that still clung to the workout clothes Laila hadn't got around to washing after her last gym session; rubbing Laila's citrus moisturiser into her neck and cheeks; dabbing Laila's perfume behind her ears and under her breasts, until Laila's scent was all over her, mingling with Tara's own.

It wasn't perfect, as plans went; it couldn't be, when Jimmy's ears were so sharp they could catch a grass blade breaking underfoot from a hundred paces, when his eyes were as clever as a barn owl's in the dark. But it would be – *might* be – enough to confuse him, to throw him off his game, if only for a minute or two. Long enough to buy Laila the time she'd need to take the shot.

The gun had been another surprise, for Laila at least. Another secret Tara had kept hidden in the attic, with her photos and her sketches: a fully-loaded service pistol, a Colt, plundered from the ruined body of an American airman in the early '60s. She'd never understood why she'd kept it; why she'd felt compelled to carry it with her from one home to another, one *marriage* to another. Perhaps she'd always known she'd need it, somewhere down the line; that eventually a real threat would show itself, and the weapons she'd been born with – the claws and teeth and strength and speed – would prove painfully insufficient.

She'd brought it down from the attic, along with the lockbox. As an act of confession, contrition, or so she'd thought at the time.

It had been Laila's idea to use it on Jimmy.

"You'll have to get him in the head," Tara told her; anxious, sceptical. Laila had taken hold of the gun by then; was studying it, feeling the weight of it in her hands. "It wouldn't do much damage otherwise. You'll only get one chance – if you even get that. And it'll be black, pitch black out there."

"Understood." Laila had unloaded it; let the cartridge fall into her open palm.

"You'll have to shoot him," Tara repeated – her gaze locked on the Colt, on the ease and the confidence with which Laila seemed, inexplicably, to be handling it. "In the head."

"Yes. I get it."

"Do you know how to do that? Shoot a gun, I mean?"

Laila had flashed her a smile so condescending Tara would have found it enraging, in another set of circumstances.

"I went to Lahore every summer as a kid, did I ever tell you that? Stayed with my Uncle Hamza and his sons – weapons fanatics, all of them. They kept a display case full of Glocks and assault rifles in the basement, next to the pool table. Used to let us use the little ones for target practice down the bottom of the garden." She'd re-loaded the ammunition with a click; raised an eyebrow at Tara, who hadn't been able to help but smile back. "So, yeah. I should think I'll be alright."

It's ludicrous, this situation, Tara had thought. *Preposterous, really, if you take a bird's eye view of it. We're preposterous: a shapeshifting headmistress on the run and a civil servant from the suburbs waving a loaded gun around like Rambo, plotting to murder a monster dressed as a man while the kettle boils.*

But perhaps, she'd added to herself, preposterous though it was… it wasn't as bad as it could be, if they were in it together.

§ § §

"We're not talking about her," she told Jimmy.

"And why's that, then?" The light of the moon caught the side of his face, illuminating his profile, and she saw there was an open cut along his jawline: raw and ragged, the work of a fingernail or a serrated piece of jewellery. She wondered why she hadn't smelled the blood. "Want to keep her to yourself, do you?"

"You need to leave here. All of you. Pack up your things and move on before I lose my patience."

They were big words, big promises. He'd know full well they were empty; that she'd never be able to follow through on the threat.

Would he know she was stalling, though?

Laila would be somewhere close by now, behind a bush or hidden by the trunk of a tree; staring at Jimmy down the barrel of the pistol, waiting for the moment she could take her shot. Tara could sense her – or the faintest trace of her – underneath the suffocating fog of sweat and fragrance, through the thinly suppressed veil of her own fear and the reek of timber, salt and copper radiating off of Jimmy. That had been the plan, the promise: that Tara would track him, and then wait for Laila to arrive. Arrive, and conceal herself nearby, gun trained on her target, before Tara let her presence be known.

Pull the trigger, sweetheart. Please, just pull the damn trigger.

"You sure that's what Laila wants, are you, Tion?" he said. He touched two fingers to his chin; ran them along his wounded jaw, slowly and deliberately. There was something in his hand, something glinting silver in the moonlight; something he wanted Tara to see.

A ring: white gold and diamond, a single sapphire set in its centre. A wedding ring; the one she'd given Laila at the Town Hall up in Marylebone, with two of Laila's sisters looking on.

Laila's ring. He had Laila's ring. And if he had Laila's ring, then it stood to reason he had *Laila*, too.

Which was, she realised, probably the best-case scenario. Because if he had Laila, if he'd taken her, then Laila was, at least, still alive.

She closed her eyes, and concentrated; focused her attention, her every sensate cell on Jimmy, on the signals he was giving her.

The smell on his hands and under his nails was citrus and jasmine and rich red wine; the same smell that lingered in the runnels of the open cut that marred his jaw, the cut that Laila must have given him when he took her, when he snatched her from the house to use as yet another means of leverage while Tara was wandering the streets searching for *him*.

"You couldn't have." It came out as a snarl, more animal than human. "You didn't."

But he could, and he had, and she was certain of it.

He pressed the fingers to his jaw, keeping the ring in her line of sight.

"She's not dead," he said. "Not yet. Can't guarantee she'll stay that way for long, though. Not without her woman there to protect her. So what do you reckon, Tion? Want to be a good wife and come back with me to get her?"

8

She didn't read women's fashion magazines; had no interest in glossy photoshoots or statement jackets. Tara was as aware as anyone, though, of the image-manipulation techniques most of them relied upon to sell their wares: the erasure of lines and wrinkles in the editing suite, the augmentation of cheekbones and the thinning of waists, the restoration of a healthy glow to a washed-out complexion.

Seeing her mother staring back at her from across the caravan, she thought, was very like looking at herself in the aftermath of a digital retouching: the visible signifiers of years, maybe decades, washed away to such an extent that the casual observer, should they be asked to take a guess at the relationship between them, might well have identified Tara as the parent, and her mother as the daughter.

"You need to feed," she told Tara – the first and only thing she'd said since Jimmy had led Tara into the caravan. He was there with them still; watching their reunion with barely disguised amusement from the tiny alcove that,

Tara remembered, passed on the surface as a kitchen, but was almost never used as such. "I don't know that all the damage can be repaired," she gestured to Tara's middle-aged body, the threads of grey at her temples, "but I'll wager *some* of it's reversible."

"Worth a go," Jimmy offered. "Not like it can make things any worse, is it? I mean, look at her."

"Where's Laila?" Tara said again, in the same dull monotone she'd employed the other ten or twenty times she'd asked. She was terrified, ripples of panic vibrating through her down to the bone, and they'd already *know* she was terrified, but there was nothing to be gained by spelling it out for them over and over. "Where are you keeping her?"

"We'll send Jarlath and Cailean out to hunt," her mother continued, as if Tara hadn't spoken. "They can fill out what we have already. Are the beams in place?"

"Rian set 'em up," said Jimmy. "They're done."

The beams. Impossible to forget those.

The people Jarlath and Cailean took, whoever they were, would end up there eventually: suspended vertically between the top and bottom beams of the makeshift scaffold Jimmy would have laid out in the secluded spot of woodland where they'd pitched the tent. Like pigs on a spit or chickens strung along a rotisserie grill – those were the analogies she'd reach for now.

Nothing but meat, raw and ready for eating.

She'd just turned fifteen, the first time she ate that way: the night her mother and father had walked with her to another glade in another woodland and, saliva dripping from their muzzles, invited her to fill her belly with the flesh of the naked, hanging boy they'd led her to. Fifteen: the age they all were, when they first fed that way of their own volition; when the meat they ate was meat they killed for themselves. The age the meat began to work its magic – its undocumented but *scientifically explicable* magic, as she was inclined to think of it now – on their cells and biomolecules, slowing their physical ageing to an amble and then, over time, to a crawl.

"You broke me and your Da, when you ran away." Her mother's gaze swung back to Tara: the daughter who'd left, and never come back. It was wounded now, accusatory. "Tore our hearts asunder. And not *only* me and your Da, I should say. All of us, even young Jimmy here. We'd never known such pain."

"Where. Is. Laila?" Tara repeated.

Jimmy snorted; rolled his eyes and leaned back against the wall of the ersatz kitchen. Her mother gave every impression of not having heard her at all.

"Do you have any idea how we searched for you?" she went on. "How we looked and looked, until we thought we'd die of grief? And all the while you were out there, hiding from us with that dark girl and the one before her, the papist boy in the fancy suits?"

"Mark?" The casual reference jolted Tara off-course and away from Laila. "What does *Mark* have to do with anything?"

And how, she thought but didn't add, *do you know about him, anyway? What* else *do you know, Mam?*

Jimmy snorted again, longer and louder.

"How'd you think we found you?" he said. "Carried a bit of a torch for you, that one, all the way to the end. Kept pictures of you all over his phone, and one of the two of you on your wedding day folded up in his pocket. And thank Fulla he did, eh? Else we'd never have known who he was to you, or how we'd go about finding you."

The throwaway past tense of it hit Tara like a punch to the head: the finality of *carried* and *folded* and *kept* blurring her vision, setting her ears to buzz and ring.

"You took him." She directed the question to her mother, not to Jimmy. "Murdered him."

"Not what you'd call *by design*," Jimmy answered – her mother seeming not to think it worthy of a response. "Brendan come across him over in Polstead, passed out drunk down a side street. None of us would've given him a second thought if Bren hadn't gone rifling through his suit after and seen *you* in there. After that," he pulled back his shoulders proudly, for a second less wolf than swollen, self-satisfied bullfrog, "it just needed a bit of detective work, a bit of prodding and poking around... and there you were."

Something drifted in through the caravan windows from outside: a noise, or the subtle, whispering suggestion of one. A stretching and creaking, like rope fibres chafing against wood; like knots tightening over skin.

A cry, muffled. A woman: hurting, but with too much pride to let herself show weakness.

Laila.

"Where is she?" Tara looked from Jimmy to her mother and then back again – Mark and the horrors he must have suffered in the last minutes of his life pushed aside by a renewed anxiety for her wife, for what was more than likely happening to *her* right in that moment. He was dead, and she'd grieve – would *need* to grieve. But... old grief, grief for a man she used to know, grief that would begin to heal over and scab as soon as it tasted the air... that could come later. For now, she had more pressing concerns; fresher and more debilitating griefs to forestall.

Jimmy and her mother had heard what she'd heard, there could be no doubt about it; heard it, probably, more clearly than Tara had. And they *knew* she'd heard it, too: the return of that smug, self-satisfied grin to Jimmy's fat mouth told her as much, though her mother sat impassive.

"Where's who?" said Jimmy, through his smirk.

She felt her nostrils flare and widen of their own accord; felt the tips of her incisors lengthen and descend towards her lower lip as her rage swelled and crested and threatened to take her over wholesale.

Three times in a weekend, her rational mind reminded her, even as a more primal compulsion pressed it into silence. *No change for years, for decades, and suddenly you're letting it happen three times in a weekend.*

You're welcoming *it*.

"Take me to her," she growled. And it *was* a growl: more sound than speech, and unintelligible to another kind of audience.

"To *who*?" Jimmy was close to outright laughter now, as amused – or so she suspected – by Tara's inability to control herself as by the demand itself.

"Stop." Tara's mother held up a hand to quieten him, and the grin fell away. "You want to see the girl, Tion?" she asked Tara – softly, with a meaning hanging from the words that Tara couldn't quite parse. "Then see her you shall. Seems to me that it's a fine idea, now I think on it. A very fine idea. In fact," she stood, rising to her full height until the top of her head touched the caravan's low ceiling, "if young Jimmy here can lead the way... I believe I shall take you there myself."

9

It had been Laila Tara had heard, back in the caravan. And the way Tara had envisaged them holding her had been, she saw on entering the clearing – flanked by her mother on one side, and Jimmy on the other – near-on prophetic in its accuracy.

Laila… wasn't naked, not quite. They'd removed the outermost layers of her clothing: the jeans and boots and jacket she'd been wearing when she'd left the house, a few hours and a thousand years ago, but had left on her shirt and vest, her socks and bra and underwear. Not, Tara thought, because they cared at all about her dignity, but because they'd rather not be put to the inconvenience of chewing through leather and heavy denim, when the time came.

She was upright, the ropes around her chest and thighs binding her to Jimmy's beam: a thick wooden stake that ran from the top of the scaffold to the bottom. They were bowline knots, that held her – more secure than ties at the wrist or ankles. Much harder to break free of, however much you struggled.

There were other beams too, to her left and right; other scaffolds, all of them empty. Waiting, Tara supposed, to be filled with whomever Cailean and Jarlath brought back from the hunt.

Laila's mouth fell open on seeing Tara. But she said nothing. She'd have been told to stay quiet; would have been threatened into it. Tara could well imagine the kind of threats her captors would have thrown her way.

And those captors... they were keeping an eye on her, a very close eye. There were eleven of them altogether, that Tara could count. People she'd known once; people she recognised. People she remembered fondly, despite herself: Jocasta the knife thrower, and Gordon, who'd let Tara strap him to the Wheel of Death; Eamon, who'd taught her to read; Sandrine, who'd kept her entertained as a child with impromptu spells of juggling and ventriloquism.

Most were human-shaped, although a few had changed already: Lili and Rut, twin sisters a decade Tara's junior; Iain, who sang badly but who played the flute and the fiddle as well as any musician Tara had heard out in the world; grey-coated Sim, who'd lived through the birth of the Kingdom of Alba and could recall with perfect clarity the crowning of Malcolm I.

Every one of them turned their heads to Tara and her escorts as they approached.

Her mother came to a stop by the scaffold, directly in front of Laila, and Jimmy followed her lead.

I could keep moving, Tara told herself. *If I'm fast, and I make the change midway, I could do it: dive onto the scaffold, tear off the ropes, pull her onto my back and run.*

Except...

They'd never let me, would they? I'd never move fast enough to get past them – past Jimmy and my mother, let alone the rest.

They'd rip me to pieces. Or... no, that's not quite right, is it? They'd rip Laila to pieces, and they'd make me watch.

"Tion." Her mother's voice stilled the thoughts; vibrated along the notches of her spine, calling her to attention as irresistibly as a dog-whistle. "Tion, you need to feed."

"What?" Tara looked to Laila, utterly trapped and silently terrified, and then to her mother – the stomach-churning absurdity of the suggestion she *feed* breaking the spell, shocking her out of the paralysis she'd felt beginning to creep into her bones. "No! Jesus, no!"

Her mother didn't so much as flinch at the violence of the reaction.

"This has gone on long enough," she said, impassive but implacable. The way she'd been when Tara had been young and, too naive to know better, had asked to play with her father's torches or one of Jocasta's knives. "You've had your fun, out there," she indicated the trees at the perimeter of the clearing, the towns and cities beyond the forest, "and you can see on your face what it's done to you. But it's time to stop it now. *Past* time."

And Tara understood: for her mother, it was a done deal. Tara feeding on Laila, as far as her mother was concerned – feeding on her own *wife* - was an inevitability; would be as unconscious an action for Tara as lifting a fork to eat in a restaurant when the main course arrived.

Not because of any pressure exerted on her by the presence of Sim and Jocasta and the rest. Not even because of the weight of familial expectation, the impossible-to-deny demands of a community so desperate to draw her back into the fold they were prepared to ruin her to get their way.

Because it was *what was done*; it was *what they did*.

Because humans, full-blood humans... they were meat, only ever meat. You could play with them a little, if you absolutely had to, the way you'd cuddle a lamb in a field at shearing time before you sent it away to be slaughtered. But they weren't real, not really; not the way *you* were real. They didn't feel, the way you felt; didn't matter, the way you did.

They were meat; it was the nature of them. And you were hungry. Always, always hungry.

"You still know what to do, I take it?" her mother added.

Tara looked again at Laila; at her mother and Jimmy; at their crowd of onlookers.

And yes: she *did* know, after all.

She wouldn't have been fast enough to close the gap between her body and Laila's without Jimmy intervening, and the others following suit; that much was true. But her mother was nearer, less than a foot separating her from Tara. And that distance, at least, Tara could clear unimpeded.

She sprung left on the balls of her feet, changing as she lunged: senses sharpening, ears twitching, canines sharpening to needles. Her teeth were buried in her mother's neck before anyone but her had registered what was happening: slicing through brawn and muscle with the ease of a boning knife.

Hot blood flooded her mouth, full-flavoured and satisfying.

She'd missed this: this power, this pleasure.

Her mother howled and Tara swallowed, letting the blood wash over her tongue and palate. The others were circling her now, Jimmy and Sim and the rest, all of them changed or changing – surprise and caution slowing the speed of their advancement to a light-pawed tread. It wouldn't last, though. They'd come for her, close in on her, and soon.

She was sure of this. But, as wave upon wave of the blood – her mother's blood, blood that might just as well have been Tara's own – wet her lips and swamped her taste buds, she found she didn't care at all.

It wasn't just the delight of it, the absolute intoxication. Distracted though she was by the sheer force of *that*, she was aware too – albeit only dimly – of another, second change beginning to overwhelm her. A physical change; a reshaping of the structure of her bones and skin and tissue.

She was... growing: that was the only word for it. Widening and lengthening: her limbs stretching to twice and then three times their original size, her haunches thickening, her jaws and vertebrae and cranium and the matter that surrounded them expanding to accommodate the swelling of her organs, the elongating of the teeth still working at her mother's dying flesh.

And as she grew, the others seemed, correspondingly, to shrink, until she was looking not *up* at them, but *down*. Until, despite their number, they held no fear for her at all.

Jimmy moved first, reaching for her with his claws. Tara let her mother's body drop to the ground – a longer drop, she noticed, than it ought to have been, than it *would* have been before – and struck out, catching him in mid-air at the muzzle and crushing his skull, as he fell, beneath the pads of an impossibly heavy forepaw.

She heard the bones crunch and splinter, felt the fluid seep into his fur. And then he was still.

A scream, neither human nor entirely animal, ruptured the air around her, followed by another, and another. Their echoes passed along the circle like a stadium wave – through Sandrine and Eamon and one-eyed Fin, who'd never lost a fight.

They scattered, fleeing this way and that into the woods in a flurry of leaves and bark.

All of them but Laila, who was staring at Tara – at the thing Tara had become – with something like awe. Laila and old Sim, who padded not away from Tara but towards her, his head lowered.

In deference, she realised. In submission. Exactly as the creatures in the sketches she'd kept had bowed to the Ancient. To their king.

Aglaeca, he growled. *Aglaeca, my lady. You've been missed.*

She reared up, her own head raised to the night sky.

Yes, she told him, baring her teeth. *Yes, I know.*

§ § §

At the edges of the clearing, shaded by oak trees older even than she was, the red-haired woman nodded to herself in tacit approval. Events hadn't unfolded quite as she'd anticipated they might, it was true – but they would do for her purposes, she thought. They would certainly do.

PART IV
GALLOW

1

There's a patch of grass behind the recycling bins in the car park of the bed and breakfast. It's carpet-like in its softness, and the cat has opted for this as her waiting spot.

She isn't hiding, exactly; no-one here, she thinks, would give a second glance to a stray black cat yawning and stretching and sunning itself out in the open. It's why she's settled on this form for her surveillance assignments; why it's the one she defaults to when she's in the mood for anonymity, which she so frequently is.

But she dislikes discomfort, dislikes it intensely. And a choice, for her, between a soft, warm patch of grass exempt from public haunt and the sharp basalt edges of a gravelled driveway... well, it's barely a choice at all.

She'd felt the motor car approach some minutes back, caught the hum of the engine and the sweet, spoiled-egg tang of the exhaust, but is surprised by the *look* of it when it swings left into the car park. It's rusted and dented, verging on dilapidated: the wing mirrors held together by duct-tape, thickly but inelegantly applied, and the passenger door painted not the faded blue of the chassis but a glaring uranium yellow. The kind of vehicle that might, perhaps, trundle relatively inconspicuously along the dual carriageways of Brighton or Crawley, or even St. Leonard's, but which is apt to attract a good deal of attention among the Audis and Range Rovers and BMWs that clog the streets of this particular parish.

The driver surprises her too, when he finally succeeds in packing away the wires of his portable satellite and ventures out to brave the daylight.

He's young: that's her first observation. What could possibly have drawn a young man here, to a place like this? And not just drawn him, surely – *compelled* him to come. This settlement, she understands better than anyone – better than *almost* anyone – is most assuredly not a place one stumbles upon unwittingly; such stumbling, in fact, would be a virtual impossibility. It *exists*, of course; in purely physical, purely topographic terms, it unequivocally *is*. But, as of these last few weeks, it's existed… off the map, so to speak: cloaked in magics of a class designed to repel the casual interloper, to guide them away with the subtle but inexorable force of a magnet. Ones that urge disoriented motorists to drive *around* the village rather than through it; that induce the knowledge of its precise location to slip, imperceptibly, from the grasp of the navigator even as they squint and goggle at the atlas.

Technically, *technically* – the boy ought not to have been able to find it at all.

He's small and slight, which only adds to the impression of his youth. His shoulders are narrow, swamped by the distressed black leather of his jacket; the fringe of his dirty blond hair hangs down into his eyes, shielding them from scrutiny. There's stubble on his cheeks, the beginnings of a beard – but cultivated, she imagines, in an effort to age him, to pre-empt interrogation on his date of birth at the liquor store or the cigarette counter. He's old enough to drive, evidently – but no older than his early twenties. A student, perhaps.

What, therefore, she asks herself again, could a boy like this possibly be doing here?

He trudges around to the back of the motor car, the soles of his pristine white training-shoes displacing shards of gravel with every step; lifts open the boot and pulls out a rucksack. It's a large one, of the sort favoured by hikers and campers and outdoorsmen, and packed tightly – bursting, in fact, at its heavy-duty seams.

A rucksack suggesting, she deduces, that this will not be a flying visit, an overnight affair, but rather that the boy intends to stay. To bed down for a spell in town.

This – this is interesting. An unexpected development, perhaps even an unwelcome one.

But then again, perhaps not.

In either case: the cat now has a mission. Has places to be, and intel to report.

The patch of grass is softer now, and warmer still, warmed and softened by the heat and press of her recumbent body. Nevertheless, she breaks free of it: arches her back and, with a twitch of the legs and a shake of the tail, darts back to her cottage to share the news.

2

The bag was bulky, unwieldy. Jonas had regretted bringing so much with him almost the second he hit the motorway. So many unnecessary t-shirts, stuffed in amongst the belts and shower gels and deodorant sticks; so many paperbacks he likely wouldn't have a chance to open, let alone to read.

Boxer shorts, clean jeans, toothbrush; laptop, phone, Testogel. These were the things he needed, the things he couldn't go without. Everything else he could've picked up on the road and saved himself the effort of packing. There had to be a supermarket or a corner shop, even in a place like this. Even if it locked its doors at 5pm on the dot and the manager pretended not to see you until you cleared your throat.

He slung the rucksack over both shoulders and, knees bowing under the weight of it, inched across the driveway like a tortoise until he reached the white-pillared porch that served, he assumed, as the B&B's guest entrance.

A woman answered before he could touch a finger to the bell: tall and thin and fifty-something, gold hoops from an earlier era decorating both her ears and blood red nails extending like talons from her cuticles.

She took him in: up and down and up again, the quick once-over he'd grown accustomed to receiving from strangers thrown off-kilter by his height, the softness of his features, the resurgent sprinkling of acne that peppered his cheeks and chin. Then smiled broadly, apparently delighted to see him.

"You'll be Jonas, my love?" Leaving him no conversational gap in which to supply an answer, she extended a hand towards him across the threshold, virtually tugging him inside when he took it. "We thought we might've lost you on the A23. Get stuck in traffic, did you?"

He shook his head. Getting out of Brixton had been a hassle, a steady stream of white vans and motorhomes slowing his pace to a crawl until he was south of Coulsdon, but there'd been remarkably few other cars on the road once he'd skirted Pease Pottage, and none at all for at least a mile before he'd eventually passed the sign welcoming visitors to Gallow.

"Just a careful driver," he said, smiling back at her with a little-boy-lost flutter of the eyelashes he'd been told brought out the maternal instincts in a certain kind of older woman. It would pay, he thought, to keep her on side as much as he could, if he was going to be staying in what was effectively her house for the next few days.

Besides, he might have to actually *talk* to her at some point; interview her, even. She didn't seem the fanatical type, from the earrings and the nail varnish – nor from the discreet but emphatic rainbow flag sticker she or someone in her household had taped to the front window, come to that – but it was a small town, and she lived here, so chances were she knew *something* worth capturing.

If she trusted him enough to let him in on it, anyway.

"We've put you in the attic room," she told him, leading him along the hallway and deeper into the house. It was a big place, larger on the inside than it had seemed from the driveway: Victorian but well preserved, all high ceilings and hardwood floors that echoed underfoot. The kind of place he'd like to own himself one day, though the odds of that – as Dan loved to remind him, whenever they talked even in abstract terms about the future – were vanishingly small, if he stayed in academia. "The penthouse, we call it," she added, with an artificial chuckle he was sure she'd tacked on for his benefit. "There's a king size and a single up there, and the sofa folds out, so we usually keep it for families with kids, but the way things have been this month…"

She trailed off; conscious, maybe, of having given away too much about the current state of her business. And worse still: about what this might in turn imply about the quality of the hospitality on offer.

"Things been quiet?" He followed her up the stairs, the weight of the rucksack forcing him down into a simian crouch so low he was half tempted to tackle the final few steps on all fours.

She turned her head to look at him. Scrutinised him, as if working out whether he was someone who might look sympathetically on a downturn in custom – or whether he might, conversely, be disposed to broadcast whatever secrets she confided in him across the darker hospitality-themed reaches of social media or weaponise them in the form of a TripAdvisor review. Then, seemingly satisfied with whatever guilelessness or moral rectitude she saw in him, nodded.

"As the grave," she said softly. "Twenty-three years ago it was, when I moved down here from Wakefield, and I've never known it so dead, even this time of year. Truth be told, chick, you're the first guest we've had all month – the first *reservation*, if we're being *really* honest. I don't know what the hell's going on."

"It gets… busy, then? Normally?" He tried to keep the incredulity out of his voice, with only limited success. What, after all, could possibly entice the casual holidaymaker or mini-breaker to Gallow – a place he'd struggled at first to pinpoint not only on Google Maps but on the paper A-Z he kept in the car for emergencies, the one he reached for only when more modern technologies failed him? There were no landmarks here, no sites of historic interest or notable natural beauty. It was just... another nowhere place, out in the sticks: moderately wealthy, very white, and – at least at present – socially conservative to the point of violence.

"Oh, yes. It's the location. Close enough to Brighton and Eastbourne that you can nip down to the seaside easy, but nothing like as expensive as either of them two. They're not coming for Gallow, the tourists. They're coming for the access. Only now... well, now they're not, are they? As of right this moment, they're not coming at all."

She took a left at the top of the stairs, guiding him towards an open door leading to what he guessed was his room: a wide, wood-panelled space distinguished by shaggy turquoise rugs, the promised multiplicity of beds and a footprint larger by several square feet than the studio he'd been renting back in Coldharbour Lane.

"And here we are," she told him, shifting aside to let him in. "There's no phone up here, but the password for the internet's taped to the little fridge under the desk, and Glen and I are only downstairs if you need us. It'll do you alright, will it?"

"Brilliantly, thanks." He let the rucksack slip from his shoulders and drop to the floor. It fell open, spilling half a dozen or more of the belongings it held into the deep recesses of the nearest rug: shampoo, moisturiser, boiled sweets and tortilla chips, a library copy of Mary Douglas' Purity & Danger... and, to his horror, the spare silicone packer he'd thrown in at the last minute, just in case.

His gaze darted downward, automatically. The packer stared back at him, thickly veined and limp and – unlike his regular model – at least two shades lighter than his own skin, and he felt the blood rush to his cheeks and a familiar knot begin to form in his stomach.

She'd see it; there was no question she'd see it. You couldn't miss it. But would she know *what* she was seeing? Understand what it meant?

"I'll leave you to get your bearings, my love," she said, her eyes flicking down to the rug along the same trajectory as his had, before returning immediately to his face. *She* didn't blush; didn't so much as stutter. She seemed, in fact, entirely unaffected by the contents of his bag. Perhaps she *didn't* know, then; perhaps he'd got lucky, and she *hadn't* understood. "We're on the ground floor, as I say, so just shout if you want us for owt."

She stepped backwards and out of the doorway, crossed five paces to the top of the stairs, and then hesitated.

"Please don't think I'm meddling." She looked him dead in the eye; bit her lip. "And you can tell me to mind my own business if you must, but Glen and I... it seems to me we've got what you might call a duty of care, when it comes to our guests. A responsibility, if you get what I'm saying. And if you're open to a bit of friendly advice – you ought to mind yourself, when you're out in town. It's a nice place, Gallow, it is, but it's not exactly, you know... *open-minded.* Not the most progressive, when it comes to different ways of living, different ways of thinking. They've got some very old-fashioned views, some of the people 'round here, *very* old-fashioned – and they're getting worse lately, not better. Worse, and louder. Getting dangerous, if you ask me. So just... mind yourself, alright? Keep your head down. And for God's sake, steer clear of St. Stephen's church, if you ever happen across it. I don't know exactly what it is they're up to over there, when they're not shouting the odds at the headmistress over at Hummingbird – that's the primary school up the road. But they're up to *something.* And I'll tell you now... whatever it is, it's nothing good."

3

The journey home takes no time at all in this body, lithe and quick as she finds it by comparison to some of the other forms she's taken. She tends towards impatience, and in this respect the feline species suit her perfectly, the smaller cats especially. She read once about another, faster creature – a kind of antelope, horned and hoofed, its movements tight as a spring – but has never yet found an opportunity to mimic its shape and stride. Perhaps one day, she thinks. In another time, another place.

It's not easy to open the door like this, though. So she goes around the back of the cottage, to the summer house Miranda has appropriated as a kill room-cum-storage facility for the exenterated carcasses she's made of the men and women she's been hunting; the ones she's yet to dispose of in the lake on the outskirts of the town.

Miranda is in there, tending to the almost-living topiary she's so hellbent on creating in amongst her more commercially viable wood-and-metal sculptures: paring the upper layers of skin from the freshest of the dead with a hunting knife. Languidly, casually; so casually, she might have been stripping the peel from an apple at the dining table.

She always was an artist, Miranda, the cat thinks. Long before she ever considered selling the fruits of her labour to the money men of Canary Wharf and the Square Mile to finance her lifestyle: the houses and the travel, the obsidian blades from Hokkaido and the handsaws from Uppsala.

She hears the cat enter; extricates the knife from the flesh of today's corpse and spins around to greet her, blackish blood dripping from the tip of the blade to her gloveless wrist.

The cat takes her cue, and changes. Draws the dark fur back into her own flesh, the tail into the base of her spine, the dew claws into her feet; elongates the bones and muscle of her back, flattens her ears, shakes out her hair and straightens up, chin set.

"Who's this?" she says, glancing to the half-skinned corpse. Her teeth, smaller and flatter now, try nevertheless to curl over her bottom lip as she speaks, heedless of their new dimensions. They're milk teeth; a child's teeth in a child's mouth, fewer and more brittle than the adult sets she's sported in her prior human forms. The lower left incisor, she notes, is beginning to loosen already, wobbling uncertainly with every flick of her tongue.

"He's Ewart's," Miranda tells her, virtually spitting out the old identifier – abandoned of late for the more contemporary *Howard*. "A churchman."

"But of course." The cat-who-is-no-longer-a-cat grins; warms herself on the news. She takes easily to pleasure: it's what, she believes, led Miranda to alight on *Sunny* as the sobriquet they'd use for her in Gallow. A nod to the no-longer-a-cat's propensity for delight, albeit – as is ever the way with Miranda lately – a sardonic one.

Her name, her *real* name is... somewhat harder to pronounce. Although Miranda, to her credit, never stops trying.

"There's a new boy," she adds, resisting the urge to clean her paws with her tongue. "Checking into the Marchmonts' lodging house even as we speak."

"For St. Stephen's?" Miranda's ears prick up, insomuch as human-shaped ears ever can. Her bare fingers tighten around the knife.

"No." Sunny – for she might as well call *herself* that, might she not, if it's the moniker she's to be lumbered with, out here? – accentuates the *no* with a shrug. "They have a kind of... smell, the church people, wouldn't you say? And he... didn't."

"Then how did he get *in*?" Miranda sounds alarmed now, as well she might. It was she, not Sunny, who arranged for the protections around the town; she who saw to it that no-one new could get through, no-one not already connected to Gallow in some significant way.

If the protections have failed, then the failing is Miranda's.

But *new*, Sunny thinks, is a nebulous term, an elastic term. It can be stretched to accommodate a host of possibilities, even as it keeps out the journalists and outside-police whose meddling Miranda had so feared at the beginning: the real lawmen, those more capable and potentially more of a fly in the ointment than the small-town paqūdus. Even as it warded off whatever other associates or acolytes or sympathisers Ewart is likely to have accumulated, over the years.

"I'm afraid your guess is as good as mine," Sunny says, and yawns. It might be a consequence of the prolonged periods she's been spending in the cat's body – and moreover in the child's, whose racing metabolism incinerates every calorie she feeds it with the fervour of a starving greyhound. Or it might simply be that she's weary and overdue one of the season-long naps she's taken to enjoying, these last few centuries. But she's exhausted, suddenly. She could take to her bed – the sling-like hammock Miranda has secured to the radiator in the sitting room, or the unicorn-themed divan Miranda continues to find so amusing in the context of Sunny's bedroom – and sleep solidly for a month.

"Watch him." Sunny raises an eyebrow at this, and Miranda immediately backtracks, softening the command to a more politic request. "Please."

"As you will it, so shall it be," Sunny replies, with a parody of a courtier's bow – one too good-humoured to be read as a rebuke, but with a hint of something caustic at the edges. A reminder, unspoken, that Miranda's *will* alone is insufficient to compel Sunny to action; that the dynamic between them is very far from master/servant. Because though Sunny may sometimes look like a child, in this place and time, and though she may sometimes look like an animal, she is nobody's daughter, and most certainly nobody's familiar.

"If he broke through, if he's managed to *get* here, we need to understand how. To stop it happening again."

I see, Sunny thinks. We *do, do we?*

"Indeed," she says instead, the very picture of helpfulness.

"There's something else, also," Miranda goes on – hesitantly, as if afraid to push Sunny too far. "I was hoping I might persuade you to... keep a closer eye on the church. Not on Ewart, but on the church itself."

"The building?" This surprises Sunny. Much of her reconnaissance thus far has been restricted to Ewart, and latterly to Ewart and his most recent Girl Friday: a perpetually sneering town gossip and busybody named Elspeth Palmer, who has seemed to Sunny to do little but attend unnecessary parish meetings and follow Ewart around with the unchecked zeal of a Boston Terrier.

"Yes. I've been hearing... rumours. About Ewart – what he's cooking up this time. Nothing concrete yet, but I'd be interested to know who's been visiting St. Stephen's lately, and to what end. Whether it's been attracting any... new blood from the village."

Her eyes dart across to the coagulated tissues that still cling to the corpse, and she licks her lips. Sunny has known her too long and too well to regard the gesture as accidental.

"Interesting," Sunny says, her curiosity roused despite the indifference her tone suggests. "And dare I ask what these rumours might be?"

Miranda relays them. And Sunny, so rarely shocked by anything these last few centuries, feels her mouth fall open in astonishment.

4

From: jonas.thurman@slu.ac.uk

To: danthemighty@crackle.com

Subject: Gallow

Greetings, from the arse-crack of beyond!

(Why did I decide to come here, again? And why, sweet prince, did you not put just a *soupçon* more effort into talking me out of coming?)

You requested regular updates, and never let it be said that I'm not a man of my word, so here goes…

I'll start with the good news: the B&B is lovely. Clean and super roomy, with more beds than you can stick a stick at, and one of those rainforest showers you're always on about in the en-suite. You'd really like it here, I think. As long as neither of us ever left the room.

The landlady's a bit of a doll too, which I suppose is another plus. She reminds me of... well, maybe not *my* mum and definitely not yours, but *somebody's* mum. A bit of a Brady Bunch type, like she'd pack you off to school with a hug and a lunchbox full of fresh fruit but still come and land a punch on the playground bully if he ever messed with you. You get what I mean?

She knows about me – found out *literally* two minutes after I'd checked in, and no, I will *not* be telling you how, because it's embarrassing even by my standards and I'd rather not spend the rest of our lives listening to you retool my humiliation as a dinner party anecdote, thank you very much. And she's been brilliant about it. Not asked any dodgy questions or made anything into a big deal, although she *has* said a couple of things that have made me a bit... I don't know, uneasy?

Not things about me, to be clear – about the town. But I'll come back to that.

And so, onto the bad news...

(I'll warn you now - there's a lot of it).

I spoke to Louis last night (or this morning, I suppose, from his perspective – he's back in Manila) and he said he'd "forgotten" to tell Dad I was coming to Gallow, but he was sure it'd be fine if I dropped by and "surprised" the old man. "Surprised" him, for fuck's sake! I know you've never met him, but has anything I've ever said about my father given you the impression he's the kind of guy who likes surprises? He hasn't answered my calls or replied to any of my texts in a year. It's not like he's going to be expecting to find me on his doorstep.

(Also, as long as we're on the subject of things Louis has done lately to piss me off... He kept calling me "Joe," which he knows I hate – I assume because it's close enough to my deadname that he doesn't have to try too hard or worry about slipping up? He doesn't mean anything by it, I know, but it's a fucking pain regardless).

I'm still going to go and talk to Dad, I am – I'm here now, and I've got myself psyched up for seeing him, so I might as well. But it'll be a million times harder than it would have been if Louis had just done what he was supposed to do and taken five fucking minutes out of his life to pick up the phone and let the old man know I'd be in town.

But that particular shitstorm can wait until tomorrow.

Today's bad news – or maybe I mean odd and slightly disconcerting news? – is more...

Jonas tailed off – his fingers hovering, stalled, over the keys of the laptop.

He wanted to tell Dan about the day he'd had, the things he'd seen – but to do it in a way that wouldn't raise alarm bells. Wouldn't lead Dan to wonder whether Jonas had lost his mind or been replaced by whatever kind of pod-person did the rounds in the coastal southeast.

And therein lay the problem.

The tenor of their conversations, public and intimate alike, tended towards sarcasm, towards the mordant and the satirical. Towards the downplaying of emotional impact.

For Jonas, this was – or so his therapist had very convincingly assured him – a hangover from his pre-coming out days, when barbed self-deprecation was more survival strategy than stylistic device. For Dan it was, by his own admission, A Public School Thing, as difficult to shake in adulthood as the unintentional crispness of his vowels and his propensity to reel off Latin catchphrases in moments of high stress. And it meant that even the faintest insinuation of sincerity from one fell on the ears of the other like a klaxon: an irrefutable signal that something was very, very wrong.

Except, what Jonas had to say... he wasn't sure he *could* spin it sarcastically; that he could keep the requisite distance and clear-headedness. It was too odd, what had happened, and it had him unsettled.

Had him, if he was honest with himself, quite a lot more than *a bit uneasy*.

§ § §

It had seemed like such a good idea, at first blush.

He'd been at home in the flat when it had hit him, on a video-chat with Louis: a long, meandering conversation made even more so by the weed Louis had smoked to bring himself down after a weekend of partying in Bali. Jonas had been trying to extricate himself from the call; had been pondering which excuse, of the many available to him, would suggest both that he missed his brother's physical presence in the UK, and that – with departmental pressure mounting to refine an appropriate research question for his PhD, and Dan's mother coming down to London the following weekend – he didn't have time right at that moment to listen to snatches of half-remembered anecdotes about how many Arak Attack cocktails Big Andy could put away or what Debs had got up to at the Wet 'N' Wild Party.

"Wait," Louis had said, sensing Jonas's eagerness to be free of him. "Listen. I haven't told you what Dad told me when I rang him the other day."

"What?" Jonas's pulse had quickened; it often did lately, at even the vaguest mention of their father. "What about him? What did he say?"

Louis had paused to take a long, deep drag on the joint he was – Jonas had assumed – still smoking.

"He said," another pause, then another drag, followed by a round of chest-rattling coughs as the weed and tobacco hit his lungs, "there's been some weird shit going on at the school across the road from his bungalow. Religious shit."

"What does that mean?" Jonas had asked. He'd neither seen nor spoken to their father in the time since the old man and his wife, Jonas' stepmother, had relocated to Gallow from Bexleyheath six months earlier, and he'd known nothing at all about the old man's new house, much less about the school with which it apparently shared a street. "What kind of religious shit?"

"Protests. There's this church – an evangelical place, you get me? And they're, like, really angry at the school. Holding demos angry. Dad says they're there every day, Monday to Friday, shouting at people when they try to go inside."

"At a *school*? A *school* managed to piss off a church?"

"Sort of. But not the school exactly, right? What the school is teaching the kids. The, like... curriculum. They're doing this..." Louis had stalled again, mid-sentence – not, Jonas realised later, because of the weed, but because he was embarrassed. "This... sex education class. For kids. And the church is trying to stop it."

"Yeah?" Jonas had begun to get a sense of where Louis was heading. And of why, moreover, he'd been struggling to get there.

"Yeah. But not, you know... regular sex education. Like... gay stuff."

"Gay sex?" He'd known that wasn't what Louis had meant, exactly. But if the question made him uneasy, Jonas had reasoned, then surely Louis *deserved* to be uneasy, at least a little?

"No! Jesus. Not *sex* sex. Fuck's sake, Joe, they're, like, five years old, they're not gonna be learning about *that*. It'll be, you know... Tango Has Two Mummies, or whatever. Same-sex parenting and pronouns and... other stuff."

"Other stuff?" A part of Jonas had felt like a dick for pushing, but a louder and more frustrated part of him had screamed – rightly or wrongly – that Louis had to learn; that he'd have to work through his discomfort sometime, and *there and then* was as a good a time as any. "*Trans* stuff, you mean?"

Stoned and hungover though he was, Louis had been ruffled.

"Fucking hell, do you have to make *everything* about...? *Yes*, trans stuff. Gender and identity... stuff."

"*Stuff.* Right. Gotcha."

Louis had hung up not long afterwards, pleading exhaustion. But for all that his discomfort – and the unspoken prejudices that drove it – had irritated Jonas, the bit about Gallow and its apoplectic churchgoers had got him thinking.

He needed a research *plan* almost as much as he needed a research *question*: Hamish, his supervisor, was getting quite insistent about it. The initial proposal he'd submitted to the university (*Understanding the Drivers of Anti-LGBT Attitudes in British Public Discourse: A Cultural Studies Perspective)* had been enough to secure him funding from the sociology department – but had been accepted on the understanding that Jonas would, before too long, identify an actual cohort of people to study, and an actual location in which to conduct his fieldwork.

And the primary school in Gallow, which had sounded from Louis's brief description like a simmering hotbed of religiously inflected homophobic lunacy, could be just what he was looking for.

He hadn't told Hamish what he'd had in mind – or Alice, his other supervisor, a perennially power-suited Canadian specialist in queer linguistics, whose role had been restricted thus far to sitting motionless in the corner of Hamish's office and watching silently but sternly while Jonas reeled off whatever half-baked notion he'd brought with him into *that* week's supervision. Better, he'd thought, to scope out the place first, to see if it was a viable option before saying or doing anything that might lead inexorably to his having to produce a rationale for choosing Gallow as a fieldwork site – and worse, having to present that rationale to a departmental ethics committee.

He'd assumed, because everything was, that the protests would be online, or that they would at the very least have made the news: parcelled up, maybe, as an underdog tale of a plucky village school fighting back against the forces of theocratic oppression in the Guardian, or as a dog whistle take on political correctness run amok in the Mail, or even as a local interest feature in whichever low-circulation paper routinely covered those events that unfolded in the greater Gallow area. But there was nothing: not a story, not a hashtag, not a hastily shot video uploaded from the mobile of a citizen-journalist on the ground.

It was weird.

He'd tried harder, dug deeper, but come up just as empty as before. Which had left him, as he'd seen it, two alternatives: give up the ghost and hope another likely candidate for in-field research presented itself... or find out wherever Gallow was on the map, and get his arse down there to scope the situation out first-hand.

Go and visit his dad and Fiona while he was there, maybe. If he could pluck up the courage; if the old man was open to more than just slamming the door in his son's face.

§ § §

He forced his fingers back down to the keyboard.

… more worrying, I suppose.

Here's the thing. I went down to the school early this morning to get a look at the protests and see what the church was up to. Not *into* the school, I should add – it wouldn't look great, would it, a young bloke with no kids trying to sidle into the playground in a town like this? But outside it, by the gates, when the parents were doing drop-off. I figured with that many people knocking around, I could get lost in the crowd. Blend in a bit.

They were there, the church people, like twenty of them, and it was pretty fucking scary actually. They weren't just the shouting, though that on its own would have been enough to freak me out normally. No, they were all chanting different things in different rhythms, mostly off-key, so you couldn't really hear what anyone was saying. Imagine listening to some really bad Gregorian chanting played backwards on a turntable, and you're halfway there.

Still: you could *feel* how angry they were, even if you couldn't tell exactly what they were angry *about*. And if the signs they were waving around are anything to go by, then they *really* fucking hate us.

(One of the parents seemed really upset, actually – this woman with a little boy. They had to physically push through a crowd of church people to get in, and both of them looked like they were about to cry. So much for *protecting kids*, or whatever the fuck it is that church says it's trying to do).

Anyway.

The protestors... they had this leader. A priest or a vicar, I think. He wore a dog-collar, though I wouldn't have said he *looked* much like a vicar. More like a rugby player, or something? A soldier? He had a sort of... Jason Statham thing going on. My first thought, if we're being completely truthful, was that he was, you know... too hot for the priesthood. Definitely too hot to be whipping a load of yummy mummies up into a homophobic frenzy outside an infant school.

I wish I could tell you I wasn't staring, but I think maybe I *was*, a bit. It was hard not to, and not just because of the way he looked. He had... I don't know what you'd call it. Presence? Charisma? It was obvious he was the one in charge, that he was calling the shots, but he didn't seem like he was *doing* anything. The woman next to him had a megaphone, and the rest of them were chanting and yelling and waving their signs around like maniacs, but he just stood there with his arms folded, watching and smiling.

He was side-on to me, so I was mostly seeing him in profile: his nose and cheek and jaw and shoulder.

His neck.

He was a solid guy, really built but tapered, your classic V-shape. So his neck was *thick*. A serious surface area to play with if he ever decided to get inked.

He was tall too, much taller than me, so that neck... it was pretty much exactly in my line of sight. I could see everything: every vein, every muscle, every tendon and ligament, every inch of skin.

And this is going to sound mental, I know. But I swear to God, D... under that, under all of that, there was something moving.

Something rippling. Writhing, like a snake. Like an eel underwater.

Jonas hesitated again. It *did* sound crazy; *he* sounded crazy.

Then again: so what if he did? After what he'd seen, what he *thought* he'd seen... did it matter how he sounded, how sane he did or didn't seem to his own boyfriend?

Besides: it was an email, only an email, wasn't it? It was ephemeral; deniable, up until the very moment he hit send.

For now, secure in the knowledge he could delete it all at a single stroke, he could write anything he wanted. Anything he needed to be rid of, to drag out of his head and onto the page.

I know what you're going to ask, he continued, as if addressing not Dan but his own teenage diary. Was it a twitch, or a pulse, or a muscle going into spasm? Something completely normal, completely innocuous, made to seem more sinister than it was by the context or a trick of the light?

Am I so anxious about my dad and what he'll say when I knock on his door that I'm beginning to hallucinate? Has this church thing triggered me, somehow? Sent me spiralling?

And the answer is: no. I know what I saw. There was something *there* under that guy's skin, alive and moving – something alien, parasitic. Part of him but *not* part of him, you know?

Or maybe you don't. I'm not sure *I* do.

I don't think I spoke. I was scared shitless, and I probably did open my mouth to say something – to scream, even – but I don't remember making any kind of noise. Even if I had, you wouldn't have heard it, over the shouting and the chanting and the woman with the megaphone.

But it didn't matter. The vicar... he turned around anyway. Looked straight at me.

Looked straight at me and smiled, like he knew what I'd just seen.

Like he wanted me to see it.

5

To the interested parties of Gallow, and there have been mercifully few of them thus far, she's Miranda's daughter: a brooding, sallow creature of six or seven years, bound like others of her apparent age to attend a school wherein she might learn the English alphabet and, should she prove sufficiently entertaining to an audience of her peers, the rudiments of friendship.

It's become her habit, however, to slip out of the classroom and away from Hummingbird once the register has been taken. There's little to be gleaned of Ewart or his lackeys from the children; she's known this from the start. And the children's teacher – a green-eyed Celtic girl, so young-looking it seems remarkable she's been allowed to do the job – is painfully easy to thrall, such that Sunny is faintly embarrassed whenever the need to hoodwink her arises.

It's become her habit also to return to Miranda's cottage immediately thereafter, for rest and food and sundry replenishments, before venturing out anew – on four legs, in the interests of discretion, rather than two – to sample whichever of the secrets of the town and its denizens should reveal themselves to her that morning. To taste them on her tongue.

Not today, however.

Today, she'd observed through the windows from across the field as she'd neared the cottage, Miranda has company: a hollow-cheeked, familiar-looking blonde swigging nervously from a coffee cup, her legs dangling from the fingertips of the malformed scrap of synecdochic hardwood Miranda has the audacity to call an easy chair. One of the Hummingbird parents, perhaps. Not one whose name Sunny can call immediately to mind but then, she's had little incentive to memorise the identity of *every* mother and father she's ever seen lingering by the school's much-gated entrance.

Miranda has made no mention of guests, prior or anticipated, and certainly not of the kind of guest who might be treated to a hot drink in the parlour. The only visitors to the cottage of whom Sunny's been aware, these past weeks, have gone directly to the summer house in the back garden, whence none have yet returned.

What Miranda intends to do with *this* one once the coffee has been drunk is anyone's guess, though Sunny will certainly be asking her later. Once the woman, whoever she might be, has taken her leave.

Sunny has no use for strangers, much less for strangers who might seek to stroke her fur and scoop her up into their laps – as she imagines this one would, were Sunny to traipse indoors in this body, this skin. Nor has she use for those queries liable to arise – *who she is to Miranda, what she's doing out of school at this hour* – were she to show herself in human dress.

Today, therefore – and with no small amount of displeasure – she's forsaking her usual morning routine: her carpaccio and mustard, her saucerful of apple juice, her rejuvenating nap across the uppermost shelves of the bookcase. Forsaking it in favour of Miranda's newest mission: the watch-keeping at St. Stephen's and the surveillance of its congregants.

She's come to rest in the branches of a gnarled yew tree: the largest and leafiest in the churchyard, conveniently positioned beside the church building proper. It affords her an unimpeded view of the crucifix-strewn backroom serving currently as Ewart's office, and of Ewart himself, who sits writing at a foldaway desk within. The tree's proximity to the office ensures, moreover, that should Ewart speak, she will hear whatever words he utters as clearly as she would were they in the room together. The old yew grows flush against the weathered limestone brick of the exterior church wall, and Ewart – his hubris showing – has left the window open on its latch.

Who, in any event, would question the presence of a neighbourhood cat in a village churchyard?

For minutes or hours Ewart sits, scribbling and scratching and scanning the lines he's written, and Sunny feels her eyes begin to close, her muscles loosen and unfurl in a precursor to sleep.

Then suddenly, a knock from somewhere just beyond the office: a hesitant tap of joint on wood.

Ewart, too, has a visitor.

"Come on in," he answers, amiable to a fault, and Sunny feels a twinge of envy at his ease with modern idiom, how successfully – how seamlessly – he's adapted to this time and place.

The door opens, and the visitor reveals himself: a tall man, long-limbed and thoroughly unprepossessing, perhaps thirty-five but bald and stooped enough to pass for a decade older. He wears poorly cut blue jeans with a cheap leather belt; a brown merino sweater that might be fashionable on another kind of body but could never be on his.

She realises, upon reviewing this visual data, that she knows him: that she's seen him before at Hummingbird, and more than once.

Another moment of concentration, and she has an appellation: *Mr Bantry* (forename unknown, at least to her). The deputy headteacher, second-in-command to Mrs. Blacklock (forename Tara, domestic arrangements and extracurricular proclivities detailed and documented for Miranda at a length even Sunny considers exhaustive).

"Reverend Howard?" Bantry says, inching into the room with the caution of a man afraid of being swallowed by a sinkhole.

"Just Tim, please," says Ewart, still thoroughly genial. "What can I do for you?"

He doesn't, Sunny notes, invite Bantry to sit.

"I've been thinking about what you said. When you called." Bantry doesn't look at Ewart as he speaks; keeps his eyes on the ground and his jaw clenched tight. Waiting, Sunny thinks, for the sinkhole to open under him.

"Oh, yes?" Ewart turns around in his seat until they're face-to-face. He's smiling: a handsome stretch-and-pull of the muscles at his mouth, one with which Sunny is all too familiar. Rarely do kindness or compassion follow the smile's emergence. "Which... aspect?"

Bantry clasps his hands together; brings them to hover protectively over his groin, as if bracing himself to receive a swift, sharp kick to the vitals. "The... rapprochement, I think you called it?" His voice is shaking; he sounds to Sunny not only nervous but guilty. It strikes her that he, like her, is playing truant this morning; that he, like her, ought right now to be inside the Hummingbird gates, cloistered there until mid-afternoon. "How we might be able to... work together?"

Ewart's smile broadens, so wide it could devour the world.

"Wonderful news!" He rises from his desk; walks across to Bantry and claps a companionable hand on the man's thin shoulder, just that bit too hard. "I was hoping you'd see the light."

"I don't want to go behind anyone's back," Bantry stutters, as Ewart releases his hold. "Tara's been good to me, very good. But the thing is, the *thing* is... I don't disagree with what you're doing, you and your people here. The protests, and so on. This new relationship education curriculum, the children learning about… homosexuality and so on. It makes me uncomfortable, very uncomfortable. Really doesn't sit right with me, not at all."

Curious, Sunny thinks. She takes no moral position herself on the matter, nor on very much of anything… but she would, if pressed, have identified Bantry himself as homosexual. If not as a *gay man*, as in today's parlance, then perhaps as an *erastes*: a boy-lover, of the kind she knew so well in Syracuse and Sparta.

"Tara," he continues, "she's very competent, *very* competent. Very well-liked. But you know, don't you, that she's a…" He sputters to a momentary halt – struggling, Sunny suspects, to say the necessary word aloud in a house of God. "A *lesbian*. And you can't tell me that isn't colouring her judgement? Isn't leading her to make certain decisions that another head wouldn't, in her position?"

"Absolutely. Absolutely." Ewart clears his throat. "I should think it goes without saying that we share your concerns there. I'm aware of how our objections have been framed by Mrs. Blacklock – and by some other of your colleagues, no doubt. But we're interested solely in the wellbeing of the children. In their happiness, their spiritual welfare. And if we can look to you to help us safeguard them…"

"It can't be anything public," Bantry says, interrupting Ewart mid-flow with an assertiveness Sunny wouldn't have expected of someone otherwise so timid. "I can't be seen to be endorsing your message. Your tactics. I'd be putting my job on the line."

"I understand," Ewart replies – the soft, appeasing tone he adopts equally surprising to Sunny, in its way. "And be assured that starting another war with Hummingbird… it's not what we want, either. Not at all. We – I – had very much assumed that whatever help you chose to give us would be given… discreetly."

Bantry swallows, the motion sending his Adam's apple plunging up and down the loose skin of his gullet like a seesaw in a hurricane. "But you're looking to… build bridges?"

"Oh, yes." Ewart lowers himself back into his chair; finally urges Bantry to avail himself of the visitor's seat beside his own with an expansive wave of the hand. "Again: our primary concern, our *only* concern is the children. And as... let's say *overeager* as some of us here might be when it comes to direct action... the rest of us recognise very well the value of cooperation. We want to work *with* you, Alastair. Not against you."

"I can't do much about the lesson plans. They're Tara's purview. And not even hers, really, it's the trust that decides that kind of thing. The governors. We teach what they tell us to teach. More or less."

"Completely understood. We're already... *in conversation*, you might say, with the board of trustees. And we've reached out a hand to Mrs. Blacklock, so I'm hopeful she'll come to grasp eventually that we aren't the enemy, however she might feel about us in this second."

"Then why did you ring *me*?" Bantry's face creases: eyebrows furrowed, nose wrinkled, mouth pursed to a wrinkled O. He looks, Sunny thinks, almost comically puzzled. "What is it you think I can do for you?"

Ewart's smile is positively serpentine now; the illusion of his humanity, Sunny thinks, close to shattered by the white points of the teeth that caress his lower lip, the suddenly vertical slant to his reddening pupils. Has Bantry noticed the changes in him yet, she wonders? Or will it take longer for Bantry's mind to accept the accumulating evidence of his own eyes?

"We'd like to... gift you something," Ewart says. "For the school. For the children. As a kind of... peace offering. Mrs. Blacklock would slam the door in our faces if we were to go through her, of course, but we thought *you* might be more amenable to the gesture. That you might accept it in the spirit in which it's offered."

"What kind of gift?"

Bantry is sceptical; suspicious of Ewart, of what scheme he and his cabal might be hatching. Perhaps something of Ewart's appearance – of what Ewart *is*, below the skin – is beginning to sink in, to penetrate Bantry's viscera and nerve-endings if not his knowing wits.

"I suspect you'll find it rather silly." Ewart sounds bashful; sheepish, even. Like so much of what he says and does, it's entirely affected. Play-acting, for Bantry's benefit. "One of the St. Stephen's ladies, she's written a hymn for the children. Nothing political, before you ask. Just a hymn. A little bit *Morning Has Broken*, a little bit *All Things Bright and Beautiful*, if you can imagine that. I was hoping I might induce you to, let's say… sing it with the children in assembly? Perhaps give a bit of an introduction about what it is and who it's from, so they know that we're here for them and we care, and that we're not at all the monsters their parents might have told them."

"A… hymn?"

Bantry's puzzlement returns, which Sunny considers entirely reasonable. She's bordering on puzzled herself.

"Let me read it to you," Ewart says, reaching for a thickly creased sheet of lined paper buried beneath a pile of others on his desk. "I don't have the music to hand, but I have the words here, written down. A kind of poem, you know?"

Bantry starts to protest, to tell Ewart there's no need, that he doesn't *need* to hear it… but it's too late. Ewart has already begun to read aloud from his paper, clear and stentorian.

Sunny listens; follows along with the words as he speaks them.

Realises: these words, they're not the adulterated verses of a psalm or the lyrics of a children's song. They're words she knows, powerful words; words with which she's well-acquainted.

She thinks back to what Miranda told her in the summer house, the rumour she'd heard and relayed; understands immediately that the rumour, wheresoever it came from and shocking as she'd found it, was only half the truth.

Ewart… he isn't coming for the children. He isn't out to harm them, to hurt them – not, at least, in the manner Miranda's rumour had suggested.

No. He's weaponising them.

6

The front room reeked of vinegar and herbs: basil, and calendula, and others Jonas didn't recognise. The curtains, maroon velvet and ostentatiously fringed, had been drawn against the midday sun; what little light there was emanated from below the green glass hood of a notary lamp gathering dust on the side table.

And then there were the amulets: palm-shaped – palm-*sized* – Hands of Miriam in innumerable shades of turquoise hanging from what felt to Jonas like every spare inch of wall, every patch of ceiling, each one sporting a single lidless eye in its centre.

The overall effect from Jonas' perspective was of a fortune-teller's stall, squatting unhappily at the end of a rundown pier in a seaside town long left to ruin – the domain, perhaps, of an ageing, nicotine-stained clairvoyant who had herself seen better days.

It was his stepmother's handiwork, he thought. It had to be. His father had never so much as touched wood or thrown salt over his shoulder in

Jonas' presence; the old man didn't, as far as Jonas was aware, have a single superstitious bone in his dry accountant's body. Fiona conversely had always been something of a kook, casting runes and hoarding tarot cards and professing low-level psychic abilities. Jonas could only assume she'd gotten weirder, now the menopause was taking hold.

"Are these Fi's?" he said, pointing to the nearest of the Hands.

His father shrugged; pulled deep on his Panetella and exhaled a dense, earthy cloud of cigar smoke. "Don't bloody ask me. Woman's been mad on them all month. Stuck them all over the house. Stunk out the place, too, with all this...," he gestured around the room with the cigar, "dried sage and parsley. Made everything smell like the rear end of a chicken."

"I suppose she's got her reasons."

"I suppose she has." The old man took a final puff of the cigar and stubbed it out into the empty ashtray by his elbow: a homemade-looking black ceramic pot with a pentagram carved into the bottom. He leaned back into his armchair, clicked his tongue against the roof of his mouth and sighed. "What is it you want, anyway? Why are you here?"

Jonas had anticipated the question, or something like it, from the moment his father had answered the door. Doug Thurman was nothing if not predictable: expecting anything else of him would be like waiting around for a polar bear to fly. But the rejection implicit in it made Jonas flinch, regardless; made his breath catch in his chest and a dull, radiating pain take root in his stomach, as if he'd been punched.

"I wanted to see you. Don't know if you've noticed, but it's been a while."

"For God's sake, do you have to be such a fucking smart-arse? I *know* it's been a while. And we *both* know why that is."

He wasn't used to it – his father swearing, swearing *at* him. It left him dazed; momentarily stupefied. He had to gather himself, *pull himself together* as the old man might have said, before he felt able to reply.

"I hoped you'd... started to see things differently. Done, I don't know... some reading or something. Talked to someone about it, so you understood better."

The scoff the old man let escape at that, Jonas thought, would stay with him until the day he died.

"*Talked* to someone? Are you serious? Do you honestly believe I want *anyone* knowing about this, about what you've done to yourself? I don't know why you've elected to do this to me, why you've made the choices you've made – why you've *put me in this bloody position* – but I can safely say, I'll be keeping it *firmly* to myself. We've only just moved here – do you think I want every man and his dog gossiping about me down the pub? About that chap at Number Thirty with the wife who thinks she's a witch and the daughter who thinks she's a boy? Get a *grip*."

There was no hope for him, Jonas realised then. No chance of the old man changing his mind or shedding any of the beliefs he'd rather repeat ad infinitum – and with ever greater bluster – than hold up to serious scrutiny. No chance, therefore, of the two of them salvaging any kind of parent-child relationship, not as things were. Straining to make one happen was just pissing in the wind; Jonas would do nothing but hurt himself, in trying.

He got to his feet. Said nothing – because what would have been the point? – and, avoiding the old man's eyes, took himself out of the room, letting his features sag and his own eyes well up when the door leading out into the hallway was safely closed behind him.

The hallway, where Fiona was waiting for him: sun-and-moon pendants swinging from her neck and long grey hair scraped back from her face by a cyan head wrap. She was starting to *look* like a carnival psychic, he thought.

"I'm glad you came, Jonas," she told him, squeezing his upper arm with a bony hand so thoroughly encircled by occult silverware that she shouldn't, logically, have been able to lift it. He took note of her use of his name and was thankful. He hadn't had her pegged as a bigot – her irrationality tended to be aimed in other directions than prejudice. But he'd miscalculated before, misjudged a smile as kindness or a pat on the back as a gesture of solidarity, and the discovery of his mistake had never failed to leave him sick and sad and aching for something he couldn't name but wanted desperately regardless.

"Not sure it was the best idea, to be honest," he said.

"He'll come around. You know what he's like, so bloody stubborn. But he's missed you. It's been hard for him, with you and your brother both gone."

"Didn't seem that way."

"Because he's got his head up his backside. He can't keep it there forever, though, can he? And I'll talk to him. I'll *keep* talking to him."

She squeezed his arm again. He leaned into the touch, afraid he might cry; a part of him wondering, as he'd so often wondered, how a woman like her – an old hippie, and certainly a flake, but without an obviously malicious bone in her body – managed to co-exist with a man like his father.

"I should go," he said eventually, wiping his reddening eyes with his sleeve.

"Back to London?"

"No. No, I'm... sticking around for a bit. In town."

"In Gallow?" She frowned, and the lines smoothed from her forehead by the head wrap temporarily returned. "What for?"

He might as well tell her the truth, he figured. What was there to lose, anymore? What difference would it make if she disapproved of his intentions? He couldn't see himself coming back here any time soon.

"It's... for my PhD." He cleared his throat, struggling to sound at least a little less like his voice was cracking; pushed the resurgent memory of the vicar and his pulsing, snake-like flesh to the furthest reaches of his conscious mind. The *false* memory, he told himself; the thing he *imagined* he'd seen, in a moment of stress and weakness and anxiety. "I've been looking at, you know... cultural narratives of discrimination. And Louis mentioned what's been going on at the school, with the church and the protests and everything, so I thought it might make a good, you know... case study."

He paused, afraid he might have lost her. That even the mildest allusion to his research topic would cause her to glaze over, as so often happened – with everyone but Dan and his supervisors, at least – when he had cause to describe it. And he had his suspicions even Dan was only feigning enthusiasm half the time.

Fiona didn't seem bored or disinterested, though. If anything, she seemed agitated. Concerned, suddenly.

"Don't." She took hold of both of his arms now; dug her fingers into the flesh there, her jewellery leaving marks in his skin he could already feel, and that would doubtless show up later in the mirror. "Please, don't."

He wanted to ask her, *why not?* To ask her what exactly she was afraid of, if she was afraid – or, if she wasn't, what kind of wasps' nest she was worried he'd be kicking, what kind of trouble she thought he'd be bringing down upon himself.

(And what it's got to do with that vicar and the crawling thing under his skin and the way his eyes looked like they were on fire when he smiled at you)

"He's the devil," she added, as if she'd ripped the unspoken question wholesale from those – *irrational, impossible, utterly insane* – thoughts he was working so hard to keep quiet, to wrap and bury until they stopped screaming to be heard. "Howard, the priest at the church. The *false* priest. He looks like a man, but he's not one, Jonas. He's the devil. The devil himself."

7

unny had been in Paris when she'd first heard the words emerge from human mouths: at the peak of the Terror, not so very long after Robespierre's *sans-culottes* had marched Madame Veto and her King to the guillotine.

Idle curiosity had led her there, her interest piqued by the twin assurances of bloodshed and political machination. And on the former promise at least, the city hadn't disappointed. Blood and rage and bile had flowed like rainwater from the Place de la Révolution to the Basilica of St. Denis, and she'd revelled in it: cheering along with the baying crowd at every cry of pain and botched decapitation; hurling florid polysyllabic blasphemies at every Girondist and lord and landowner she'd seen arrested.

The odours of the city, however, had overwhelmed her; the mingling stench of rotten vegetables and ordure, unwashed bodies and purpling corpses left too long to the elements proving too great a price of admission. So it was that she found herself tacitly eyeing her next destination – weighing the respective merits of Port-au-Prince versus Copenhagen – when, in search of a particular eyepatch-sporting gentleman who might (or so it was rumoured) be inclined to ease the passage out of France of the more moneyed would-be traveller, she'd entered the unmarked subterranean Cafe informally known as La Pleine Lune.

And had stumbled into... a kind of meeting: a throng of plain-dressed Frenchmen assembled, improbably, before a lone elderly woman looking back at them from an upright barrel, who had appeared, more improbably still, to have them entirely in her thrall.

The old woman wore what Sunny had initially believed to be religious attire: the cream habit and caramel veil of a Sister of the Carmelites of Compiegne. What she spoke, though – the measured incantation that had so thoroughly captured the attention of her audience – was nothing at all like Latin, nor French, nor any other of the languages Sunny had necessarily imbibed, riding wave after sanguinary wave of carnage across the continent.

Rather it had been, after a fashion, Sunny's mother tongue.

The nun, if nun she had been, had talked at the men for perhaps a minute before the fissure had opened, as Sunny had known it would – bringing with it the whispered inducements of the things beyond. Then the eyes, pressing and pulsing against the walls of the café: staring out through the crack from their reeking void that was neither *her* world nor *this* world, but an interstitial space between the two. A cage, of sorts; a holding cell.

The effect on the men of La Pleine Lune had been both immediate and utterly irrevocable.

They'd moved together, as what had seemed from the outside as a single, resolute entity, though each man had sought to carry out his mission in the manner of his choosing.

(Inasmuch, she'd thought at the time, as it was possible to speak of *choice* under such circumstances; of *will* or *volition* or *consent*).

One, standing so close to Sunny that she could detect the sweat of his underarms and the fisherman's cologne of his clothes, had produced a rusted hook from the inner reaches of his jacket, clasped it between his dirt-caked hands like a rosary and, with not a second's hesitation, impaled himself upon it: the point and barb of the implement piercing the flesh of his chin, and thereafter his brain, as he'd let himself fall forward.

The man beside him, meanwhile, had begun the process of opening the veins of his wrist with a blunted bradawl: chiselling at the cuff with a methodical craftsmanship Sunny had envisioned him applying to the carving of a cabinet, causing great arterial sprays to gush from him and to stain and blotch, thereafter, the writhing corpses-in-waiting of his brothers.

The man beside *him* had been less lucky: settling, in the absence of a tool appropriate for self-mutilation, for tearing at his shirt and digging his blunted fingernails into the flesh of his gut, stabbing harder and harder and deeper and deeper until he'd succeeded in piercing so many layers of visceral fat that thick, gelatinous ropes of his own innards had begun to spill from the cavern of his gut into his waiting palms. He'd held them there momentarily; looking down as if to consider them, to ponder their size and heft. And then he'd tugged, his bare biceps twitching and flexing with the effort of pulling them free.

Sunny had scanned the cellar, left and right. Seen men clawing at their eyes until they came loose from the sockets and jamming thumbs into the glutinous holes that remained; men smashing glasses into pieces on table-tops and slitting their throats to the bone with the shards; men lying on their backs on the bloodied floor, dropping caskets heavy with wine onto their stomachs again and again until their internal organs cracked under the pressure.

Seen an orgy of suicidal violence, carefully choreographed.

And then the old nun, looking down on the slaughter and smiling. A smile like Ewart's: one that took pleasure in the chaos it had set in motion.

Sunny hadn't thought of La Pleine Lune in years, before coming to Gallow. But she thinks of it now: of the flickering candles casting shadows on stone walls dripping with cruor; of the stench of faeces vomited up from perforated bowels; the dying hands still clutching tight at the hilts of swords and the shafts of makeshift coshes.

What she'd seen there – what she and Miranda are apt to see *here*, should they fail to act on what she's overheard at Ewart's window… it's what the words do. How they work; how they've always worked, from the very beginning.

Of the exact mechanism by which they operate, she's unclear. But at base, she recognises, they serve as a kind of dog-whistle: calling out to the shame and guilt lodged deep and unacknowledged in the soul of the listener and dredging them upward. All the way upward, to the topmost surface of the listener's mind, past the inevitable strata of delusion and denial, until a swift death – and not an ignominious living – seems to them the most elegant and logical solution to the problem at hand.

(As to the appearance of the creatures of the interstice… here, she can only hypothesise. Perhaps, she thinks, the words call to *them*, too: appealing pre-emptively to their taste for pain, like a pristine body thrown to sharks that smell the blood below the skin).

It's rather clever of Ewart, using children to deliver the words, the message; she'll grant him this. Children, she's observed – certainly the younger ones she's known at Hummingbird – are largely unencumbered by the crippling guilts and immobilising shames of their adult counterparts. Not *all* their adult counterparts, she corrects herself: true believers and fanatics of all stripes, in her experience, tend to traverse their corners of the world comparatively free from those feelings of personal culpability she's seen plague the more existentially uncertain. Ironically, she thinks, Ewart's own congregation – those, in any event, who really *have* put their faith in his Old Testament doctrine – might also prove convenient vessels; useful, guiltless mouthpieces for his genocidal communiqué.

Though quite how Deputy Head Bantry's mind will hold up against the weight of those words, she wouldn't like to say.

8

know your Dad doesn't like it," Fiona said, the gold and silver bangles on her forearms clinking like a door chime with every indignant flick of her wrist. "He thinks I've got a screw loose lately."

Looking around the potting shed she'd evidently been using as a workroom, Jonas found he couldn't altogether disagree with that appraisal.

If the living room inside the bungalow was a fortune teller's stall, the shed could have passed for the police-precinct setting of an American cop show. Along every stretch of wall, Fiona – certainly Fiona, and certainly *not* his father – had affixed a length of cork panelling, creating in Jonas the sensation of having been captured in the belly of a large, three-dimensional pin board. To the panels she'd secured with adhesive tape a mosaic of paper and card: handwritten lines and printed notes in digitised fonts, photographs and sketches and sun-faded polaroids. All arranged, if the degree of wear and discolouration were any indication, in a rough chronological order.

The older items, the woodcuts and watercolour reproductions and portions of manuscript that might have been ripped from the pages of a long-lost diary: their subject-matter he found difficult to discern, in the absence of the glasses he wore to drive and watch television. The newer ones were clearer, though; *their* contents more readily identifiable, despite his near-sightedness.

In every photograph, every drawing, he saw the same face: the vicar from the church across the road. The man with a writhing serpent under his skin; the man Fi had called the devil.

"What are... these?" he asked, in his most soothing voice. The one he'd use on his brother when they were kids; when Louis was rocking back and forth on his bed, knees clutched to his chest, convinced – after too much skunk or too many pills or a bad batch of mushrooms – that the pulsating, gelatinous mass of shadows only he could see was preparing to descend on him from the ceiling.

"You don't have to take that tone with me," Fiona said, more sharply than Jonas had expected. "I know what this looks like. But I've got nowhere else to put it all. I can't very well keep it in the house, can I?"

No, Jonas thought. *No, you really can't. Not if you want to avoid Dad calling the GP and having you carted away like Blanche DuBois.*

A part of him was pleased, though; curiously moved that she'd taken him into her confidence, however bizarre and detached from reality that confidence might be.

"It's evidence," she continued. "About Howard. Proof of what he is."

"Which is... the devil."

He was all too aware of how *he* sounded; knew she'd assume he was mocking her. He wasn't, though – not exactly. Maybe *devil* wasn't right, wasn't the word he'd have reached for or the assumption he'd have leapt to. But there was *something* wrong with Howard, wasn't there? Jonas had seen it for himself, or thought he had.

"Which is the devil." She held up a finger to forestall any immediate follow-up questions; walked the very small distance to the oldest of the papers and removed one, very carefully, from the board. "And we could spend all day going back and forth on it, me trying to convince you I'm not losing my marbles. Or you could have a look at this."

She prised open the clenched fingers of his right hand and laid the paper, just as carefully, onto the palm. It was a portrait; an engraving, Jonas thought.

"Who's this?" he asked instinctively, though the question was redundant. The hair was longer, tousled and down below his ears, and the collar was high, the black cassock and thick white cravat of a Georgian clergyman covering the subject's upper body. But it was, unmistakably, the vicar. Howard.

"This is from 1829," Fiona said. "He went by Ewart then, Thomas Ewart. When he sat for this picture, he was the rector of Cardwell, up near Grimsby. Ever heard of Cardwell, Jonas?"

Jonas shook his head.

"No, you wouldn't have. It doesn't exist anymore, is the thing. Cardwell – it's abandoned now. A ghost town. Everyone who lived there, every one of Thomas Ewart's parishioners... they died, somewhere in the spring of 1831. Walked into the sea and drowned themselves – all of them, all at once."

§ § §

He'd been aware for as long as he could remember that Fiona's friends were very different than the other adults he and Louis knew; that the loose-knit network of women she chatted with online and met up with in Oxford and Brighton and Bath were, to his and Louis's acute embarrassment, self-identified witches.

Mostly, he'd gathered, they tended towards what he thought of as the *homeopathic* end of – for want of a word that didn't make him wince – witchcraft: healing magnets and medicinal tinctures, ley lines and handfasting ceremonies and aura cleanses, the odd bit of Goddess worship when the stars aligned. Nothing dark; nothing sinister. For all Fi's talk about Samhain and ritual circles and Books of Shadows, and despite her somewhat toe-curling tendency to refer to her *coven*, the whole thing seemed to him about as eldritch as a charity bake sale.

Still, it made sense to him that she'd reach out to these same friends, afterwards; that she'd ask them to help her understand what she might have seen when, out walking early one weekday morning, she'd spotted a very handsome stranger – later introduced to her as the Reverend Tim Howard – approach an older, dog-collared gentleman tending the flowers in the churchyard at St. Stephen's and, after a brief but apparently perfectly pleasant conversation, grab hold of the elderly man's ears and tear his head from his body, so quickly and so effortlessly he might have been plucking a daisy from the grass.

"It was the old vicar," she told Jonas. "The one who was in charge before Howard replaced him. Mycroft, Stan Mycroft. We hadn't been here long enough to know him much, but people seemed to like him well enough. It got reported on, by the way, the death – they said he'd been in an accident on the road out to Great Kilner. It was all over the paper the next day. Said he'd swerved so hard he'd sent the car rolling over and got dragged out through the windscreen. Decapitated himself like that actress in the '60s. Jayne something?"

"Mansfield," said Jonas, his mind elsewhere.

"Right. But it was a lie, wasn't it? A great big lie. Because I'd *seen* what had happened to him, at that church. Seen it with my own two eyes."

Reasoning, however, that the evidence of her own two eyes would be far from enough to persuade the local constabulary to investigate a murder that was, even she had to admit, a physical impossibility – and reasoning moreover that her husband, an eminently stolid and sensible sort, really *might* try to have her sectioned if she shared her story with him – she turned, in something of a panic, to her sister-witches, at home and abroad. Who reassured her, as she must have hoped they would, that she was entirely sane; that what she'd seen in the churchyard *wasn't* impossible; and that, between them, they'd get to the bottom of it, just as soon as they could.

"It didn't take them long," Fi said. "Howard came slithering into Gallow full-time that same week, and he was filling Stan Mycroft's boots up at the church within the fortnight. All I had to do was get a picture of him and send it over to the girls to look at. We've got a WhatsApp group," she added.

From Colorado to the Cotswolds, the witches sprang into action: reading and researching, cross-referencing and compiling. There were several librarians and archivists among their number, woman well-versed in image searches and comparisons. In a matter of days, they'd tracked down a headshot that might have been a match for Howard, albeit one that raised more questions than it answered. It had been taken from an article in the long-defunct *Des Moines Comet & Star* – one that detailed the sudden disappearance, in August 1936, of more than half the residents of the tiny Iowa town of Charity, together with its de factor Mayor and spiritual leader, the Reverend Tommy Horton.

"It was him, no doubt about it." Fiona pointed down to the piece of paper Jonas still held in his hand: the reproduced engraving of what was undeniably Tim Howard's face, apparently superimposed onto the torso of a 19th century preacher. "Sometime between now and *then*," she pressed a finger to the edge of the paper, "he must've gone over to the States. And when he did…"

The Charity vanishings, according to the *Comet & Star's* rather sensationalist reporting, had happened literally overnight. On the evening of August 23rd, the town was home to no fewer than two hundred residents, men and women and children, spread out across some sixty-five properties over twenty kilometres of predominantly agricultural land; by the morning of August 24th, forty of the houses were empty, their occupants never to be seen again.

"God knows what he did to them," Fi said. "What he got them to do to themselves. But whatever it was, he'd done it before. Done it over and over again."

Further matches followed, from other articles buried in other archives, in English and Spanish and Russian and Hindi, with some dating back to the early 1800s – and including reports of the mass suicides at Cardwell.

Wherever Tim Howard – or Thomas Ewart, or Tommy Horton, or any of the dozen other pseudonyms he'd adopted over the centuries – had travelled, he'd brought death. Stabbings, drownings, arsons, shootings: all had trailed in his wake.

No-one before Fiona and her friends though, it seemed, had seen fit to connect each ostensibly disparate event; nor had anyone attributed the incidents in Cardwell and Charity – and in Ottawa, and Chittorgarh, Rajasthan and Vyborg during the Finnish Civil War – to the presence of the pale, blue-eyed Christian who appeared on the scene just before each tragedy occurred, and dematerialised almost instantly thereafter.

"You really think it's the same person?" Jonas asked – finding himself, despite his own predisposition towards scepticism in the face of absurdity, very nearly believing what he was hearing. "That the vicar, the actual *vicar* over the road... he's been doing all this since, I don't know... George III?"

"No." She took the paper from Jonas' hand; fixed it back onto the empty spot on the wall. "He's been doing it longer. Much, much longer. Cardwell might be the first time anyone took note of it... but it's far from the first time it happened."

"You said he was the devil. Why? Why would you think that?"

(*because of those eyes, why do you think? those eyes and that smile and the snakes under his skin*)

Fi stared up at the cork board and its body of evidence, her expression unreadable.

"I never used to believe in it," she said softly. "God and Lucifer and heaven and hell, all that *Paradise Lost* stuff. But he had horns, Jonas. When I saw him, stood in that graveyard, holding Stan Mycroft's head in his hands like a football trophy – there were horns thick as antlers coming out of his temples. And when he opened his mouth, when he opened his mouth to lick the blood from what was left of that poor old sod's neck… I got a look at his tongue. His *forked* tongue. So… *you* tell *me*. You see something that looks like a man, but with horns like a stag and a tongue like a snake, and you find out he's been around murdering people for what might as well be forever – what would *you* say he was, if not the devil?"

9

Miranda is alone when Sunny returns to the cottage – the blonde woman gone, whatever tête-à-tête they'd been enjoying disbanded or adjourned.

She's back in the summer house, making a Michelangelo of the freshest of her bodies with a chisel and a craft knife: another man, his arms and legs and chest – or what remains of them, at this latter stage of the process – a two-dimensional tapestry of coloured inks and East Asian calligraphic flourishes. So absorbed is she in her work that Sunny has to sniff and crack her once-more-human knuckles before Miranda notices she's there.

"You've been out a while," Miranda says.

"You had a friend over. I rather thought I'd leave you to it."

How best, she wonders, to break the news? Clearly it can't wait; clearly action must be taken. Deputy Head Bantry cannot be allowed to deliver his message to the children in his care. He must be stopped; ideally, given what he knows – but ought *not* to know – he must be put down. Ended.

Sunny would seize the baton if she could – would take it delightedly, with gusto. That she can't, that she never will be able to… it galls her, galls her terribly.

"She's gone." Miranda cleans the blood from the chisel with a handkerchief already stained rigid with gore; wipes the blade of the knife with the same, and tucks both knife and chisel into the tool belt at her waist. "For hours now."

No further information about the visitor is forthcoming: who she is, how she found her way to the cottage, what interest Miranda has in her.

Later, Sunny thinks. Later, perhaps, she'll make it her business to find out.

For now, there are more pressing matters to address. Whoever this mysterious guest of Miranda's might be, she'll keep.

"We have a problem," she says. "With Ewart. I believe I know what he's been up to. What he intends to do, at the school. And I must warn you, it isn't quite what you thought."

Miranda touches a hand to her lips; licks an errant drop of the tattooed man's blood from the friction ridges of her index finger.

"It isn't?"

"It isn't." Sunny shakes her head, sending greasy clumps of unwashed child-hair whipping back and forth across her cheeks. "It's worse, I'm afraid. Much, much worse."

§ § §

Sunny isn't able to kill, in this world. There are laws in place in her own world that proscribe it: stringent laws, all too readily applied by the powers that be, explicitly prohibiting the doling-out of unsanctioned death. But *were* she able to, she believes, it's entirely possible she might have struck Ewart down where he stood the very first night they met.

He was nothing but human then: a man, and only a man, though blessed with greater might and moral certitude than other men of the age.

She, conversely, was a god.

Her worshippers were few, by comparison to the thousand-strong cults she'd once gathered to her in Anatolia and the Levant, but they'd been ardent in their devotion, as scrupulous and diligent as any Phoenician in their rituals and sacrifices. Their coven numbered twelve, in the beginning, and twenty-seven by the time Ewart descended on them: all women, neither so crazed nor so decrepit with years as the Puritans insisted, but better-read and brighter than the men who were ostensibly their keepers. Canny enough to evade detection by the amateur witch-hunters who stalked the moors and fells of Jacobean Lancashire.

It was in the pages of a book they'd learned of her existence, and thereafter of the means by which to attract her attention: a magician's grimoire bound in warrior's skin, once the property – or so it was rumoured – of Bolingbroke the necromancer. And it was in those same pages that Ewart, as canny as any of the women but more ruthless by far, had found a way to do the same.

That the witch-hunters of the day were cast, long after the fact, as moral crusaders and soldiers of Christ brought Sunny a modicum of dark amusement, still. The ones she'd known were rogues and opportunists. Conmen, with nothing more to distinguish them from the farmers so many of them would otherwise have been but an indifference to suffering and the stomach to hang spinsters and torch grandmothers alive on the pyre for the price of two cows and a stallion.

Ewart was different, though.

He'd been a preacher before his conversion to the cause: not a lawyer like Hopkins or a landlord like Stearne, but a bona fide Presbyterian cleric. A true believer; obsessed with sin and utterly intent on its eradication. On burning it away.

He and his hunters-for-hire had been drawn to the site of Sunny's almost-temple – a craggy, winding slope of a village called Lock's Head – by the usual glut of unsubstantiated rumours: that the dark arts were practiced there, and bloodletting, and fornication, by practitioners so brazen in their godlessness that they eschewed even Sunday prayers at the parish chapel. They received neither hospitality nor assistance from the townsfolk, nor the presiding Justice of the Peace – but somehow, with his bloodhound's nose for sin, Ewart found the women anyway.

The women, and – concealed behind a wall panel in the High Priestess's small, ramshackle house – the book.

He and his pack of hunters had destroyed the women, of course: strangled and hanged and flayed them, the latter a personal touch of his own that would remind Sunny, centuries later, of what the American lawmen who specialised in the stalking and capture of serial killers came to call a *signature*.

And then, armed with the book and the knowledge held therein, he'd summoned her. Called her to him; bound her to the world she had hitherto visited only as it suited her, and demanded that she make him… if not quite like her, then something better than he was, something more than human. Not a god, perhaps, but a demigod; a halfling, a portion of her life-force siphoned into him.

She'd hated him for it; tried with all she had to resist. But the lines of the book were an edict, not an argument; a noose that had grown tighter and tighter around her neck the harder she'd resisted.

Eventually, defeated, she'd had no choice but to give him what he'd asked for.

§ § §

"The *children*?"

Miranda is horrified; aghast, one hand quite literally clasped to her breast in shock. It's not, Sunny thinks, the reaction one might expect from a woman who only a moment before had shucked the outer layers of flesh from a corpse with the ease of a master chef de-husking an ear of corn.

"The children. It's ingenious, really. They're less volatile than the adults, spiritually at least. More *pure*, you know? Or that's how he'd put it, I'm sure."

"I see." Miranda's hair has broken loose from its band; a strand of it dangles down, shielding her eyes. She pushes it back into place, smearing sticky, half-dried blood across her forehead in the process. "So we must stop him, then. This Bantry."

"There's no *we* about it, dear. I can't, you know that. It's you, all you. I understand he isn't one of your... shall we say *direct targets*, like our friend here." She gestures to the tattooed man strung up on the silver branches of Miranda's ersatz tree, to the curling ribbons of his skin. "But *you* must stop him, not me. The best *I* can do is watch from the side-lines while you tear him to pieces."

10

Jonas had grown up in cities, as per the dictates of his father's career: Manchester, then Bristol, and finally London. He'd never had cause therefore to shoe a horse, nor indeed to carry a horseshoe about his person.

Nevertheless, he carried one now; thrust as far down as had been physically possible, and long past what had been comfortable, into the back pocket of his jeans. It was a sad-looking thing, rusted to a chestnut brown and bent so far out of its original shape that it might have been an ancient sickle or the head of an Iron Age weapon. And it was, by Fiona's account, nearly five hundred years old.

"You remember hearing me and your dad talk about Mother Shipton?" she'd asked him, when she'd forced it into his resisting hand just before he'd said his goodbyes. "We took you and your brother to see her Cave when you were kids, that summer we stayed in Harrogate."

He *had* remembered. Not just the petrifying well that housed the cave, unforgettably oppressive though the place and the calcified ornaments that decorated it had been, but the stories Fi had told him and Louis in the car on the way: about Shipton, 16th century Yorkshire's answer to Nostradamus; about her doomsday prophecies and her healing potions; about the rumours that had driven her to live out the last of her years alone in the woods, away from the whispers of her former neighbours. The old hunchbacked witch had scared him then; had cast a lingering shadow over the remainder of the family holiday. She frightened him a little, still.

"Vaguely, I think," he'd lied.

"Bullshit. I saw the look on your face just then. But it doesn't matter if you do or you don't. What matters is, that horseshoe you're holding like it's burning your fingers? It was hers."

He'd stared down at it; tried to imagine what uses Shipton might have put it to, and what use moreover Fi thought *he* could possibly have for it now. They were protective charms, weren't they, horseshoes – back in the day, anyway? People hung them over their front doors to ward off evil, or something like that.

"My friend Nadine sent it, all the way from New Orleans," Fi had continued. "Said *she'd* got it from a lady out in Reykjavik. Got *them*, actually – there were two of them she sent, after she found out what was going on over here. One for me, and one for your Dad, since he insists on us staying put here. They're to keep us safe – from Howard and his people."

"Okay. And you're giving it to me...?"

"Because me and your Dad don't need two of them between us. And because I *know* you, Jonas Thurman. I might not be your mother, but I know well enough what you're like when someone tells you not to do something. It's like a red rag to a bull. I'd get down on my knees right here, right now and beg you if I thought it'd make you get out of Gallow and back to London quicker. But it wouldn't, would it? I'm absolutely terrified for you, and that's the truth. I know what Howard is, as well, and I know what he can do, the same as you do now. But if you *must* stick around here, and I can't persuade you to do otherwise, then I'm going to do everything in my power to keep you upright and in one piece. So take the bloody horseshoe, alright? Just *take it*."

And maybe Fi *did* have a screw loose, and maybe she *had* disappeared too far down a very specific rabbit-hole of occult conspiracy theories; he wasn't sure at all he believed half of what she'd told him in the shed, in spite of what she'd shown him and what he'd seen for himself outside the gates of the school. He wasn't religious, never had been – and if he didn't buy the idea of a benevolent god, then how could he possibly reconcile himself to the existence of a devil, of *the* devil, let alone one who'd chosen to bed down in the same sleepy, off the map little town his parents had retired to?

But she did know Jonas; had been spot-on in her assessment of his character.

He *should* leave Gallow, PhD or none. There'd be other research topics, other rabble-rousing homophobes to observe from a discreet distance. Ones with neither glowing eyes nor snakes under their skin; ones who were nothing but the common-or-garden human variety of devil. There'd be other towns, too; towns a thousand metaphorical miles from his father's judgement.

He didn't *want* to leave, though. Didn't want to feel he'd been driven away from a mystery so big and so strange he suspected it would haunt him for the rest of his life if he didn't at least try to unravel it. And so what if it was dangerous, if it was risky? His whole *life* was a risk, a roll of the fucking dice: every trip to the shops fraught with worry that the wrong type of angry cis dude would clock him as shorter and softer than a man ought to be; every toilet in every pub and restaurant a battleground; every dinner out or late-night walk by the river with Dan an opportunity for the drunk City boys piling out of the pubs to take out the day's frustrations on the queers in their sight-line. Hell, Jonas' own *father* had him down as a deluded embarrassment, a shameful secret.

So, if Fi *was* in her right mind, and Howard – or Ewart, or whoever he was – really *did* turn out to be the devil...well, so fucking what?

He was angry, he realised, slamming shut the car door and buckling himself into his seatbelt with a trembling hand. Furious, actually.

Too furious to be thinking clearly, to be capable of rational decision making? Probably.

But that didn't mean he was wrong. It didn't mean he *should* leave Gallow.

He started the engine; reversed the car out of his father's driveway and set off down the road. He'd go back to the B&B, for the rest of the afternoon at least. Email Dan; practice some breathing exercises; gather his thoughts.

Then he'd decide what to do: whether to stick around or go.

He'd made it perhaps four hundred metres from the house and past the primary school when the man in the baggy brown sweater stepped out in front of him. Collided with the bumper and rolled, with sickening slowness, over the bonnet.

11

Bantry isn't difficult to find. The smell of camphor and fresh sweat cleaves to him like clingfilm; the contrails of guilt he leaves in his wake are very nearly visible.

Miranda sees him first: sees him stepping out into the road like the walking dead, like a shambling zombie from an old *giallo*. He's muttering to himself: a string of contextless denials, negative on negative.

Shouldn't wouldn't didn't mustn't can't.

Isn't. Wouldn't ever.

No.

"What's wrong with him?" she asks Sunny.

"The words." Sunny cranes her neck to get a closer look at him, at what he's become. Her vision is frustratingly clouded, in this child's body; it might, she thinks, be worth her while to return soon to a form with senses more acute than this one has to offer. "The words Ewart gave to him, to pass on to the children – they're breaking him. Eating him up, from the inside-out."

"How? I thought the parents were the targets, and he and the children were just the messengers? The… what did you call them? The delivery mechanism?"

"They are. They were." Sunny recalls again the basement of La Pleine Lune; the Parisian revolutionaries driven to suicidal madness by the spell cast on them there, by the unbearable shame and intolerable self-knowledge the old nun's incantations dredged to the surface of their minds. "But that only works, you see, when that vessel is a true believer – when he believes himself blameless, believes his own soul spotless. Or," she adds, "when, like the children, they're burdened with no real guilt to begin with. Our Mr Bantry, I suspect, may not have been quite so pure a spirit as Ewart would have had him be. A faulty weapon, you might say. Ewart pulled the trigger, in his office; what you see now is the pressure building in the barrel, right before the gun explodes."

"What will he do?"

"Kill himself, I'd imagine. Providing, if I may, a rather neat solution to the most immediate of our problems in the process."

She allows herself a brief, satisfied smile. Sometimes, she thinks – just sometimes – this world and its more serendipitous calamities can take one quite by surprise.

She's still smiling, still delighting in her apparent good fortune, when the car appears as if from nowhere on the road before them, striking Bantry at the belly, and the man goes flying.

12

onas stopped the car immediately: jammed his foot on the brake so hard he worried his chest would smash against the steering wheel.

He hadn't been going fast, he told himself, his pulse beating a staccato in the side of his neck. He'd been doing fifteen – twenty, tops – when he hit the guy.

When the guy had hit *him*.

He unbuckled the belt that pinned him in place; shoulder-barged open the door and half-rolled onto the road, one hand already wrapped around his phone. He'd call... someone. He'd have to. An ambulance, or the police – even Fiona, if he had to. Someone – anyone – with the wherewithal to help.

Because he'd need help, wouldn't he, the man in the sweater? Jonas had been driving slowly, and the impact had been less, far less, than it could have been – but you didn't get knocked over by a car and then just dust yourself off and walk away. At best there'd be bleeding, some bruising and concussion; torn skin and broken limbs.

The worst-case scenario... it didn't bear thinking about.

He hadn't been in the wrong: that was what he needed to remember. The man had shuffled out – *jumped* out – in front of *him*, and from nowhere. Not even the keenest pair of eyes would have noticed him coming.

There was nothing Jonas could have done differently. Nothing.

The bonnet was damaged, he saw that immediately: a concave pit the size of a medicine ball denting the metal. A portion of the front bumper had come loose from its fastenings; pencil-thin fissures radiated out from the centre of the left headlight.

But the man – the man was nowhere.

Cautiously, stomach somersaulting and cold chills that were probably the early stages of shock beginning to grip his muscles, Jonas circled the car. On the right side there was only a strip of unoccupied pavement and a shallow grass verge; to the rear, nothing but open road.

He was turning to examine the left when *something* ploughed into him from behind: struck him just below the ribs and threw him face-down onto the concrete. He was aware of a back-tooth cracking as he collided with the ground; heard, then felt the crunch of his nose as it hit the ground.

And a voice – first above him, muttering and indistinct, then clearer and louder in his ear as the body generating the sound forced itself on top of his.

"Filthy filthy dirty shame of it disgusting do you hear me, Alastair? disgusting what you've been doing shouldn't mustn't mustn't ever not again sick you are sick in the head..."

It spilled into Jonas like imagist poetry, like a conjugation: fragmented, punctuated not by any logical break in word order but by the speaker's need to periodically draw breath. And Alastair? Who was Alastair? This person pinning him down, assaulting him with incoherent epithets, with actual physical violence – did they think *Jonas* was Alastair?

The pressure on his back and upper arms intensified, his assailant dropping more of their weight onto him to keep him still. He'd have to fight, he realised; use his hips and what little space there was between him and the body covering his own to break free, if he wanted to keep from suffocating.

He'd done a little self-defence training: weekend workshops in Krav Maga and Brazilian jujitsu organised by the university's LGBT society, the occasional evening class at a gym in Camden. Nothing to have left him particularly tough or well-versed in martial arts, but just enough that he knew, at least in principle, that the best way – maybe the only way – to get himself out of his present situation was to curl; to roll; and then, all being well, to run.

He arched his back; managed, somehow, to dislodge his attacker. He rolled, intending to spring upright, but overreached, his own momentum carrying him further, until he was belly-up. And then whoever had been above him was again on top of him, straddling him – both their hands clawed and tight around Jonas' throat.

He began to choke almost immediately. But not before he had the chance to really see the man; to take in the face and frame of the stranger who apparently wanted him dead.

The man was sweating: not drops but *lashes* of perspiration trickling from his balding forehead to his nose, past his twitching lips and into his open mouth. His eyes were wide and manic, unblinking; the dilated pupils and convulsing facial muscles suggested to Jonas an ageing clubber in the grip of a dance-floor ketamine overdose. His complexion was chalk-white but peppered with purpling welts, as if he'd been beaten. To Jonas, trapped beneath him in the middle of the road, he was monstrous.

His cheeks were the worst of it, though: both of them riven with scratches so deep and so bloody Jonas might have believed them the work of an animal, a wildcat or a large dog with a savage streak, had he not been privy to so close-up a view of the strips of raw skin that trailed from the man's fingernails.

He's been clawing at himself with those fingers. Gouging chunks out of his own face.

The man's breath was stale, coppery – weak, spittle-laced gusts of it hitting Jonas' mouth, also open, as he whispered and mumbled and cursed.

"Disgusting bloody disgusting, sick it is so sick, would march you off to see the priest right now if it wasn't for the shame of it, did you even think about us did you me and your dad? He'd die if he knew just about die I tell you..."

His grip tightened further, digging harder into Jonas' neck, the fingers seeking purchase on Jonas' windpipe.

I've got about half a minute before I pass out, Jonas thought. *Before he cuts my throat with those nails and plucks out my eyes while I'm bleeding to death.*

There was no moving the man now; no way of loosening his grip. Jonas' arms were trapped, palms flush against his hips.

Against the pockets of his jeans.

It was instinct, pure instinct that made him reach for the horseshoe; made him wrench it out from the pocket with force enough to rip the fabric and thrust it up into the ranting man's own throat.

Where it began to glow, the metal turning from a rusted orange to a polished, luminous gold.

The ranting man screamed at the contact, for just a second: a scream cut short by the liquid gurgling that replaced it as the rim of the horseshoe sliced into the muscle, severing his windpipe, and then on, deeper down through layer after layer of flesh.

The shredding fingertips flew to his gullet, trying – Jonas thought – to staunch the bleeding, and Jonas allowed his own hold on the impromptu weapon to release.

The horseshoe wouldn't let him. Wouldn't *let him* let go.

It could have been a psychic's moving glass or the planchette of a Ouija board for all the control he had over it, over the trajectory of its movement. It cut and cut, despite his efforts: deeper and deeper through the man's throat until it hit bone, then continued to slice, a cleaver through a leg of lamb.

Jonas screwed shut his eyes. Knew what was coming, and didn't want to see it.

He couldn't help but feel it, though. The river of hot, stinking blood soaking his hands, saturating his clothes; the slackening of the man's body on top of him, and then – suddenly – not; the rush of air across his knuckles as the horseshoe passed through the back of the man's neck and his head detached, finally, from its spinal cord and fell to the ground with a soft, wet slap.

He'd keep his eyes closed, he thought. Keep his eyes closed and stay right there in the road beside the body until someone came, until someone found him. Found them both.

"Get up."

Jonas opened his eyes. There was blood in them, too; warm blood, beginning to coagulate around the lids.

"Up, please. This is a quiet bit of the world, but *someone* will doubtless be along soon, and I'm sure none of us want them to see... this."

Two figures hovered over him. Strangers: a tall, red-haired woman in an opera cape, and a little girl, no older than eight or nine.

"What?" he said, dazed. "I don't... what?"

"*Must* I repeat myself endlessly?" It was, impossibly, the little girl and not the woman who spoke – her voice inflected with the plummy, faintly ironic edge of a dowager duchess burdened with a perennially raised eyebrow. "You. Need. To. Get. Up. Before someone *else* finds you."

He blinked, uncertain. A week before, he'd have dismissed their presence as a hallucination, as unlikely as the snakes he'd seen writhing below Tim Howard's skin. But that was then, and this was now, and who knew *what* the hell was possible anymore, in this place?

"Who are you?" he asked them, not sure any answer at all would satisfy him.

"Friends." It was the woman who spoke this time; the woman who, unlike the little girl, looked down at him with something like sympathy. "Or... well, if not now, then eventually, perhaps. We've been watching you, from across the way. You and Mr Bantry – that man you just killed. We saw what you did. What you were *capable* of doing. I think, perhaps, we may be able to help you... understand yourself a little better. And that possibly, eventually – you may be able to help us, in return."

PART V
MIRANDA

I

Oak Wood, Carndonagh – County Donegal, Ireland, 1927

They'd invited only nine guests to the ceremony: a powerful figure, and one that coincided happily with the number of women in their immediate circle.

It was a warm day, as they'd hoped and prayed it would be; as they'd sought from the Goddess with every gift of wild garlic, violet and meadowsweet they'd left at the Rock. Siobhan's hair was free of its braid, her blonde curls reaching to her hips; her gown was long and loose, the ivory cotton cinched only at the waist. Her feet were bare, and Miranda's too: both sets resting, not unpleasantly, on the soft moss blanketing the forest floor, almost but not quite touching at the toes.

Side-by-side they stood: elbow to elbow and wrist to wrist, eyes mostly straight ahead on Mother Saoirse as she offered up the blessing they'd agreed on together, the three of them. Siobhan stealing occasional glances at

Miranda, and Miranda at Siobhan; each one breaking into tiny, irrepressible smiles when they caught the other looking.

Mother Saoirse took the last of the ropes, pulled it taut and laid it over their clasped hands, tying them. Miranda's smile widened; behind them, the other women set to singing.

"Together," Saoirse said, looping the rope's edges into a knot. "*Trí do lámha a cheangal, ceangal tú do chroí freisin...*"

The singing stopped, abruptly. One of the women – Miranda thought it might have been the youngest of them, Rada – let out a short, sharp cry.

She couldn't turn to look, not without taking Siobhan with her; any sudden movement would send both of them tumbling to the ground. But the panicked widening of Saoirse's wrinkled eyes and the way the Mother's knuckles gripped and whitened around the rope told Miranda something had gone terribly awry.

"Mira?" Siobhan said – sounding... perhaps not frightened, but on the cusp of something that might easily become fear. "Mira, what is it? What's going on?"

Another cry rang out across the wood: louder and more penetrating than its predecessor, pitched too high and held too long to be an expression of anything but distress. Saoirse let the knotted rope drop, her fingers grasping for the paper-dry rushes of the Brigid's cross that fell from her neck.

And, knees bent to steady herself and upper body bound so completely to Siobhan's they might have been a pair of conjoined twins, Miranda turned – and, turning, drew them both into a kind of hell.

They were five: four of them men, or creatures at the very least man-shaped, ranging left and right about the fifth, who was nothing like a man at all. The men – the almost-men – were in a frenzy: scratching and striking at the witnesses with nails sharp as talons, grabbing blindly at the women's limbs and tearing wildly at the cloth of their dresses, at the flesh below. One had his teeth sunk deep into Sister Clodagh's throat and appeared to be sucking at the blood that flowed from the wound he'd made there; another held Rada – who was no longer crying out or screaming – in a choke-hold so tight Miranda wondered how the girl was still breathing, the muscles twitching and rippling like jumping worms under the skin of his forearms.

The fifth of them, though, stood apart from the fray: watching the carnage unfold with a coolly detached interest that reminded Miranda, perversely, of a spectator at a hurling game. He – for the thing had on the bearing and the buttoned dress-coat of a gentleman, despite his appearance – teetered on legs as thickly-furred as a ram's, but that tapered down to cleft hooves where his ankles ought to have begun; from his shaven *ceann* there sprouted two white, horn-like protuberances reminiscent of the antlers of a stag, the bony tips of each coated in a viscid chartreuse liquid she felt for sure was venom.

"*An diabhal*," she heard Saoirse whisper. "The Dark One."

The horned thing cocked his head, apparently listening. His eyes, red and slitted as a snake's, flickered past Miranda to the Mother behind her, and then across to Siobhan and Miranda herself, where it lingered. He took them in: their dresses and the flowers in their hair, their bare feet on the soil, the lengths upon lengths of rope and coloured string that bound them indivisibly together. Wrinkled his nose and spat.

"Leo," he called, to the nearest of his men – the accent English, quietly commanding. "Patrick. Come."

The twitching man who had Rada released his hold; threw her down onto the twig-littered moss, where she rolled and, finally, was still.

"Sir?" He straightened, recalibrating his spine into a posture that would have done a soldier proud. A second man joined him, fang-like canines puncturing his lower lip and wet blood smeared in artless circles about his chin and jaw.

"There." The creature thrust a pink and unexpectedly human hand outward. "The younger two."

She felt Siobhan reaching for her, digging tremulous fingers into her lower back: crying now, and shaking. Miranda wanted to comfort her, to soothe her, but found she couldn't; that she had nothing to give.

It's us, she realised, her own throat seizing and closing shut as surely as Rada's had already. *They're coming for us.*

"Sir?" the first man asked again.

The creature looked directly at Miranda then; held her eyes and smiled, obscenely.

"Bring them here," he said, smile widening. "Both of them. To me."

2

Gallow, 2019

The handle of the cleaver was hot in Jodie's grip, warmed by the sweat of her skin and by Elspeth Palmer's blood as it coagulated to paste in her palm and the grooves between her fingers.

Something wasn't right.

It wasn't the fact itself of Elspeth's death: Jodie had wanted that, had *known* she wanted it – and wanted, moreover, to be the one who brought it about – since the moment she'd slipped the blade out of Miranda's hand and into her own.

Nor was it that Jodie had killed, intentionally and with what Laura might have called *malice aforethought*. That she'd taken the blade and driven it, over and over, into Elspeth's helpless, shackled body: into her stomach and chest and shoulders, her neck and cheeks and the membranous tissues of her eyeballs.

It was the blood. Or rather, the *colour* of the blood, a bilious yellow-green, and the squirming, nematodic organisms that infested it: tiny and as densely packed as parasites in the thickening puddles expanding in concentric circles at Elspeth's feet.

"They're harmless," Miranda said. She'd stayed silent through the killing, watching from the shadows of her corpse tree with her thumbs tucked demurely into the pockets of her butcher's apron; the sudden return of her voice, in the coppery silence of the summer house, made Jodie jump so violently in fright she almost dropped the cleaver. "Disgusting, but harmless, if you keep them away from open wounds."

"What *are* they?" Jodie bent to examine the parasite-things, swallowing her disgust at the sour stench of the blood, at the proximity of what remained of Elspeth. She shouldn't, she thought distantly, have found her focus drawn to so comparatively small a detail in what was, in effect, an abattoir; and after what she'd done, the unimaginable threshold she'd crossed. But they were so *strange* – the parasites, and the fluid in which they swam. Strange, and somehow alien; entirely unlike any creature Jodie had seen before.

"An infection. A kind of... bacteria, I suppose. The same strain that did for Rick and Tanya here." Miranda gestured to the skinless figures hanging from the branches of the silver tree, the scooped-out remnants of what had once been Henry Fielding's dad and Freddie Tate's dour mother. "Though Elspeth was much further along in the process than either of them, which makes me wonder if she was the one responsible for spreading the contaminant through St. Stephen's. Our Patient Zero."

"They were... ill?" A wave of nausea passed through Jodie, followed immediately thereafter by an ice-cold dizziness and an understanding, a *real* understanding, of what she'd done in this almost-stranger's kill-room. The gravity of it.

She'd murdered someone. Someone she'd loathed, yes; someone she'd wanted dead, wanted to suffer the way Connor had suffered, every time she'd walked him – both of them in tears – past the signs and the yelling and the *hatred* through the gates of that bloody school. You couldn't just do that, though, could you? You couldn't just... take a person out of circulation because you'd decided they didn't deserve to live.

And what *about* Connor – had she even stopped to think about him before she'd picked up Miranda's hatchet and gone to town on Elspeth? If anyone found out what she'd done – and of *course* they'd find out, you couldn't get away with carving someone up like that, especially not when the police were already looking for them... she'd be arrested. There'd be a trial; a story in the papers. Not even the Oxbridge QCs Laura had known at law school would be able to convince a jury to acquit her: she'd done nothing at all to cover her tracks. The evidence against her would be overwhelming. She'd lose Laura; lose Connor. Be allowed to see him once a fortnight across a table in a grey-walled visiting room surveilled by guards and grim-eyed psychopaths, not able even to hug him goodbye without permission. If Laura would even bring him in to visit her; if she didn't serve Jodie with an injunction or a no contact order the second she got a look at the case file, at the confession Jodie would inevitably make under interrogation.

What had she done? What the *fuck* had she done?

"It's not *entirely* accurate to call it an illness." It wasn't Miranda who answered, but rather a second voice: a child's voice, high-pitched and light. Jodie bolted upright from her crouching position; spun around and saw it *was* a child, in the summer house doorway. Miranda's daughter, Sunny. "Though it's as good a metaphor as any. I prefer to think of it as a contagion, myself." The little girl yawned and stretched – lazily, Jodie thought, as if she'd been roused from a nap against her will. "All *you* need to worry about is what it *does* – the effect it has on its host. The way it effaces their... *humanity*, shall we say? Makes them just enough like Ewart to be useful. To be pliable foot-soldiers."

"Ewart?" Jodie's head swam, new confusion blending with the older sickness and threatening to double her over. And what *was* this child, who spoke like Noël Coward and could stare out into a cabinet of mutilated bodies with barely a flicker of interest? "Who's Ewart?"

"Ah." The little girl grimaced; shook her head in a parody of disappointment. "Miranda has left you in the dark, I see."

"I was about to tell her," Miranda replied. Slightly defensively, was Jodie's impression – as if she'd been chastised.

"Tell me *what*?" Jodie looked directly at Miranda now. Miranda, her last surviving link to her old, familiar life in an ever-expanding ocean of insanity.

"I didn't intend..." Miranda began, hesitantly. "That is, it wasn't..."

The child looked to Miranda, then to Jodie, then back to Miranda again, eyebrow arched.

"Really, Mira? *This* one? Now?" Miranda said nothing – her gaze, Jodie noticed, now turned downward to the bloodied floor in what Jodie at least read as embarrassment. "I see." The child shook her head a second time and, apparently heedless of the gore-drenched weapon Jodie still clutched in her fist, began to walk towards her. "Well," she continued, to Jodie this time. "I don't know what you *have* been told, but if Miranda here has yet to contextualise... all of *this* for you," she pointed to the silver tree, to the bodies hanging there, "then I'm afraid I may have some bad news. There's something of an apocalypse brewing, in this strange little town of yours. And you, my dear, have just joined the Resistance."

3

Oak Wood, Carndonagh – County Donegal, Ireland, 1927

Miranda lay on her side under the oak tree, knees clutched to her chest. It was full dark now, the wood illuminated by nothing but stars.

Above her, necks throttled and stretched by Mother Saoirse's binding rope, the bodies swayed from the old oak's branches. She could count them, every one, even in the dark.

Rada. Clodagh. Aisling and Briannon and Saoirse herself.

And Siobhan: her throat shredded by the ragged teeth of the flax and every inch of perfect skin stripped from her body.

He'd made Miranda watch as he'd flayed her, the devil with the face of a man; had his *saighdiúiri* hold Miranda still as he tore into her lover's stomach with his talons, as he peeled away Siobhan's flesh with nothing but his teeth and licked at her blood with his serpent's tongue. They'd been tied together, through it all, tethered at the arms and hands and wrists: Miranda helpless, vision turned almost to black with rage and terror, and Siobhan thrashing and screaming at her side. Fighting it, at first; fighting *him*. Pleading for mercy, until the pain became unbearable, then pleading, finally, for release.

He'd let her die, in the end. Snapped her spine with a crack that had made Miranda wish she had the means to deafen herself, then cut Siobhan loose from her ties and passed her along to his men to be strung up with the others.

"For the wages of sin is death," he'd told Miranda, as she'd fallen to the earth, "but the gift of God is eternal life, through Jesus Christ our Lord. See, and know."

He'd spat again, as if clearing his mouth of the taste of something rotten, and Miranda had squeezed shut her eyes against him, against the horror of it all. Kept them closed; poured every inch of her will into deadening her ears and nose, suppressing the evidence of her other senses, though the stench of blood and early putrefaction had remained, impossible to ignore.

When she'd opened them, the devil and his men were gone, and she was alone in the wood with only the dead for company.

Hours passed. The sun set, and darkness crept in through the leaves and branches, turning the dripping bodies from full colour to monochrome, and then to shadow. Miranda tried to force herself into a state of non-existence; to let her mind become a blank space hacked from the matter of the world and set adrift in an empyrean elephant's graveyard.

From the tree, Siobhan watched over her; her eyeless, skinless face set in immutable judgement.

"Are you able to move?"

The question came from somewhere close by; to the left of her, by the Rock in the sight of which Saoirse had secured her to Siobhan.

Miranda shuffled sideways along the ground; scanned the darkness as best she could, but saw nothing, no one.

"Do you need help?" the same voice asked. Closer still, now. Almost upon her.

She looked up, arching her back and rising onto her shoulders.

Someone stood over her: an unfamiliar figure, short and hunched and draped in shawls. An old woman – an old woman who seemed, incredibly, unmoved by the devastation around her. Could she not *see* the bodies? Not *smell* the slaughter, the decay?

"Who are you?" The words were slurred, Miranda's lips sticky with blood. She sounded dazed; intoxicated, even to herself. "What do you want?"

The old woman squatted beside her, surprisingly limber for her years; ran the outside edge of a weathered, papery hand along Miranda's jaw.

"You'll survive," she said. Her accent, Miranda realised, was not dissimilar to the devil's: too young and too crisp to belong to the wrinkled, geriatric visage behind the head-shawl. "It may not feel like it in this moment, but you will. He left you alive so you could witness, so you could see – it's as important to him as the act itself, the witnessing. The seeing and the knowing – what I daresay he'd call *the recognition of the sin*. But what you've seen here, on this day, what you've endured… it *will* pass. And when it does, you shall want redress. My word on it, you shall."

Miranda blinked, twice.

"You'll want revenge on him, the animal who did this to you. To your woman." The old girl's eyes flitted upward to the night sky, to the death-tree. "And as things stand, I'm afraid, you may struggle to achieve it to your satisfaction. He's a clever one, you see. Clever *and* powerful, alas."

"Why…" Miranda hesitated. Pulled herself into a sitting position, until she and the old woman were face to face; cleared her throat and tasted the blood on her lips. "Why are telling me this?"

"Why?" the old woman said. "Because you, Miranda – you can be powerful too. I have the means to make you so, if you should want it. And then between us, I believe, we shall be well equipped to, if you'll forgive the idiom, *bring the bastard down*."

4

Gallow, 2019

Apocalypse?" Jodie put a thumb to the ridge of her eyebrow and pressed down, hard. It alleviated neither the tension behind her eyes nor the churning in her belly. "Apocalypse as in, the end of the world?"

"Indeed." The child nodded.

"And it's something to do with... this?" She wasn't sure what *this* she meant: Miranda's corpse-tree, or the dead woman shackled to the wall, the woman she'd killed with her own two hands; the parasites in the blood seeping into the summer house floor and whatever their presence denoted, or something else altogether, the cumulative total of all of these things and more.

But the child seemed to understand the intent behind the question anyway. Seemed to know instinctively that Jodie wasn't only asking for an explanation for the apparently imminent apocalypse and how she, Jodie, was supposed to prevent it, but for a story and a meaning: something through which she could make sense of the things she'd heard and seen, the things she'd done.

"Miranda," she said, her eyes still on Jodie, "why don't you take your friend back into the house and show her through to the bathroom? There are things she'd like to ask us, I suspect. Things she'd like to know. And it might make her more comfortable to… clean herself up a touch, before we begin."

§ § §

They led her to the bathroom. Gave her thick white towels and a dressing gown – green silk, more expensive and luxuriant than any she was used to – and left the shower running, before abandoning her to her own devices; both Miranda and the child understanding, too – without her needing to utter a word – that the sight of clear bathwater turning to pink and then red around her naked body as Elspeth's blood sluiced from her skin would be too much for Jodie to bear, would send her spiralling into a full-blown panic attack, if not into outright catatonia.

Under the prickling heat of the shower, she washed – thinking, as she sluiced Elspeth from her hair and face and arms, not of Connor or Laura, nor even of Miranda and her daughter, but of Tim Howard and his followers and the spittle flying from their mouths as they shrieked and chanted at the Hummingbird gates.

She was scared, that much was certain: scared of the consequences of her actions, of what she'd discovered she was capable of when she was pushed. But was she *sorry* for any of what had happened in the summer house? Was it only self-preservation and the inevitable destruction of the life and the family she'd built that made her regret it?

And if it was: what did that make her?

They were waiting for her when she left the bathroom, Miranda and the child: Miranda with a cup of steaming tea, and the child with empty hands and a reluctant smile.

"Shall we move to the sitting room?" she said, as if she were inviting Jodie to retire for brandy and cigars after a dinner party. "I daresay there are questions you'd like addressed, and Miranda and I certainly have things to share, since she's drafted you into the cause." She shot Miranda a look that Jodie would have interpreted as a rebuke had it come from an adult and not a girl no older than Connor, and Miranda grimaced.

"Okay," Jodie answered. "Okay."

She followed them through the hall and along the stairs to the sitting room, where the child began to talk. And where Jodie – hook-like coils of dread and panic taking deeper and deeper root in her with every hammer-blow of revelation – got both the explanation she'd been promised and the story she'd been sure she needed.

§ § §

Later, much later, when Miranda and the child had left her to think over what she'd learned and to decide for herself what she wanted to do next, the door to the sitting room opened and a new stranger poked his shaggy blond head around it: a boy, or perhaps a man on the cusp of his twenties, in the baggy jeans and hooded sweatshirt of a teenager at a skatepark. He looked unassuming, and crucially, from Jodie's perspective, entirely human – though she was acutely aware, after hearing the little girl recount a history of magic and witch-hunting and demonology with the slightly bored ease of one revisiting What They Did On Their Holidays for a teacher, and after *seeing* the kid transform herself from an under-ten to a black cat and then back again, that she could trust her own judgment of anything or anyone about as far as she could throw it. The boy could be a werewolf or an extra-terrestrial shapeshifter, for all Jodie knew.

"Can I come in?" he asked – and waited, she noticed, for her to murmur a *sure* of assent before entering the room.

He was shorter than her, and slight. But something about his posture and the way he carried himself put her in mind of a coiled spring or the idling engine of a race car in the moment just before acceleration: an untapped reservoir of potential energy and latent exuberance. He was like a lion cub, she thought – but a lion cub who'd recently discovered he could go out hunting buffalo whenever the urge took him.

"Jonas," he said, offering her his hand to shake. "And you're... Jodie? Sunny mentioned you were in here. That she and Miranda had, you know... had a word. About the church and the vicar. Howard? Or Ewart, I suppose. That's his real name, I think – the one he was using at the beginning."

"*Had a word*?" She laughed; a harsh, bitter chuckle that was entirely unlike any of her usual expressions of mirth. "Is that what we're calling it?"

"It's a lot, I get that." He didn't look away; didn't falter. She hadn't fazed him, then, she thought. He'd been prepared for her reaction. "*I* still have trouble getting my head 'round it, and I've *seen* it – seen what that... hex or whatever can do to people. What it can make them do to themselves."

"Right. You've seen it. Okay. And you don't think perhaps it's all a little bit, I don't know... insane?"

More insane than hacking someone to death with a meat cleaver because they called you names in the street? Even if she was supposed to have been some sort of snake-vampire thing with leeches in her blood...?

"At first? Absolutely. But then..." The boy spun ninety degrees, until he was facing one of Miranda's sculptures – the wooden chair with splayed fingers for a backrest Jodie remembered from her first visit to the cottage. He flipped one of his hands palm-up; flicked his own fingers in a *come hither* gesture, and the legs of the chair began to rise from the floor, entirely unaided, until it hovered half a foot above the floor. "Then it turned out I could do stuff like this. And I had to, you know... update my priors a bit."

5

Killea – County Donegal, Ireland, 1927

t's too much!" Miranda was screaming; clawing at the skin of her chest as she spoke. "I can feel it everywhere, burning me up. How do you *bear* it?"

The cat, who had been watching her from what she considered a sufficiently safe distance of five feet, arched her back and stretched forward. And continued to stretch – her body shifting and shedding and lengthening until it resembled the body not of a cat but of an old woman bent into a yogic pose, her forehead resting on the ground and the outline of her shoulders eclipsed by heavy knitted shawls.

She raised her chin, as spry as she'd been the night she'd found Miranda in the forest; drew back her shoulders and levered herself upright

"You really ought to calm down," she said. "What is it you expect to achieve, with all this gnashing and wailing?"

"It *hurts*!" There were tears in Miranda's eyes; tears streaking like the lines of a tiger across her red-spattered cheeks.

"We discussed this." The old woman was calm, unperturbed. "It's the becoming. The body struggles to tolerate the necessary adaptations, the changes in the bone and blood. It has a tendency to fight them, tooth and nail, while the change is underway. Eventually the pain will lessen."

"You did this!" Miranda was wailing now, her howl rising up like a siren through the bright green canopy overhead.

"And you *chose* it. I offered you this, and you seized upon it. You would do well not to pretend thing were otherwise."

"I feel as if I'm *dying*!"

"Yes. In a sense, you are. But you are infinitely stronger now than ever you might have been, had you remained human. You will never know age or ill-health, as you most certainly would have, under other circumstances. Moreover: when this transitional phase passes, as inevitably it will... you will be better equipped than any creature on this earth to wipe Thomas Ewart from the face of it. Which was, as I recall, exactly what you wanted."

The invocation of the devil's name, his *true* name, seemed to galvanise Miranda, to steel her spine, and she fell silent.

"*Thank* you." The old woman scratched her head. "And, since we're here..." She pointed upwards, to the tree immediately above them; to the skinless, half-dismembered body Miranda had hung from its lowest branches. A petty thief and would-be rapist with a prettier face than his character deserved, albeit a face now entirely decimated by Miranda's teeth and nails – unlucky enough to have chanced upon them in the forest while Miranda slept through the worst of her pain, and too stupid to have fled while the possibility of fleeing still existed. "What is it you propose to do about *that*?"

6

Gallow, 2019

Jonas rotated his head a quarter-circle, and the chair descended to the floor with a scrape of wood on floorboard.

"So, yeah," he said – seeming to Jodie a little sheepish, a little embarrassed by his own exhibitionism. "That's a thing I can do now, I guess."

Jodie was, she found, entirely lost for words. Her own transgressions notwithstanding – and God knew, there were enough of *them* to gloss over – she'd heard and seen so many strange and frightening things since entering the cottage that day, she'd assumed she'd become more or less inured to any further shock or horror.

The vicar at St. Stephen's was a kind of demon, fluent in what sounded – from the description she'd gotten from Miranda's daughter, who wasn't *actually* a cat but could apparently turn into one at will – like the syntax and the lexicon of hell, or at least of *a* hell?

Okay. Implausible, but okay.

And that same vicar... he was planning on using that language, that hell-speech, to turn the kids at Hummingbird – Jodie's *own son* among them – into an armoury of loaded guns, primed to turn on their parents and any other adult in the vicinity with sin in their heart, whatever *that* meant?

Sure. Why not?

And Sunny and Miranda, they were the only ones who could stop this slaughter of the not-so-innocent, apparently with Jodie's help?

Fine. *Fine.*

Levitating furniture, though – it was a bridge too far, the final absurdity.

"It wasn't... something I *knew* I could do," Jonas added, filling the silence. "Before, I mean." He laughed. "Before last week, actually."

She regained her voice, finally. "Last week? What happened last week?"

"What *didn't*?" Another small laugh; another amused shake of his shaggy head. "Long story short, I got caught up in a *very* weird situation, ended up having to fight off one of Howard's zombies with a fucking *horseshoe*, and found out in the process that I was a... God, I don't even want to *say* it, it sounds so ridiculous. A warlock. Sorcerer. Necromancer? Something like that. A, you know... man-witch, type thing."

Against all odds, the *man-witch* made her smile, though she attributed this in large part to Jonas' awkwardly bemused delivery – in other circumstances, she thought, she'd probably like the kid a lot.

"Zombies?" she said. There was so much to unpack in what he'd just told her, so much to make her head pound and her vision swim – but if she had to start somewhere, in this brave new world of devils and warlocks and dismembered corpses, then why *not* start with zombies?

"That's how I've been thinking of them – Howard's victims. Not the ones he bites, the ones he infects with whatever's in his blood – they're probably more like vampires, if we're looking for analogies. I mean the *other* ones – the ones he casts his spell on, who hear the words and lose their minds. They're still upright and moving around, until they tear themselves to pieces anyway, but there's nobody *in* there. Something else is doing the driving."

"Jesus." She shuddered, an all-body spasm that set her teeth rattling.

"Yeah." Jonas was sombre, for a second. Then his frown became a grin, broad and mischievous. "Good thing I'm a man-witch, right?"

She laughed too then; couldn't help it.

"And what does it entail, this being a man-witch? Do you have to study for it, or…?"

"Sunny says it's in the blood." The grin vanished, abruptly. "Or it can be. It came from my mother, probably – I don't remember much about her, she died when I was little, but she was into that sort of thing, I think. Magic or Wicca or whatever. My stepmum is too, funnily enough, though my dad is about as far removed from it as you could possibly imagine. He *hates* that shit. But then, my brother… I don't know. Could be he's got a touch of something too, now I think about it. He used to *see* things, when we were kids. Things that weren't there. Shadows and monsters, stuff like that. I figured they were hallucinations, because he smoked so much weed and spent so much time off his face, but I wonder now if he was just self-medicating, you know? Trying to keep things *out*, not invite them in." He paused. "Anyway. Not important right now. Main thing is: man-witch; ergo, weird-ass late-onset superpowers; ergo, here to help. And when I say *help*, I mean: put Howard and all those poor fuckers he's turned in the ground while someone still can."

"His… what did you call them? Vampires?"

"It's not a perfect analogy, I know. But Howard's M.O.… There's something very *Dracula* about it, from what Sunny's told me. Move somewhere, build himself an army of diehard-zealot Renfields, use them to knock off everyone he sees as sinners, and then fuck off somewhere else to start all over again. He tends to leave the Renfields to die in his dust – they never last long, after he's gone. And he's been doing it for centuries, the sick fuck. Actual centuries. It's about time *somebody* stopped him."

"And that's you, is it?"

"You too, if you're up for it. And Sunny and Miranda, obviously. *Mostly* Sunny and Miranda, probably."

"Right." She thought back to the hanging bodies in the summer house; the smell of rot in the air, and Miranda pleading with her to understand. *We couldn't just let them carry* on *hurting us, could we?* Then further back still, to Rick Fielding and his motorbikes and the pleasantries she'd exchanged with him on the school run in the days before the protests – before Tim Howard had got his hooks into him, and Rick had made up his mind that she and Laura were Unclean. "And it doesn't bother you at all, that Miranda's got a screw loose? That she's been skinning people alive in her workshop and turning the bodies into installation art?"

(and not just chopping them up with a cleaver like you, you mean?)

"They're not people." Jonas shifted position in his seat, evidently uncomfortable with the line of questioning. "You can't talk about them as if they're people, not once they've been turned. They're... something else, and they wouldn't think twice about ripping your throat out if Howard gave them the nod. Miranda... she's got her issues, anyone can see that. But her heart's in the right place. Kind of. Besides: what choice have we got, right? She and Sunny are the only ones strong enough to take that fucker head-on, and I for one don't want the world to end just because I was squeamish about who I had to team up with to keep it from ending. The enemy of my enemy is my friend, and all that."

There it was again, she thought: the end of the world. The apocalypse. Did he really believe it, really think that was on the horizon if they didn't act on what they knew?

"Why *the world*?" she said. "That was how they put it, too – Sunny and Miranda. *The end of the world*. But why? It's bad for *us*, I get that – bad for Gallow and Hummingbird. The *world*, though? The whole world? I don't see how what Howard's doing would affect anyone in *Brighton*, let alone any further out."

"They didn't tell you?" Jonas looked worried now, his smooth brow furrowing in consternation. "Jodie, this isn't just about Gallow or the school. Hummingbird, what he's trying to do with the kids... it's a testing ground for Howard. A dry run. He pulls it off, and he's rolling it out everywhere – Berlin to Taipei. *Broadcasting* it – Sunny says he's got someone installed already at a kids' TV network, just waiting to push the button and take his message wide. Take his *words* wide. And if he does that... well, we're all fucked, aren't we? Every single one of us."

7

*Common Land Just Beyond the Church of St. Mary of the Castle
– Whatton, Derbyshire, 1958*

The squirrel picked its way through the woodland, shrivelled leaves crunching under the weight of its hind paws with every step. Periodically, it froze in its tracks, ears pricked and tail raised; wrinkled its nose as if to sniff the air, scanned the tree-trunks in its immediate line of sight and then, satisfied, moved on.

A quarter of a mile in, it found what it was looking for: a man, legless and flayed and hanging from a chestnut tree, the raw stumps of his feet threatening to scrape the dirt below.

There were no other people in the forest; the squirrel was sure of that now. And so, in the absence of any human audience, it twitched a whisker, scratched one bulging cheek with a pensive claw and changed: rippling and cycling through a plethora of shapes and sizes before settling on the form it had begun to favour best since the advent of the Classical Hollywood era.

It – though really it was *she* now, unequivocally *she* – was young, perhaps twenty-five or thereabouts; full in the breasts and lips and fuller still in the hips. Her blonde hair was thick, her eyelashes as long as a gazelle's; she might have passed for Jayne Mansfield from a distance but for her loose-fitting blouse and belted slacks, both of which she'd found to be more practical and more comfortable than any self-consciously feminine alternative.

Bipedally attired, she walked towards the hanging body for a closer look, all the while knowing that no closer look was needed. It was Miranda's handiwork. They always were.

In the still-bleeding hollow of his skinless neck, she saw it: the trigger. The red rag that must have loosened Miranda's tenuous hold over her sanity and sent her spiralling, yet again, into violence.

It was a dog-collar, or rather the tattered vestiges of one; the vestment of a churchman. The bulk of its fabric was gone, torn free from the shreds of dark-stained shirt that clung to the dead man's waist and adhered like the tassels of a grass-skirt to the sticky tissues of his thighs – by Miranda, no doubt. She was strong, now; her veins pulsing with the power the woman who was not Jayne Mansfield, nor even really a woman, had given her. Strong enough, evidently, to pull not just cloth but flesh apart with the merest swipe of her fingertip.

Strong, and unstable. And as impossible to pin down as a leaf in the breeze since she'd run from the Donegal forest that had – in a fashion – birthed her, three decades before.

All the woman who was not Jayne Mansfield could do was follow in her wake and clean up the mess Miranda left behind.

She reached up to the noose that held the corpse and, with an effortless swipe of her own fingers, tugged it – and an accompanying wave of horse chestnuts, still in their shells – free of the branch Miranda had used to secure it. The corpse fell, hitting the woodland-bed of leaves with a dry crack, and the conkers rained down on it, reminding the woman who was not Jayne

Mansfield for a moment of the revolutionaries she'd known in Paris: angry men and angrier women who'd pelt an aristo's body with rotten fruit and spoiled vegetables long after its head had been carried away from the guillotine in a basket.

She'd find Miranda, she told herself – as she always told herself. Eventually, she'd find her.

The corpse shuddered on the ground. Not, she realised on peering down at where it lay, in a belated death throe, but because its blood was crawling with parasites: the same undulating flatworms she'd observed in the remains of so many other of Miranda's victims. They seemed to look back at her as she watched them, rearing up towards her like a battalion of miniature cobras. They recognised her, she thought. As well they might.

Miranda was still tracking him, then, even in her madness; still chasing down Ewart and the newest of his acolytes alone. Alone, and with none of the help she'd need to actually *find* him and serve him his dues.

It was infuriating; quite infuriating.

The woman who was not Jayne Mansfield allowed herself a sigh, the weight of the world on her slender shoulders. Then she rolled up the sleeves of her blouse, bent to the leaf-strewn earth and began, with inhuman speed and no tool but her hands, to dig the clergyman a grave.

8

Gallow, 2019

My son," Jodie said – able suddenly to think only of Connor, of Connor and Laura arriving back from a burger-bar lunch and the afternoon shopping trip to Arundel that invariably followed Sunday morning football practice to find an empty house and Jodie missing. "I need to call my son. My wife. They don't know where I am."

"What will you tell them?" Jonas leaned back further in Miranda's monstrosity of a chair, regarding her with curiosity. "Not the truth, I assume?"

"Jesus, no." She imagined Laura's face, were Jodie to begin even to broach what she'd done, what she'd learned – what her eyes had been opened to in the cottage since that morning. The look of anxious concern Laura would wear as Jodie regaled her with the story of the demon vicar and the shapeshifting child and the worms in Elspeth Palmer's blood; the surreptitious calls she'd make later to the GP and her psychologist friend Harriet – possibly even to her own solicitor or the police – when Jodie left to use the bathroom. "But… something. I have to tell them something. I can't just… not go home. I need to get Connor ready for bed – he likes me to read him his book after Laura's given him his bath. And we have plans tomorrow; we're taking him to the farm park after school. I have to be there."

The look Jonas gave her in return was kind but pitying.

"I don't think that's going to be possible," he told her, gently. "Not tonight, anyway. Howard… he's moving fast. Really fucking fast. He's already had one crack at getting to the kids through the guy I… you know. With the horseshoe." He blushed. "And Sunny thinks he already has someone lined up to take *that* guy's place. Another… what would you call it? Loudspeaker? So, *we* need to move fast too."

"Okay. And this means I can't see my son tonight… why?"

"Fuck's sake – Miranda hasn't told you *anything*, has she?" The boy grabbed at a tuft of his own hair, apparently as exasperated with Miranda as Sunny had been. "I'm sorry – but she should have done, she fucking *should* have done if she was trying to recruit you for this bullshit."

"What, Jonas? What should she have told me?"

"When I say we need to move fast…" The boy swallowed, nervous now. "I *mean* fast. Miranda taking that woman she's been keeping in her studio, Howard's red right hand, and getting her out of the way… that was step one of the plan she and Sunny have been hatching. Step two is going after Howard directly – *actually* going after him, head on. And as far as I know… they want to do that, like, now. Tonight."

"So?"

"So… if you're with us, if you're on board – you'll be coming too. I don't exactly know what…"

A voice rang out, in the hallway just beyond the door: a woman's voice, one Jodie thought she recognised, whispering about having *found something*.

Then the door was opening, and *two* women were pushing their way inside the living room, Sunny and Miranda immediately behind them.

One was short, slight, South Asian; a few years Jodie's senior, her grey-black hair scraped back from her face and deep, dark circles carved into the skin below her eyes. She looked, to Jodie, in very desperate need of a good night's sleep.

The other, to Jodie's great surprise, was Tara Blacklock: the headmistress at Connor's school.

§ § §

"Tara's *sionnach*," Sunny said, as if this explained everything.

The tired-looking woman, now leaning back against the wall with her hands in the pockets of her leather jacket like a caricature of a teenage delinquent, snorted in derision. *Tara's wife Laila*: that was how Sunny had introduced her, though for Jodie – who was sure she'd met the woman before – no introduction had been necessary.

Sunny had neglected to offer so much as a scrap of further qualifying detail as to why Laila – or Tara – might be there in Miranda's cottage in the first place.

"*Sionnach*?" Jodie said, the instinctive deference and excessive politeness she usually felt compelled to demonstrate in the presence of Connor's teachers evaporated. "I don't know what that is."

"And why *should* you?" Tara folded her arms – sounding, Jodie thought, as strident and authoritative as she ever had at the helm of a parents' evening or a Hummingbird Open Day. "It's not a term *we* use to describe ourselves. I don't see why it's one *you* ought to be familiar with."

"You've heard of werewolves?" This was Miranda; standing close – uncomfortably close – to Jodie in the now-cramped living room, the top of her right thigh virtually pressed against Jodie's. She was watching her, too; Jodie could feel the burn of it, the intensity of her stare. "Tara's people, they're something rather like that, though more vulpine than lupine, as I understand it. *Sionnach...* it simply means *fox*, in Scots Gaelic. In Irish too, in fact," she added – and Jodie could have sworn there was something wistful, even melancholy in her voice then. Something faintly bereft. "The *sionnach* – they're shifters. A kind of... were*fox*, I suppose."

"Could we not, please?" Tara's tone had hardened further; taken on a disciplinarian timbre that made Jodie's heart go out to any misbehaving child who ever found themselves in her office. "It's not a word I enjoy, especially not currently. This... situation is absurd enough as it is. I'd prefer not to add any John Carpenter hyperbole into the mix, and I'm sure Laila is with me on that."

"Is it any more absurd than the reality, though?" Laila smiled at Tara; tender, even in her exhaustion. "Seems like quite an accurate appraisal, from the little I've seen of what you can do."

"You *know* that's not the point."

"Ladies." Sunny clapped her hands together, silencing the women. It was a disorienting gesture to witness from a child, Jodie considered; more disorienting still when you knew what that child really was, behind the mask it wore. "Might this perhaps wait? We have more pressing concerns than taxonomical minutiae."

"You're a werewolf?" Jodie asked Tara, sufficiently incredulous to ignore Sunny entirely. "My son's headteacher is a werewolf? Sorry, were*fox*."

"I only found out recently myself, if that makes you feel any better." Laila shot her wife another half-smile, this one more admonishing and altogether less affectionate than the first. "I know a lot of marriages have secrets, but they tend to be a bit more prosaic. It's gambling addictions and one-night stands most women worry about, isn't it? Not discovering their wives are the Queens of the Werepeople."

"Laila." It was intended as a warning shot, Jodie thought; as a rebuke. But

Tara was so obviously anxious about upsetting Laila – because, Jodie assumed, things between them were still so delicate, so *raw* – it came off as pleading.

"Yes," said Sunny, some of her impatience seeming to dissipate, "that came as quite the shock to us too, didn't it, Mira? We were aware of the *sionnach* connection, of course – one can smell it from a mile away. But that Tara would turn out to be the *Ancient*, of all things... frankly, we couldn't have asked for better."

"The Ancient?" This, it appeared, was to be Jodie's role in the conversation: to listen but fail to understand what she'd heard, to ask what was almost certainly a question nobody else needed answering, and then to wait for one of the others to furnish her with an explanation amounting to more than just riddles and allusions to phenomena she'd had no reason to ever imagine existed. Not even Jonas had chimed in to help her out since the women had entered the room.

"Is *not* something we need to dwell on," Tara said. "To Sunny's point: we really do have other fish to fry." She scrutinised Jodie for a moment. "Wait – you're one of Connor Campbell's mums, aren't you? I *thought* we'd met – outside of school, I mean. Your wife... Laura, isn't it?... she's at Bhaskar & Hardy. Something to do with conveyancing? Bloody hell. I can't wait to hear how *you* got caught up in all this."

"Small town living." Laila rolled her eyes. "You can't beat it."

"You said you found something?" Miranda switched her attention to Tara. "About St. Stephen's?"

"*Under* St. Stephen's," Laila corrected her. "We think that's where Tim Howard's been going in the evenings, when he's not in his office or out doing something with his coterie of psychopaths. Where he's been sleeping."

"There are tunnels there," Tara added. "Below the church. They're not in the building plans, we checked with the council and the heritage association. They're there, though. I had a... friend go and look. He didn't go inside, not all the way – it didn't seem sensible, with Howard knocking around. But he saw enough. Saw Howard go down there, too. There's an access point in the cemetery."

"A friend?" Sunny arched an eyebrow – another disquieting expression on her child's features. "Who?"

"An *old* friend. Someone I trust."

Another *sionnach*, Jodie thought. Who better than a fox, or someone who *looked* like a fox from time to time, to go sniffing around a graveyard in the early hours?

"That's where he lives? Under the church?" Miranda was all intensity again, suddenly; absolutely laser focused on what Tara and Laila were suggesting.

"I don't know about *lives*," Laila said. "But if Jonas is right," she nodded at the boy, "and he *is* a bit like Dracula... I'd put money on those tunnels being his crypt."

"I see." Miranda looked to Sunny, as if for confirmation, but the child's face was impassive, unreadable. "Then there, I suppose, is where we must go."

9

Kilburn – London, 2018

Wouldn't you rather it was *him* up there?"

Startled, Miranda released her grip on the chisel she'd been using. It fell, spattering the hard stone floor with blood and flecks of tissue.

The woman who had never been Jayne Mansfield – and who currently, in any case, more closely resembled the country singer Patsy Cline, circa 1961 – completed her descent, taking the final stairs leading down to the basement with exaggerated care.

Miranda had learned, she saw immediately; had evolved during her period in the wilderness. Had become… sophisticated, *creative* in the execution of her desires.

There were *tools*, for one thing, where once there'd been only nails and teeth and rage. Not only the chisel but a positive *array* of implements laid out along the workbench that spanned the length of one wall: hunting knives and spatulas, claw hammers and machetes, thick hessian cord and razor-edged cheese wire, cleaned and polished and sharp as an artisan's dream.

And Miranda herself was different too, or so it appeared to the woman who was not Patsy Cline, and who had never been Jayne Mansfield. More efficient: organised and clinical rather than haphazard. She wore protective clothing, now: gloves and a heavy leather apron and industrial steel-toe boots, a far cry from the gore-soaked linen dresses and bare feet she'd favoured in the earliest days of her career.

Were the ersatz Cline to settle on an idiomatic summation of the change she saw in Miranda, the word she'd alight on would be: *together*. Not manic, nor wild with untrammelled grief, but poised. Controlled.

Perhaps, she thought, these decades had been good for Miranda; had helped to sculpt her into the instrument she'd need to be, to stand any chance of toppling Ewart. Perhaps everything happened for a reason, after all.

"How did you find me?"

Not *who are you?* No; Miranda knew that already, knew it instinctively. And why wouldn't she? Certainly, the woman who was not Patsy Cline would have recognised *Miranda* regardless of any changes in her outward appearance, just as she would recognise Ewart behind any visage, any costume. There was a connection between them, between the woman who was not Patsy Cline and the ones she had sired. They could sense one another, particularly up close – as easily and as automatically as a man might focus in on the adult face of a boy he once knew at school across a crowded Tube carriage.

Though Miranda, of course, hadn't aged a day.

"You hardly made it easy. But I'm rather doggedly persistent, when I need to be."

"And what do you want?" Miranda crouched, her eyes never leaving the ersatz Cline's, and retrieved the chisel.

"Nothing more than that on which we originally agreed: to hunt down Ewart and destroy him. If, that is, destroying him is still... on your agenda?"

Miranda walked backwards two steps from the makeshift wooden gallows and the body she'd been working on, giving the woman who was not Patsy Cline an unimpeded view of the wounds she'd thus far inflicted: the peeled skin, the absent scalp, the incisions at the chest and stomach. The body was male, she saw – male and older than she might have expected, perhaps seventy-five or eighty. Blood parasites jerked and writhed across his every open wound.

"What do *you* think?" Miranda said.

The man on the gallows moaned, softly; still not quite dead enough to have fallen silent.

"I *think*," the woman who was not Patsy Cline replied, "you've made your point. And I *think*, moreover, I may have some welcome news for you, if you'd care to stay in one place long enough for me to break it."

"Which is?"

"Ewart. I believe I know where he is, or rather where he intends to be, which is surely better still. So why don't you… finish up what you're doing down here, and we can sit down with a cup of tea and work out together what we might do with this information? I'm happy to wait."

10

Gallow, 2019

They'd go in through the chapel. There was another entrance to the tunnels there, Tara had said: historically an escape hatch for endangered holy men and other nonconformist fugitives in need of protection under Elizabeth I and her successors. If they could break into the church unseen, they could access whatever tunnel network lay below it; and could thereafter, she was confident, rely on their collective intelligence and her own (apparently better than average) sensitivity to sound and smell to locate Tim Howard, wherever he might be hiding.

On what would happen after *that*, both Tara and Sunny had been vague – though Jodie had been left very much with the sense that a plan *was* in place. Just not one she was privy to.

Which was, she told herself, immaterial anyway, because there was no way in hell she was going down into any of those tunnels, much less with a view to murdering a vicar she didn't know for sure really *was* the monster all the rest of them believed.

"I'm not doing this," she said aloud. "I'm just not. It's insane."

Laila looked up from her phone. Only the two of them were left in the living room now, she and Jodie. Jonas had left to ring his step-mum; Tara to speak with whatever vulpine Deep Throat had passed along to her their knowledge of the tunnels, and Sunny and Miranda to the summer house, to do... whatever needed to be done with Elspeth Palmer's body. But Laila, it seemed, had nowhere else to be.

"Of course you're doing it," she said. "Don't be ridiculous."

She shook her head dismissively and returned to the phone.

"No." Jodie tried to sound firmer, more decisive. "I'm not. I need to be at home with my wife and my son and the TV on. Not here, in this madness. And definitely not underground hunting imaginary demons."

"Oh?" Laila pushed a button on the phone; the screen faded to black, and she slipped it into her jacket pocket. "And you'd be comfortable with that decision, would you? Given what you know?"

"I don't *know* anything. Not the way you're suggesting."

"You're a liar. You've seen what Sunny is, you've seen that boy Jonas do his magic tricks – you wouldn't still be here if you hadn't. You can't need *more* proof that what they're telling you is true."

"I don't know what I've seen. And even if I *did* know, even if I *was* sure – that wouldn't prove anything about *Howard*, would it? It still wouldn't be a good enough reason to saddle up to fight a war against the local priest in a Tudor tunnel."

"I see. You want *evidence*." Laila snaked a hand back into the pocket, and the phone came back into view.

"You say that like it's unreasonable."

"Not at all. I'm a policy analyst, I *adore* evidence. It's just not always easy to come by."

She tapped in what Jodie assumed was a passcode; traced a finger across the phone's display.

"Here." She passed the phone across to Jodie. "Watch this. It'll help."

Jodie took it, reluctantly. A single image filled the screen, the paused opening still from a video.

It was a kitchen: the kitchen of what must have been a house or flat, shot at a vertiginously Expressionist angle through what looked like an open window. In it two men stood, side-by-side and static, beside a dining table. One was tall, late thirties, his head shaved down to a light grey fuzz and his mouth caught in the moment of speaking; Jodie thought she recognised him from the protests. The other was Tim Howard.

"This happened a couple of days ago," Laila said. "Tara's had one of her... friends keep an eye on the people from that church, just in case. Thankfully he's got pretty good at holding a camera in his mouth."

"Who's he?" Jodie pointed to the tall man in the video – electing, for her own peace of mind, to leave the mouth/camera question for a later date.

"Gavin something? I'll check with Tara, she knows them all." She gestured to the screen. "You ready?"

"Probably not," Jodie said. And pressed play.

On-screen, the men began to move. There was no sound, but it was clear what was going on was an argument. Howard was calm, his posture nonthreatening and his action-hero jaw relaxed; Gavin, by contrast, was disturbed, his complexion scarlet and arms flapping in agitation.

"I don't know what they were talking about," Laila said, before she could ask. "But look."

Wordlessly, Howard placed a hand on Gavin's shoulder and gently squeezed it. Gavin seemed to settle for a moment at the touch, gesticulating limbs stilling and returning to his sides. The red in his cheeks receded, the excess blood-flow draining until he was the colour of whipped cream.

Whereupon Howard... changed.

Jodie wondered for a second if what she was seeing was a fault within the footage; an optical illusion created by Tara's lieutenant and their camerawork, their unorthodox approach to mise-en-scène. Then she remembered Sunny, and the way the air around *her* had seemed to pucker and shimmer like a mirage in the desert as she'd shifted; remembered the sweep of Jonas' wrist and the rattle of the chair as he'd lifted it off the ground without so much as touching it.

Remembered the worms in Elspeth's wounds and the smell of her dying under Miranda's knife in Jodie's hand.

And thought: perhaps it *was* real, after all.

Howard's eyes were the first to change: their Paul Newman blue becoming a burning cinnabar so bright it could have been the reflection of a bonfire in a concave mirror. His neck and collarbone began to ripple and writhe, slowly and then violently, as if whatever lived below the skin was preparing to burst free of it. Two spiked, bone-like lumps rose up from the smooth flesh of his forehead, one above each eyebrow, and continued to grow and swell and sharpen, until they seemed less like the horns she'd taken them to be and more like the spiny antlers of a deer. But *wet*, somehow: glistening with an unidentifiable slime that might have been mucus but might just as easily have been poison.

His lips parted, and the tongue that emerged was as forked as a Komodo dragon's.

Jodie's breath caught in her chest and stayed there, trapped, until her ribs began to ache. Howard was going to kill Gavin, she understood; tear him in two as she watched, and lick the bones clean with that lizard's tongue.

But he didn't.

Instead, his hand still clamped to Gavin's shoulder, he leaned in and... whispered something in the other man's ear. Gavin's face was frozen, horror-struck; a death-mask carved from pale wax. Unmoving, even as the tips of Howard's tongue darted back and forth across his neck and mastoid process, intimate as a lover's kiss.

Abruptly, Howard stopped whatever he'd been doing. Stepped back from Gavin, until there was a gap of several feet between them, and, or so it seemed to Jodie... waited.

"What's he doing?" she said – but before Laila could answer, Gavin was in motion: snatching a dessert fork from the drying rack beside the sink and plunging it into the socket of his left eye.

Jodie screamed, softly, though her own eyes stayed fixed to the screen.

In the kitchen, Gavin wrenched the fork from the socket, and the eyeball with it: pinkish blood and yellow fluid seeping down his cheek from the orange string of the optic nerve. He reached up and pulled the eyeball free of the tines of the fork – Jodie could well imagine the sucking sound it must have made as it detached – and, with the impatience of a man digging into a sponge pudding to release the molten caramel inside, stabbed himself again, this time in the groin.

Laila, perhaps sensing she'd taken all she could of the death scene, removed the phone from Jodie's curled fist and slid it back into her pocket.

"That's what we're up against," she said. "That's what he can do – what he *will* do, if we let him. Not just to the odd person here and there, either: to everyone. Everyone he thinks has it coming. And he'll use every kid he can get his hands on to do it, *including* your son. So, go on: tell me again you won't help us. Tell me again you want to go home."

11

Gallow, Before

Sunny was talking. Something about Gallow, about necromancy and bodies at the bottom of a lake: bodies far, far older than the ones Miranda had disposed of in the water at the edge of town.

Miranda scarcely heard her, though. Not because the new height disparity between them meant Miranda had to bend at the waist to listen whenever Sunny spoke; nor because the chanting and hollering of the Godfolk at the school gates tended to drown out all other sounds in their vicinity.

No: it was the woman, hurrying towards the gates – and the Godfolk – with the small boy at her heels. The woman who, Miranda assured herself, wasn't Siobhan, *couldn't be* Siobhan, despite all evidence to the contrary.

The physical resemblance was uncanny. It had been years, yes – decades, too many decades – but Miranda would never as long as she lived forget the planes of Siobhan's face or the vanilla-blonde flow of her hair down her back.

And they *moved* the same: the woman's gait the very replica of Siobhan's, down to the nervous, slightly self-effacing dip of her head as she walked.

More confusing even than the way she looked, though, was the way she smelled. Miranda had learned to trust in the accuracy of her senses – her senses as they were now, not as they'd been when Siobhan had been with her, been at her side. And the stranger... she *smelled* like Siobhan, smelled exactly like her even from this distance. Like pine needles and sea salt, heather and dew.

How was that possible, that she should not only look like her, but *smell* like her, too? How?

Unless...

Could Siobhan have found a way to come back? Back to Miranda? They'd been tied, after all; been bound together, before the devil had ripped them apart. They belonged to one another, always. If there *were* a way back from wherever Siobhan had been... Siobhan have found it, Miranda was sure. Certainly, *Miranda* would have found it. Would have broken herself into pieces with the effort of trying.

She stopped the thought in its tracks.

"*What* about the lake?" she said, aware that Sunny was no longer talking but had quietened in anticipation of a response.

Sunny's dense child's eyebrows knotted, disapproving, in the centre of her brow. "I wonder, would it not save us both valuable time, were you to admit you've heard not a word I've said?"

"I'm sorry." Miranda turned away from the stranger, and back to Sunny. "Please, continue."

"I assume by *continue* you mean *recap*?" Sunny tutted. "I said, that's where he put the women, when he was finished with them. In that lake of yours."

"Who did?" The stranger handed the small boy beside her a duffel bag, the same make and model Miranda herself had purchased for Sunny on her enrolment at Hummingbird; a bag designed, Miranda believed, to hold plimsolls and other miscellaneous sportswear items. In the corner of her eye, she saw the stranger drop a kiss to the top of the small boy's head, place a hand at the small of his back and propel him through the gates.

"Osric the Noose," Sunny said. "You've heard nothing, have you? Not a single solitary thing."

"I was..." The lie died in Miranda's mouth; it wouldn't pay, she knew by now, to argue the toss. "Osric – no. I caught that part."

She hadn't, exactly. But she was intimately acquainted with the story of Osric the Noose: Sunny had made sure of that.

Osric, they'd learned upon familiarising themselves with Gallow and its history, had made a home in the town – known then as Storton – sometime in the early 1130s, establishing himself first as a stonemason and thereafter a blacksmith – and trading out of an elaborate forge built on the site of what was now the school. In the privacy of that forge, between 1140 and 1153, he'd killed an estimated thirty-seven women snatched from villages across the county and beyond: hanging them from a scaffold of his own design until they were close to death and then extracting the hearts from their ribs with a pair of heated tongs. When finally he was caught, the body of a local merchant's daughter still fresh in his gibbet, he'd claimed to have been doing nothing less than God's work: the women, he'd said, were whores and sinners, abominations under Heaven, and removing them constituted therefore a divinely-ordained public service for which he ought, by rights, to receive gratitude, not punishment.

Storton's council of elders had disagreed, and Osric was himself sentenced to be hanged – *his* hanging giving rise, in the fullness of time, to the town's change of name. The remains of his victims had never been recovered.

"I was *saying*," Sunny continued, "that it looks as if he threw the bodies in that pond you've been using – King Edmund's Lake. Quite the coincidence, yes?"

"Not really." The blonde woman, looking so much like Siobhan it brought a pain to Miranda's chest, waved the boy goodbye through the gaps in the gate; turned and began to walk away, past the heckles of the Godfolk.

"No?" Sunny rolled her eyes. "I see. In any case, that was hardly the point I intended to make. My point – as you'd know, had you been listening – is that Osric may be the reason for Ewart's selection of Gallow as a venue. I'm increasingly of the belief that he may have chosen it for its... symbolic value."

"Oh?" The woman's pace was slow, muted; defensive, as if the Godfolk's jeers were pebbles thrown at her back. Miranda had a sudden, terrible urge to protect her; to take her in her arms and keep her safe. "And does this change anything, in terms of our plans?"

"Not a whit. But it's useful information regardless. I consider any insight into Ewart's state of mind a valuable commodity."

"Certainly." Miranda watched the woman go, until she disappeared from view. Would she be back to Hummingbird tomorrow? Surely she would, if the boy was her child; surely she'd *have* to be. She'd be at the gates every weekday morning of the school year, just as Miranda would. They would be side by side, dropping off their charges. And that being the case... Miranda would find a reason to talk to her. To find out who she really was; who she might once have been. "You're right, of course," she added. "Very valuable. Very valuable indeed."

12

Gallow, 2019

There was little opportunity for privacy, once Sunny and Miranda came back from… whatever they'd been doing with the body. Things thereafter moved quickly. Quickly enough that Jodie had no choice but to push any lingering doubts to the back of her mind and get on with preparing to go out to the tunnels to confront Tim Howard.

To kill him, you mean, she reminded herself. *He's not going to leave without a fight, is he?*

Nevertheless, she found time – while Jonas experimented with levitating other pieces of furniture and Laila helped herself to an array of small blades from the miniature armoury Miranda and Sunny had constructed in a corner of the kitchen – to sneak back upstairs to the bathroom and call Laura.

Laura wouldn't answer, of course. Her work phone she kept with her day and night, the volume on the ring tone set to high, lest an anxious client need her at 11pm on a Saturday – but her personal phone she ignored at weekends, rarely even bothering to unplug it from the charger by the bed. And this – finally, after years of Jodie chastising her for it, reminding her that the parent of a young child really *should* keep a phone on her at all times, in case of emergency... it came as a relief. Because it meant Jodie's call would go to voicemail, and Jodie would be able to leave a message saying all the things she needed to without fear of interruption. Of follow-up questions she wasn't equipped to answer.

Except... she didn't. The answerphone kicked in, she opened her mouth to speak... and nothing came. No *I'm sorry things have been so tense between us lately and I haven't known what to do about it*; no *I love you, and I wish that had been enough to make us both happy*. Not even a *please look after Connor, if I don't come home.*

Nothing.

She cancelled the call, and slunk back down the stairs, disgusted with herself.

"Did you manage to do what you needed to do?"

She turned; looked behind her and saw Laila lingering in the hallway, her jeans and jacket pockets bulging with borrowed weaponry.

"No." Jodie intended to leave it there; *should* have left it there. But something about Laila's knowing, mock-casual delivery, the suggestion that she knew exactly what Jodie had been doing, or rather had failed to do... it irked her, and she lashed out. "What about you – did you get enough knives from that cupboard? Imagine they'll do you a *lot* of good against an actual demon."

"I have to try something." Laila shrugged, not rising to the bait. "Even if it *is* just the illusion of preparation."

"I suppose it doesn't matter for you, does it?" Jodie was filled with bitterness, suddenly; overwhelmed by her own bile. "You've got your woman looking out for you down there. What did you call her, the Queen of the

Werewolves? *You're* fine. Boy Wonder in the living room, too. It's just me who's signed up to be the cannon fodder."

"You're stronger than you think. And the odds are pretty good, wouldn't you say? Six against one, and at least two of that six strike me as more than a match for that horn-headed bastard. Besides," she added, "do you honestly think Miranda's going to let anything happen to you, if she can help it? You must've seen the way she looks at you."

"She doesn't *look at me* like anything. We're friends. Or *were* friends – I don't know *what* we are now. She's not going to be jumping in front of any bullets for me."

After what she's been doing in the studio? She'd probably be shooting the gun herself.

"We'll see," Laila said, with that same infuriating knowingness. "We'll see."

§ § §

Jodie missed fifteen calls from Laura that afternoon: calls intended, no doubt, to find out *where the hell she was, what the hell she'd been doing* and *when the hell she was coming home to her family.* Laura would have been irritated at first, Jodie knew; then outright angry at Jodie for what Laura would perceive as her selfishness in taking herself off without a word; then finally, as day drew into night and worry supplanted irritation, apprehensive and distressed – at the prospect of some nebulous *bad* having befallen Jodie, at Jodie having vanished into the ether just as Elspeth had.

Jodie let every one of the calls go to voicemail. What could she say? What was there *to* say that she hadn't already tried and failed to articulate?

They ought, Sunny had said, to leave for the tunnels as soon as it was dark enough outside for them to enter the church unobtrusively – though really, the statement was an instruction, not a suggestion, and not one of the others objected.

So, just after 8pm, they made their way to St. Stephen's, Jodie squeezed beside Sunny into the passenger seat of a green Austin Healey she hadn't known Miranda owned, and Jonas in the back of Tara and Laila's altogether more commodious Range Rover.

Jodie's experience with physical violence was, she was happy to admit, limited – certainly until very recently. But not one of the six of them, she thought, seemed anything approaching battle-ready.

Jonas had added nothing to his jeans-and-trainers ensemble but a denim jacket decorated with pin-badges; it gave him the look not of a warrior heading into the fray but of a student demonstrator getting ready to protest the closure of a local library. Tara, her purported shapeshifting powers notwithstanding, looked exactly like a headteacher in her trouser-suit and blazer, while Laila, for all her hidden knives and figure-hugging leather, wouldn't have been remotely out of place in a city council planning meeting. Miranda looked... like Miranda, riding cape and all; and Sunny, inexplicably, had elected to stay in character as the small, sallow child she'd been impersonating. Maybe, Jodie thought, she moved more quickly in that body, more nimbly. Or maybe – and this, Jodie suspected, was the more likely explanation – she was simply waiting until they approached their destination before she became... something else, something more powerful and more vicious and more predatory. A tiger, perhaps; or an elk, or a Nile crocodile. Something with claws and teeth.

It took them no time at all to reach St. Stephen's – the roads empty, even by Gallow's underpopulated standards. They parked on the road across from the churchyard, the rear of the Austin an inch from the Range Rover's bumper; crossed the street and walked in silence through the cemetery, weaving in and out of dark graves crusted with moss.

The church and the parish hall beside it were darker still, the hall padlocked and devoid of even a flicker of light – the old woman whom Jodie understood acted as a sort of informal caretaker for both buildings apparently gone for the day.

She'd expected Sunny – Sunny, or Miranda – to pry open the closed high wooden door leading inside to the chapel; possibly with a crowbar, or even the force of their bare hands. But they didn't. Instead, Jonas stepped forward and, with a wave of *his* hands, seemed to *will* the locks to open and the bolts to unfasten – then, with a final flourish, *pushed* them inwards until the whole unlit interior of the chapel was visible.

"Good work, there," Laila told him.

And, two by two, they stumbled inside.

13

Dark as it had been in the chapel, it was darker in the tunnel: dark and stiflingly warm despite the crisp coolness of the night outside. Jodie struggled to see much of anything; navigating an autonomous path through the narrow crawl-way, with its curving walls of compressed dirt, felt utterly impossible. She resolved instead to follow Miranda's lead, wherever that might take them – neither Miranda, nor Sunny or Tara, nor even Jonas showing any sign of uncertainty, of hesitation in the darkness. Only Laila, she thought – Laila, who was as human as Jodie, as *unspecial* – seemed wrong footed. And *her* hand, Jodie noticed, had been firmly gripped in Tara's since they began their descent.

She squinted, narrowing her focus to the rise and fall of Miranda's heels up ahead, and willed herself to think of the tunnels as what she knew they were, an escape hatch for endangered priests of old – and not, despite the heat and the dark and the smell of damp, undeniably organic decay that penned her in on every side, a catacomb.

She had no real understanding of the passage of time, in the artificial gloaming of the underearth. But she was aware anyway, when Miranda came abruptly to a halt at the very fore of their corporeal crocodile, of having travelled some distance from the chapel. Aware, specifically, of a kind of absence: a lack of airflow, of even the faintest shaft of exterior light.

"Why are we stopping?" Jonas' voice was barely a whisper; Jodie had to strain to hear him, even in the silence.

"They're coming." Miranda *didn't* whisper, *didn't* modulate her voice, and this in itself was alarming. "Make it brighter."

"*They?*"

"Now, please."

"But I haven't practised…"

"*Now.*" It wasn't Miranda who spoke this time, but Sunny: a Sunny who sounded, to Jodie, entirely different than the drawling, acerbic creature she'd seemed before. *This* Sunny didn't make requests; she issued orders. And moreover, Jodie knew – though she couldn't have said how – was unaccustomed to having those orders disobeyed.

Jonas shivered, or Jodie thought he did; it was impossible to tell for sure in the dark, close though she was to him. And thereafter -

(she had to blink, shake her head and blink again to confirm it)

- he began to glow: a nimbus of orange-gold radiating out from the hands he'd clasped together, palms-out, at his chest, and spreading up and down to his head and feet until it encircled them all, until the tunnel and the six of them inside it were as clearly lit, even to Jodie's imperfect human eyes, as a huddle of passengers on a railway platform at sunset.

Again, there was silence.

"There's no-one here," said Laila eventually.

And then, before Jodie could blink again, there was.

There were ten of them, at least: approaching faster than she would have imagined possible from the other, unlit end of the tunnel in a swaying, side-to-side advance that was closer to a sidewinder's slither than a forward march.

Her earliest impression, on seeing them in the newly illuminated tunnel, was: though they were no longer people in the most obviously recognisable sense, they nevertheless *had been* people, once.

Their skin, or such skin as still clung like peeling wallpaper to their grey-blue tissues was taupe and withered, desiccated as a fallen leaf. Some – whom Jodie couldn't help but think of as the *fresher* ones – had strands of hair of every variety still clinging to their scalps; the rest were bald. Though many were naked, their clothes she assumed having rotted away from their bodies, some still sported shreds of fabric over their breasts and navels and the puckered remnants of their genitals: shredded tights and moth-eaten t-shirts, half-unravelled sweatshirts and, to her horror, the silks and nylons of institutional nightgowns, of the kind worn – in her experience – only by the elderly and bed-bound.

All of them, the fresh and the decayed, were riddled all over with parasites: their muscles and fascia alive with the same red worms she'd seen in Elspeth Palmer, after she'd sliced her open.

It isn't just the people at St. Stephen's Ewart has been working on, Sunny had told her, back at the cottage – almost, she'd imagined then, as an aside, in the spirit of making conversation. *He's taken to* visiting, *beyond Gallow – doing what I'm sure* he'd *call community outreach. He's forever out at hospitals and prisons and retirement homes, talking to people... though we haven't worked out yet what he wants with them.*

Hospitals and prisons and retirement homes: holding pens for the sick, the incarcerated, people too elderly and too frail to live independently. Audience primed to be ministered to; to sit and listen to the sermons of a passionate vicar.

To fall under the spell they wouldn't know he was casting.

He's built a battalion, Jodie thought. *An army of the disposable not-quite-*

dead: the ones who didn't believe what he was selling hard enough to be viable as vessels for his messages, but who'd do as infantry, in a pinch.

He really is *a bloody vampire.*

"Tara," Sunny said – and again it was an order, a directive.

Tara murmured something under her breath, as much to Laila as to Sunny, and began to change.

Jodie had known it would be coming; had been told what Tara was, what she could do. But seeing it happen was altogether different – and nothing at all like having Sunny blur between shapes for her in the comparative comfort of Miranda's sitting room.

It was, Jodie thought – feeling curiously removed from the experience, in spite of the circumstances of its unfolding – something similar to watching a character pass from man to wolf in a horror film. The sprouting of hair from skin, coarse and reddish-brown; the mouth and nose lengthening to a sharp-toothed snout as the ears grew to points and drifted up and in; the sudden gap in her vision where the top of Tara's head had been as she dropped to all fours, tail raised.

She, of course, was more fox than wolf. But the *size* of her, the sheer muscular expanse of her neck and thighs and shoulders... She was larger by far than any fox Jodie had ever come across in the wild; larger than any *wolf* she'd ever caught a glimpse of in photographs and wildlife documentaries. There was something not entirely of the present about a living thing that size; something prehistoric, megafaunal.

Tara raised her newly formed snout and inhaled, deeply. Reared up onto her hind legs, and roared: not the bark of a fox, nor the howl of a wolf but the roar of a lion, a wounded bear.

For a moment, there was nothing. Nothing but Ewart's undead army, advancing on them with reptilian speed, so close now Jodie could have gagged on the stench of rot and ruin coming off them.

And then there was something: a returning howl from the chapel above them, and another and another, until the call-and-response of them drowned out even the slither of feet on dirt.

"They made it, then," said Laila. There was a tremor in her voice.

The undead charged.

"Up," Sunny said, with an urgency that Jodie was sure hadn't been there before. "To the chapel."

Jodie turned and sprinted back along the tunnel the way they'd come, not daring to look behind her. Laila kept pace with her; Jonas ran on ahead, lighting the way, his hands still glowing with whatever ethereal illumination he'd conjured. Tara, Miranda and Sunny, she presumed, were holding the line in the dark; keeping Ewart's soldiers at bay as the humans fled.

The tunnel steepened, the ground merging with the set of rough stone steps leading up to the hatch in the chapel floor as the gradient increased. Jonas took the steps quickly, and she followed: up, and back into St. Stephen's.

Where the foxes waited.

14

They were smaller than Tara, though still larger and fiercer than any animal she'd ever seen in the wild – each one as tall as an Irish Wolfhound and as broad as a Mastiff, thickly furred in shades of red and gold and grey.

They advanced on Jonas as a single, snarling unit: the leaner, hungrier-looking ones out front and the heavier ones along the back. Jodie counted twelve bodies blocking the aisle to the exit; twelve salivating tongues in crackling jaws. There were more of them, though; she could hear them beyond the church, howls echoing out across the graveyard.

And if they're all Tara's... how many exactly can she command? How many come calling when the Ancient clicks her fingers?

"Can you call them off?" she asked Jonas. "Get them to let us pass?"

The fox closest to her on the front line, a wiry long-legged vixen with a pure white belly, bared its teeth at her and growled. It would be the first to come for her, she thought, when they attacked. *If* they attacked.

"Call them off *how*?" Jonas said, incredulous. "What is it you think I can do here that you can't?"

The vixen dropped its weight, claws extended and eyes on Jonas – a precursor, Jodie was sure, to an inevitable lunge for the throat.

"Wait," hissed Laila from over Jodie's shoulder. "Just... wait."

Another howl rang out through the pews, rising up from the tunnel to the vaulted ceiling, and the vixen froze, mid-crouch. Jodie caught flashes of movement behind her, to her right and left... then Tara was with them in the chapel, her vast body lodged in the space between Jonas and the foxes, and the foxes were – unbelievable though it seemed to Jodie – *bowing down* before her, falling to their haunches like cattle in the rain...

"Move! Now!"

Miranda spilled out from the tunnel, Sunny at her heels. Sprinted forward in a haze of speed and seized Jodie by the hand, dragging her down the aisle, past the genuflecting foxes and into a row of stalls; flung her down onto the bench and darted forward again, into the crowded press of fur and skin.

To protect her, or so Jodie came to believe in the aftermath. To hide Jodie away as best she could and keep her some approximation of safe.

And then Howard's army was pouring from the tunnels, too: a swarm of them, far more than the ten or so there'd been before.

Tara pressed her muzzle into Laila's ribs, nudging her backwards – towards the foxes, who promptly unfroze and moved to enclose her, and away from the undead swarm. She turned 180 degrees to face the tunnel and the monsters it dislodged. And leapt.

Thereafter was chaos.

The front guard of foxes followed Tara's lead: cannonballing headfirst into the encroaching undead and shoving them down to the floor, where their skulls cracked like dry logs on an open fire against the marble inlay. Portions of torn flesh and bitten limbs, severed at the joint, flew out of the cluster of bodies and scattered on the altar; rolled along the ground and gathered at the base of the lectern. And everywhere Jodie looked, the already-dead were falling: worm-riddled blood flowing unstaunched from the teeth-marks at their throats, from the claw incisions slicing them at the chest and gut and groin.

But still they came from out of the tunnel – every undead body neutralised supplanted almost immediately by one or two or more just like it. They grabbed for the foxes with decaying arms, squeezing and digging at the muscle below the fur with blackened nails, stronger by far than anything so rotten should have been.

Jonas fought them – generating orb after orb of burning light between his cupped palms and hurling them like bowling balls at first one of the creatures, then another. Miranda fought them too: swinging at them with her fists and knocking them down with crescent kicks and roundhouses too fast and too rapidly dispatched for Jodie to be sure exactly *where* on their targets Miranda intended them to land; to be sure only that they *did* land, and with force enough to snap a spine or leave a bloody constellation of foot-shaped craters in a sunken stomach. Miranda's irises were red now, Jodie realised; and though her flesh neither writhed nor rippled, as Tim Howard's had in Laila's video, the osseous nubs of what could have been horns were visible through the broken skin of her temples.

Sunny was nowhere to be found.

The noise was cacophonous, ear-splitting. But even in the din, Jodie heard the scream when it came.

Laila.

She looked right, to the pews across the aisle, and saw a trio of the undead bearing down on Laila's body, laying supine on the bench: her legs twitching and arms flailing as the monsters tore at her, their nails raking at her clothes and exposed flesh, and the serpentine mass of their shapes obscuring Jodie's view of the rest of her.

Jodie could imagine what she'd see, though. Could picture very well the agony she'd find there, and the terror.

Another scream rang out from the pews, loud and long enough this time to carry out over the fray to Tara – who stopped dead where she stood, penned in between a bleeding, mewling fox with a stump left for a tail and an undead woman in a brown-stained dressing gown with only half a face. She roared, the shockwaves of the bellow sending the dead woman reeling backwards onto the altar, and then *vaulted*, clearing the skirmish in one bound and barrelling down the aisle, scattering fox and undead bodies in her wake.

She threw herself into the knot of living corpses thrashing over Laila on the bench, her jaws already open and dewclaws keen as Miranda's paring knife jutting from her paws; half-turned as she landed and *sliced*, severing the head of the nearest of the creatures from its body with one swipe. She bit down on the neck of another, decapitating it as cleanly as a guillotine; skewered the third with a dewclaw through the solar plexus and left it to bleed to its second death on the tiles, quaking and shuddering.

Jodie could see no more of the scene across the aisle than she could before. But the low, heartbroken wail Tara expelled as she bent her own body to the place where her wife's had been told her everything she needed to know.

Howard's soldiers had done their work. And Laila was gone.

15

Looking out from across the aisle, Jodie was sure Tara would crumble; would collapse over Laila's broken body and refuse to get up, even as the other foxes slaughtered and were slaughtered all around her.

But she didn't.

Her howling and wailing done, she lay down beside what had been Laila and whined, very softly – more dog than wolf, in her grief. She stayed there for what felt to Jodie like an eternity but might only have been a minute, then shot up, suddenly rigid – and, faster than Jodie had seen her move yet, bolted back into the thick of the fight, biting and snarling and slashing at anything and anyone in her path, undead and fox and human alike. Even Jonas and Miranda made way for her – stepping back and out of her reach before she could strike out at them, too.

She fought like something possessed; whatever power she'd wielded before amplified tenfold by a fury so great and so implacable it looked to Jodie like a kind of madness. She cut through the growing swathe of undead like they were papier-mâché, sustaining not so much as a cut to the nose in the process, until – finally – the tunnel was empty: Howard's army apparently depleted, and the upper section of the church was so densely carpeted with their corpses Jodie wouldn't have been able to cross it if she'd wanted to.

Jodie gathered her courage; climbed up onto the bench she'd been using to conceal herself from the roving dead and, raising herself up onto her knees, scanned the chapel, wall to wall. There were no undead left standing, that she could see. Only battered and bloody foxes, some limping and others already beginning to lick at their wounds; only Miranda and Jonas, surveying the impromptu battlefield – he shellshocked, and she frowning in perplexity. Only Tara, one shovel-sized paw pinning a final victim to the ground by its chest and eyes, like Jodie's, flicking left and right in search of other living bodies, other quarries.

Then Sunny, hurtling through the tunnel to the altar at the speed of a bullet. And behind her, not running but *striding* forward, Tim Howard: skin rippling like a bed of eels, antlers rising from his temples and irises blazing the red of a nuclear sunset.

Tara saw him first. Saw him, roared and lunged for him; clamped her jaws around his throat and bit down, canines sinking into the writhing flesh below the skin.

"Don't!" Miranda yelled – at her or at him, Jodie didn't know, couldn't say – but neither seemed to notice, to react.

And then Howard was grabbing Tara by the fur at the scruff of her neck and pulling her off him, frothing pink spittle and chunks Jodie thought *must* be the meat of his neck still caught in her teeth, and slamming her to the floor in a wrestler's drop.

She heard the crunch of the bone as Tara's head struck the marble.

The second he raised his knee Jodie knew what would happen next, what he intended to do. But Tara was too weak and too damaged to move, or even to roll free of his heel as he brought it down on her skull; as he stamped hard on her jaw, her muzzle, the place where her ribs jutted out from her pelt, again and again and again, until blood poured from her eyes and nose and mouth and she was entirely motionless, all breath gone from her lungs.

16

The remaining foxes cried out, as if every one of them had been kicked at once. Then they fled: running and limping and crawling over the bodies of the undead and out of the church.

"Ewart." Sunny drew herself up to her full, child's height from the squatting position she'd briefly adopted beside the heap of broken fur that had been Tara. As she stood, she changed: lengthening and stretching and *becoming,* sprouting horns like Howard's, like Miranda's, but larger and longer, so high the intertwining bones of them seemed to Jodie to stretch upward almost to the chapel's ceiling. The rest of her grew and shifted too: legs filling out and lengthening as her feet reshaped themselves to ungulate hooves, both pupils rounding and yellowing to cat's eyes as a third manifested in the middle of her forehead, and sallow olive skin shifting to an electric blue that seemed to pulse and shimmer with her every movement.

This is what she is, Jodie thought. *What she's always been, under the camouflage.*

Facing off against Howard, the way she is now... she wants to do it as herself, her real self.

"You." Howard sneered – but there was something there, below the contempt, that might have been shock. Fear, even. "I should have realised you were here. I've felt you, watching."

"Not *just* me." Sunny gestured behind her, to Miranda.

Howard squinted. Raked Miranda over, up and down; took in her reddening eyes, the beginnings of her horns, and grinned, grotesquely.

"You made another, then?"

"You don't remember?" Miranda's tongue was forked now too, Jodie saw: her every word a hiss, a spitting accusation. "All you did, *diabhal*, and you remember none of it? *Téigh ar ais go dtí ifreann áit a mbaineann tú.*"

Her flesh seemed to ripple as she cursed; to undulate, like Howard's. Like Elspeth Palmer's had, in death.

And what was *that she was speaking? Irish? Welsh?*

Miranda shoved past Sunny, and not gently – though Sunny, to Jodie's surprise, made no effort to resist, nor to retaliate in kind, but simply let herself be pushed aside.

She waved a hand – the fingers, Jodie noticed, beginning to fuse together, to harden to a nail-like keratin – and the sea of undead corpses parted for her, their limbs and torsos smashing against the chapel walls as if propelled there by the tailwind of a jet engine. Clearing her path to Howard.

"You took her from me, *diabhal*," she growled, lunging for him, driving the stiffening fingers into the wriggling pulp below his collarbone. "Everything, you took."

He grunted, his mouth and nostrils contorting in pain, and struck out at her with an elbow. It caught her just below the hairline and she tripped, reeling. She landed in the middle of the aisle, just a few feet from Jodie's pew; broke her fall with the flats of her palms and sprung back upright, snarling.

"Get out of the way!" Jonas shouted – and it took Jodie a beat to understand that he was shouting at *her*, at Jodie, that *she* was the one who needed to move, and move quickly. Another beat, and she understood why: understood, as Howard bore down on Miranda with cloven fists clenched and the tusks of his eye-teeth unsheathed, that her hiding place had made her a target. That the two of them were apt at any moment to take the fight to the benches and crush her to bone-dust in the process.

She shuffled along the bench to the far end of the pew, towards the left-hand wall and away from the aisle – quietly, she thought. But not quietly enough.

The motion, subtle as it was, turned Miranda's head – pulling her gaze left and, for a split second, out of the fight.

Howard pounced.

Miranda's neck was craned, her red eyes on Jodie – but her body faced Howard's, still. She whispered something at Jodie, something unreadable from a distance but that might have been *go*, and then jerked, suddenly: back and up, her sternum thrust forwards and her arms spread in a grim facsimile of the crucifixion scene that played out on the cross above the altar. Stomach stretched, and Howard's fist buried to the wrist in her gut: his forearm flexing as it twisted and tugged at whichever of Miranda's organs his hand had taken hold of.

She licked at her lips with the forked tip of her tongue. Blood poured from the corner of her mouth.

"Mira!" It was Sunny who called out, but Jonas who acted first: throwing one ball then another of the burning light at Howard, who batted both away with no effort at all. A third grazed Howard at the shoulder, and he bared his teeth; releasing his grip on Miranda and wrenching his hand free of her. She fell to the floor as if her strings had been cut, legs curled in on themselves and cloven fingers pawing at the ragged hole in her midsection.

Howard wiped the gore from his palm and charged, Jonas in his sights.

It defied reason, Jodie going to Miranda where she lay; was dangerous, illogical. But the way Miranda had looked at her, just before Howard attacked; the tenderness she'd shown Jodie, in the kill-room; the cool feel of Miranda's hand against her forehead after Elspeth had beaten Jodie bloody by the school gates… it was worth *something*. The accumulated weight of it: it deserved more than Jodie leaving her to die alone on the floor of a church, no matter what Miranda might have done, or to whom.

And so Jodie went to her. Crawled to her across the marble; cupped Miranda's jaw, ran a fingertip along the curve of her cheek and waited, the hiss and burn and crackle of whichever assault from Jonas Howard was deflecting fading to a muted buzz.

Miranda's eyelids fluttered open. Her eyes were green below them, the red receded to sandstone circles around the pupils.

"You're here," she said, and smiled. "*Tháinig tú ar ais chugam.* I knew you would."

"I don't…" Jodie stopped herself. What good was there in asking questions, in demanding answers? Wherever Miranda was, whoever she thought *Jodie* was… now wasn't the time to correct her, to tell her she was wrong. "Yes, I am. I'm here."

Miranda placed her own hand over Jodie's – the fingers harder than they ought to have been, but recognisably *fingers*, and nothing more.

"*Is maith an rud é tú a fheiceáil,* Siobhan. You don't know how good. It's been so hard, every day, with you gone."

She squeezed Jodie's hand, weakly.

"I'm here now," Jodie said. "It's all okay, I'm here now."

Miranda's body shuddered. Jodie looked down at the wound in her stomach and saw it was pulsing, not quite in time with her breath – the parasite worms spilling out from the frayed edges of her skin like maggots from a cut of spoiled meat.

"I knew you were." Miranda's voice was fading, her eyes beginning to shut again, though the smile hadn't left her. "I knew when I saw you that you'd done it, that you'd come back to me."

She's going, Jodie thought. And sat and listened and held her hand, until Miranda was gone.

The sounds of fighting grew louder in the background – as if someone, somewhere had turned up the volume. Jodie heard shouting – Jonas, it had to be Jonas – and then a rustling hush; a murmuring.

Howard. And was he... *praying*?

She rose from the floor, from Miranda.

Far away – or was it close by? – something cracked: a fissure spreading through a rock. A stone wall, fracturing in two.

She felt the judgement of a hundred unseen eyes across her skin, her mind. Smelled sulphur and rotting tissue; tasted burning shit on the roof of her mouth.

She gagged, blinded and deafened and sickened with herself, with the weakness and corruption that were – she knew suddenly – all she was, and all she'd ever been. In her blindness, she stumbled, tripped; fell forward, hands grasping for purchase at the thickening air.

Something tugged at her: a hand, soft as kid-gloves, pulling her away from wherever she was heading. Sunny? Whoever it was, they were speaking, she was sure. Shouting at her: something urgent, some imperative or other. But they might as well have been screaming underwater.

Another *something* gripped her: another, harder hand on her body, clawing at her biceps even as the softer hand sought to pull her in another direction altogether. The joints of both shoulders caught fire, ball and socket, and she wondered – dimly, caught already as she was in her own insensate furnace of self-loathing – if she would split in two.

She felt a sharpness at her neck. A sting.

A pain, then a blackness, as the teeth that had bitten her sank in.

17

After the blackness, a pinprick of light. Her sight came back to her, and with it came clarity, a presence of mind that, she registered now, had been absent in the moments before. She'd been unconscious, she realised; passed out on the altar. Just another body, in a makeshift mausoleum overflowing with them.

He'd bitten her. Howard had bitten her.

To turn you. He needs backup, with his army gone and Sunny and Jonas still coming for him. And there you were: blind, and lost, and vulnerable.

She pulled herself to standing. Pressed a finger to her neck, to the broken skin he'd left there; winced at the sting, the red-raw tenderness of the puncture marks.

Had he infected her already? Were his parasites in her now, coursing through her, colonising her blood the way they'd colonised Elspeth and the deconstructed men and women in Miranda's summer house?

She felt different, certainly: more lucid, more alert. Less afraid? Maybe – if only, perhaps, because the worst had happened already.

Has it, though? You're still alive, aren't you? Still here, and still breathing.

The last thought set a thin quake of panic racing down the fault-line of her spine, jolting her out of whatever reverie she'd been lost in.

Howard: where *was* he? Where had he gone?

And where, for that matter, were Sunny and Jonas?

The chapel, she saw, was empty, but for the bodies: Miranda's and Tara's and Laila's, the myriad undead and the foxes they'd butchered.

Empty, and silent.

Slowly, unsteadily, she worked her way down the aisle to the doors. Pulled them open, more easily than she'd imagined she'd be able to, and stepped out into the darkness of the graveyard.

Except... it wasn't dark out there, nor really. A faint glow illuminated the headstones and the smattering of Celtic crosses that ringed them, casting a canopy of sodium-lamp yellow over the grass and the hanging branches of the oak trees.

Jonas.

She staggered through the gravestones and around, to the back of the church, where the light grew stronger – the incandescence of it throwing moving shadows across the brickwork.

There were more graves there, row after row of them. Between the graves was Jonas: battered, barely upright but still fighting, a ball of blinding, scorching luminescence the size of a dinner plate resting on the palm of each of his hands. Not six feet from him was Howard, crouched to a defensive stance, arms covering his face in a fighter's guard – and also, to her surprise, looking as if he'd been pummelled.

He wasn't bleeding. But he'd been damaged, cut. A fine line of purple fluid oozed from his nostrils; bone extruded from his now-shirtless torso, at least two ribs broken below the muscles of his chest and the parasites that writhed there. One antler had been blasted from his head, she assumed by Jonas' projectiles, whatever they were; it hung loose and useless by his ear, that same purple fluid dripping from it like venom from the pincers of a spider, nothing but a cavity left where the cartilage had been.

He did it – Jonas actually did it, actually took a chunk out of a bloody demon. Who'd have thought a kid like that would have it in him?

But where was Sunny? Where the *fuck* was Sunny?

Another of the burning spheres flew from Jonas to Howard. Howard ducked, and it went wide, rushing past him and hitting the wing of a stone angel, which shattered. Jonas rallied; summoned another orb and lobbed it at Howard. This one was smaller, though; significantly weaker, its velocity less powerful, and it fell to the ground long before it reached Howard, scorching the grass below to baked earth and ashes.

He's losing it. The kid is losing it. He won't have long if he keeps up like this.

Howard ran at him: fast enough – even with his strength diminished – to blur the still air around them to a desert haze. Jodie, her judgement clouded by the same insufficiency of reason that had driven her towards Miranda as she lay dying, felt her own legs tense in readiness to carry her forward, to throw herself between them...

... and there, then, was Sunny: dropping from God-knew-where – from out of the sky itself, it seemed to Jodie – to bundle Jonas out of Howard's path. The pair of them rolled, curled around each other like tussling cats in a Looney Tunes cartoon, before coming to a stop between two graves and separating.

She recovered herself in a heartbeat, springing to her feet in a half-somersault and bending to retrieve Jonas, to pull him up with her.

"It's time," she told him as he found his balance – speaking low, in that same voice Jodie had heard her use before, the voice that would brook no argument. "You know what you must do."

Jonas' mouth fell open, and he paled; looking suddenly sicker and more broken even than before, if such a thing was possible.

Howard rallied, spinning to face them; to regroup before attacking again.

"Jonas," Sunny said – as a warning or a threat, Jodie didn't know. And Jonas, worse for wear though he undoubtedly was, responded. He straightened, jaw clenched and eyes boring into Howard, and began to speak, to chant: an explosion of glottal stops and fricatives in a language Jodie had never heard before and couldn't have identified if her life depended on it, but which struck her immediately as *old*. As old, perhaps, as Sunny.

Howard's whole demeanour altered, his posture tightening as his face slackened. He stalled, mid-stride, then took a step backwards, as if he'd been stunned. As if he'd walked headlong into an invisible wall and the shock had sent him reeling.

It was fear, Jodie realised. He was suddenly, desperately afraid.

She looked back at Jonas, and saw why.

Behind the boy, a battalion of women gathered, young and older: rising like mist not from the graves but from the earth itself, their forms translucent as ghosts but – she knew instinctively – every bit as solid and as real as she was.

They came clothed in what she would have thought of, had she ever had reason before to consider the matter, as Medieval peasant dress: woollen robes, coarse and voluminous, belted at the waist and reaching to the ground. A few, the younger ones, wore their long hair braided; others sported veils and headscarves, secured by knotted crowns of cotton.

Some were small and slender, others more voluptuous; some might have been mothers, grandmothers, while others still seemed barely out of adolescence.

All bore identical scars: the torn skin and deep abrasions of a hanging or a strangulation around the throat and neck, and – visible through identical holes carved out of their garments – the same sunken cavity in their chests where their hearts ought to have been.

In her hand, each carried a fist-sized lump of fleshy tissue: the missing heart, beating to the rhythm of what should have been her pulse.

"I told you," Jodie thought she heard Sunny tell Jonas as the women marched forward, towards Howard – though the boy kept right on chanting, intoning, never letting his recitation lapse. "They've been waiting."

Howard remained fixed to the spot, whatever terror he felt sprouting roots that seemed to grip the soil and hold him in place.

The ghost-women fell on him. And yes, they were solid, corporeal: grabbing at him with their free hands and pulling, tearing. They tore at his scalp, his arms, the looser skin at his jowls and Adam's apple; snapped the remaining antler from his head and yanked fistful upon fistful of bloody fur from his satyr's legs. He screamed, but it was lost immediately in the meaty Velcro ripping of skin from flesh and flesh from bone, and when one of the ghost-women reached into his mouth and began to tug at the fork of his tongue, Jodie had to look away.

When eventually she looked back, the women were gone, and there was nothing left of Howard but a patch of blood-soaked grass.

18

Later

Jodie didn't go home, afterwards, though she'd told Sunny and Jonas that she was needed there. That turning up in the middle of the night, even with Laura fuming at her disappearing act and Connor fast asleep in bed – even with blood caking the split skin of her neck and her hair steeped in the lingering base notes of death and putrefaction – would be preferable to leaving them to worry any more than they had already.

Jonas had tried to change her mind, to convince her to remain with him and Sunny at St. Stephen's until they'd finished their clean-up: until he'd cleaned and rearranged the chapel and its fixtures in a way suggestive of vandalism above violent destruction, and until Sunny – her movements quicker than the eye – had buried the undead below the soil of the graveyard.

The bodies of the foxes, he'd told Jodie – the foxes, and Tara – would be dealt with later; collected, though he hadn't said by whom. Whoever it was, she suspected, they would be persuaded to take Laila with them, too; to lay her to rest with Tara, wherever it was that creatures like the foxes rested after death. The boy would insist on it.

But Jodie had been adamant. And eventually Jonas had let her go, albeit only once she'd promised to text him the very second she was home, and call him immediately on waking the following day.

In fact, she'd destroyed her phone within minutes of leaving the church: smashed the glass and casing under her heel and then, seeing that the bulk of the device was still intact despite her efforts, taken a spare brick from a construction skip left overnight not far from Hummingbird and pounded the thing – and the circuitry inside it – to nothing but mangled metal.

Someone would find her eventually, of course. But that didn't mean she had to make it easy for them.

She ran to the lake. Her speed, while no match for Sunny's, was a noticeable improvement on any pace she'd set before, though her breath came easily and she felt none of the burn or twinge in her muscles she associated these days with exercise of any kind.

She was different now. Stronger.

There were no lights on in Wyevale Park: no street lamps, no cat's eyes, no illuminated signs. But Jodie found she could see perfectly well in the darkness; more than well enough to guide herself along the footpath to the lake.

At the edge of the water, she stopped. Took stock.

She could feel them in her now, the parasites: feel them moving, crawling through her blood and under her skin, on the way already to making her the hard, insensate thing she'd eventually become. She hated them for what they'd taken from her – what they *would* take, if she let them.

But perhaps they could be useful, too. Perhaps she could make them work *for* her; could turn the strength they'd given her to her own advantage.

She'd need it, now.

She slipped her hands into the pockets of her jeans and ran her fingers over the stones she'd filled them with, the broken chunks of brick she'd stolen from the skip.

She thought of Connor in his cabin bed, his eyes closed and hair ruffled with sleep; of Laura, who would keep him safe. And, praying she'd stay strong even as the lake closed over her, she stepped down into the water.

AFTER

Jonas cleaned the last of the pooling blood from the marble with what was left of his shirt, wrung it out in the bucket he'd found in Ewart's office and tied it back around his waist. There was so much blood drying on him already, his own and other people's – what difference would a little more make?

His sinuses ached; his cheekbones. His ears rang, no doubt from the blows he'd taken to the head; it would be days, he suspected – weeks, even – before he'd be rid of it. His wrists and ankles were sprained, though he had a sense neither were broken – and for that small mercy, at least, he was grateful.

He needed to rest, and soon. Though he couldn't imagine how he'd ever sleep again.

"This should be enough," said Sunny, surveying the remaining damage to the chapel. "We could have sprayed a little graffiti on the altar, for verisimilitude, but I didn't think to bring a can."

"Do you think she'll get home safe?" he asked her, very pointedly ignoring her effort at good humour. She wasn't like him, wasn't a person, and he understood that: she didn't see the need for sensitivity or gentleness, even in the aftermath of atrocity. But that didn't mean he had to play to her way of thinking, did it? He *was* human; *was* a person. And he was shit-scared for Jodie, as well as for himself. "She was only just standing. And after what she's been through…"

"I very much doubt she's gone home." Sunny took in the broken altar: swept her eyes – all of them, too many of them – over the crucifix, the shattered wax of the candles.

"What do you mean? She told us she was heading straight there. I wouldn't have let her go otherwise."

"No? Well. Perhaps I have it wrong, then."

She was being disingenuous; evasive, as if she was privy to information he wasn't. But he didn't have the energy to press her on it. Whatever fight he'd mustered for Howard, it was out of him now.

"She'll text me when she's in," he said, for his own benefit as much as for Sunny's. "She gave me her word on it." Then: "Are you okay? Were you able to get Miranda…?"

"In the ground with the others? Yes."

"I'm sorry."

"Are you?" It wasn't a dig, he thought. She was genuinely curious.

"Of course I am. She was your friend."

"She was a monster." Sunny's voice was flat, signifying nothing.

"Still. You're allowed to grieve. To…" He paused; adjusted his tone, his phrasing. "To wish she wasn't gone."

He might have been talking to a child; explaining grief and its percussives to a four-year-old who'd never known a loss. But there *was* something childlike about her, wasn't there? In spite of her age. Or perhaps because of it.

"I'll survive." Sunny blinked, a shiver rippling in neon streaks across her strange blue skin. And he was sorry for her, suddenly. She *would* survive; her survival had never been in question. But she'd been tied so closely to Miranda, these last months, and chasing her for longer still. Surely she'd grown used to company, to being... not quite alone?

She'd had a purpose, too, with Miranda. A mission, ever since Howard had wronged her and she'd vowed to make him pay for it. A reason for being that had seen her through centuries.

With that gone, and Miranda gone too – what would she do with herself?

"And what are *your* plans, now?" she asked him. "Will you be going back to London?"

"I suppose," he said – then faltered.

Would he go back? *Could* he?

He hadn't given Dan a date for his return, in the – vague, sometimes outright duplicitous – emails he'd sent him from Gallow, from the spare room at Miranda's cottage. Truth be told, he'd been reluctant to plan even a week ahead, since Sunny and Miranda had entered the picture: half-convinced as he'd been that he wouldn't make it through his stay, through any confrontation with Howard and his minions.

And after what he'd learned about himself, about his... capabilities in that time: he couldn't exactly rock back up to the university and carry on as normal, could he?

"I'll have to see," he finished, tripping over the words. "I might need to go and, you know... sort my head out a bit first. Work out what to do about all *this*."

He gestured down at his arms; at the hands still glowing a faint, ethereal amber at the palms and knuckles.

"It's changed you. The discovery of your powers."

"My *powers*?" He laughed. Couldn't help himself. "*All* of it has changed me. All of it. I don't even know who I am now, let alone what I'm meant to do with myself. Like," he held up the glowing palms; waved them inches from her face, "am I supposed to *use* this for something? Should I be out there, I don't know... helping people or whatever?"

"I'm afraid I'm not in a position to advise on that. *Helping people* has never been part of the job description." Her eyes narrowed, scrutinising him. "You believe you need support in navigating your new... self?"

"I mean... yeah. Fireballs and levitation haven't exactly been in *my* job description, until just lately." He paused again, as it hit him: what she might be asking him, *really* asking him. "Why – you think you might know someone?"

Maybe he'd misread her; misjudged what she was saying. Maybe there was no offer there no suggestion that she could be the guiding hand he needed, that he *would* need as the days and weeks and months went on.

Maybe she wouldn't be lonely without Miranda, after all.

But if there *was* an offer, if he *wasn't* wrong... well, maybe an arrangement like that could be doing them both a favour. For a little while, at least.

She stared back at him; tilted her head and the vast curling horns that sprung from them, as if weighing up a proposition.

"Possibly," she said, after a moment. "Possibly I do."

ACKNOWLEDGEMENTS

M uch as we might like to kid ourselves otherwise, writing a book is never a solo undertaking, and I'm enormously grateful to everyone who helped bring this one out into the world.

My thanks therefore to Steph Ellis and Alyson Faye, Catherine McCarthy, Beverley Lee and especially Lynn Love for their support and encouragement. Thanks to those who gave Hummingbird a read in its early incarnations, and whose feedback in all cases made what you've just read a better book: Lynn Love (again), April Yates and Kev Harrison.

Thanks to Hailey Piper and Laurel Hightower, for being magnificent, and to the remarkable Austrian Spencer, for being likewise.

Thanks to E and Daron, my editors and partners in crime. Long may we reign.

Thanks to Mrs Williams and the always-grisly catacombs of her imagination.

Thanks to Shauna, for putting up with me.

And thanks to you, whoever you are, for reading. I very much appreciate it.

ABOUT THE AUTHOR

TC PARKER is a writer and researcher based in the fox-ravaged wilds of Leicestershire, where she lives with her partner and family.

The author of the El Gardener feminist heist trilogy (*The Debt, The Push* and *The Remembrance*) and the horror novels *Saltblood, A Press of Feathers, Salvation Spring* and *Maiden* (with Ward Nerdlo), she's been a copywriter, a lecturer and, very briefly, an academic. Now she runs a semiotics and cultural insight agency by day and dreams up stories at night, when the kids are asleep.

Visit her online at www.tcparkerwrites.com and follow her on Twitter @tcparkerlives

www.ingramcontent.com/pod-product-compliance
Lightning Source LLC
Chambersburg PA
CBHW060945120726
47910CB00002B/498

* 9 7 8 1 0 6 8 6 6 3 8 1 9 *